D0590530

Everyman, I will go with thee, and be thy guide,
In thy most need to go by thy side.

EVERYMAN'S LIBRARY

No. 834

FICTION

MANON LESCAUT BY ABBÉ PRÉVOST
Translated by D. C. MOYLAN
and CARMEN BY PROSPER MÉRIMÉE
Translated by EDMUND H. GARRETT
INTRODUCTION *by* PHILIP HENDERSON
MEMOIR OF MÉRIMÉE *by* IMOGEN GURNEY

ANTOINE FRANÇOIS PRÉVOST D'EXILES, born on 1st. April 1697 at Hesdin, France. Ordained priest in 1726. Died at Chantilly on 23rd December 1763.

PROSPER MÉRIMÉE, born in Paris in 1803. Died at Cannes in 1870.

MANON LESCAUT
ABBÉ PRÉVOST

CARMEN
PROSPER MÉRIMÉE

LONDON: J. M. DENT & SONS LTD.
NEW YORK: E. P. DUTTON & CO. INC.

All rights reserved
Made in Great Britain
Printed by The Northumberland Press Gateshead-on-Tyne
and bound at The Temple Press Letchworth Herts
for
J. M. Dent & Sons Ltd.
Aldine House Bedford St. London
First published in this edition 1929
Last reprinted 1951

INTRODUCTION

Two men could scarcely have been more dissimilar in nature than the Abbé Prévost and Prosper Mérimée: the one, ardent, naïve, and self-contradictory: the other, reserved in his brittle scorn of humanity, "remembering to distrust," and carefully cultivating himself like some sterile flower, perfect and limited in growth. Or again, the one living life to the full, having been twice a Jesuit and twice a soldier by the age of twenty-two, and reaping a genial wisdom of experience in middle life, and the other, Inspector-General of historical monuments, holding himself back from every experience that might prove uncomfortable, and as a result being bored to death and ending his life in a state of dissatisfaction and self-protective contempt of a world which he had never really allowed himself to enter.

But, then, Mérimée was always consciously an artist, a stylist no less in life than in literature, while Prévost, even when he is so excellent a painter of nature, was, to quote Saint-Beuve, not an artist at all: he wrote just as the humour took him with a swift stream of unvarying elegance, his pen always ready and flowing, whether for an ecclesiastical history, a *Gallia Christiana*, or a tale like *Cleveland*, peopled with cannibals and demons. "Nature herself holds the pen," he declared of *Manon Lescaut*. Consciously he did not take art into account. Indeed, it is difficult to believe that *Manon* is not simply a copy of the truth, for Prévost's life, as Saint-Beuve remarks, was the first of his novels, and in some sort the material of which all the others were constructed. But the case of *Carmen* is very different. One would never dream of confusing Mérimée with Don José, although it is evident that behind the mask of such characters his real nature, hidden all through his life, is revealed. Looking at Prévost's face we see an open, good-humoured, ingenuous nature; whereas Mérimée, behind his "English" reserve, wears the smile of Mona Lisa.

Nevertheless, the two books, *Manon Lescaut* and *Carmen*, so dissimilar in their authors, are alike in aim and effect. In both we see two men reduced to very much the same state of degradation by women who dominate them by giving an unequal and spasmodic passion in return for complete surrender. The similarity continues to the end—for Don José, after killing his mistress, buries her as piously as des Grieux buried his in the sand of the desert. But we cannot help thinking that Carmen is of finer metal than her French sister, resolute and passionate as she is compared to the feather-brained little creature who at first seems incapable of any strong feeling unless it be an appetite for pleasure and a fear of poverty. But this, of course, is only the superficial side of Manon, for such natures as hers, when awakened, are capable of stronger and more

v

lasting affections than many seemingly constant women, although it is not till the end of the book, when suffering has strengthened her attachment, that it begins to appear as something not entirely trivial. At last, indeed, the story rises to a certain sublimity, due more, perhaps, to the relentless justice of circumstances than to any particularly heroic element in either of the characters.

There is certainly nothing great about des Grieux, except his passion, and even in that he droops under the powerful charms of his mistress like a flower in the excessive heat of the sun, while Manon gains our sympathy at last by her growing devotion to her lover which reveals depths in her nature hitherto unsuspected. Manon belongs to the epic courtesan tradition of Helen, Cleopatra, and Thaïs—loving with a lifelong love and remaining faithful a week, as Anatole France remarks. But Prévost's tragedy is due largely to the weakness of the chevalier who, had he been a stronger man, could, much earlier in their history, have changed the frivolity of Manon to devotion in the same way as Shakespeare's Antony, by the very magnificence of his being, changed Cleopatra, or as Paphnutius changed Thaïs. It is true that at last Manon realises the strength of her lover's passion, and then, be it noticed, she does not make such remarks as, "Do you think tenderness is compatible with starvation?" but is willing to face certain death with him in the desert. It is for a different reason that Carmen faces death at her lover's hands after her sudden swift passion has died down. To her, death is preferable to living with a man she has ceased to love, and in her fierce independence she meets it willingly. She remains unbroken, although her lover's knife has pierced her heart.

The authors of both tales, with their artful negligence, are perfect *raconteurs*, but the effect produced while reading both of them is entirely different. *Manon* excites us with its excess of emotion, the exquisite refinement of its agony; we hope and despair with the unfortunate chevalier; its tragedy is only too acute. But although an equally tragic tale is being told by Don José it all passes us by at a distance, the frigidity of the style keeps it at a distance and we realise that after all our only reason for being in Spain is to ascertain the site of the battle of Munda. We listen to José's tale to while away an odd three-quarters of an hour. Nevertheless, we do not for a moment doubt its reality. It is afterwards, a day or two afterwards perhaps, when the subject recurs to memory, that its significance dawns upon us as though we were recollecting an event of our own past experience. And so with all Mérimée's tales. They have the air of the casual anecdotes of a man of the world, instead of minutely constructed masterpieces of literature. And this is exactly what their author intended. He wanted at all costs to keep the proportion of life. He seems half-contemptuous of his creature's tragedy, and after telling it as briefly as possible he goes on to discuss something else. Like a Greek, he was totally devoid of sentiment in his art. The most violent passions of life are reflected in the flawless mirror of his mind; he is untouched by them, and he obliges us too to survey the most terrible actions with a calm eye. In his scornfully quiet manner only essentials find a place, and he leaves the bare facts to tell their own tale, psychology to manifest itself in word and gesture.

Although Mérimée's characters are so strong in their actuality that we can almost take them by the hand, the creation of Manon is all the more wonderful considering that at the time of Prévost there had been no outstanding characters in fiction at all—unless we except *The Princess of Cleves*, at which book the modern novel of character is said to begin. But even there we find nothing like Manon; no figure, that is, of her proportions. Neither, in the fiction of that period, is there any tale so natural and lifelike as *Manon*. Again, Tiberge is a most delicately drawn personality, and in him and des Grieux we see the two extremes of the author's nature. Always he clung to the moral ideal of Tiberge, but his temperament was little suited to a monastic life with its barren studies that, as he said, left his heart parched and listless. To a brother monk he writes: ". . . if I should look with the slightest favour upon certain images which present themselves only too often to my mind, and which would possess only too much power to lead me astray, even though they be half-effaced. How hard it is to pick up a little strength when one has made a habit of one's weakness, and how much it costs to fight for victory when for long past one has found it sweet to yield." After joining the Benedictines he writes: "I realised that this ardent heart of mine was still burning under the ashes. The loss of my liberty afflicted me to tears. . . . I sought consolation for six years in the pleasures of study: my books were my faithful friends, but they were as dead as myself." He suffered all the temptations of St. Anthony at this time, and finally yielded to most of them. Certainly he was suited to a monastic life no more severe than that of the Abbey of Theleme and there his heart and senses might have found tranquillity. But as it was, "he ever loved God before all things, except women," says Anatole France. He was the most superstitious, unphilosophical of men, despite his imagination. He believed in mysteries, in hell: he believed whatever he was told. But whatever happened or whatever he did his faith in God remained unshaken. At the time of working on the *Gallia Christiana*, that vast compilation of ecclesiastical history begun in 1715, he was also writing his most secular *Memoirs of a Man of Quality*, of which *Manon* is a terrible little postscript, although it was not added till some years afterwards at the age of thirty-six, when he had written *Cleveland*, and was in Holland.

How different is Mérimée! He liked to picture himself in his letters to his friends as lying on a sofa with a yellow face of boredom. He had fixed ideas, hating the church, distrusting priests, avoiding received opinions. Occasionally he allowed himself to write a story. But considering the length of his life his literary output is not large. Only one-third of it is taken up by purely creative work, the rest being translations, histories, and the reports attendant upon his position as Inspector-General of historical monuments. His *nouvelles* appeared from time to time in the *Revue de Paris*, but as he grew older he professed to value his achievements as a scholar far above his writings as an artist, notwithstanding that as an artist in his particular line he was equalled by none of his century except Balzac and Gautier at his very best.

Towards the end of his life he came more and more to put his trust in facts, the facts of history and learning, as though in them he had nothing to distrust, as though they at least could not be distorted by irrational emotion. This attitude of distrust and impassivity that he assumed in youth as a kind of mask for an emotional and deeply sensitive nature, became in later years habitual. So much so that it was conjectured by his friends that he gave way to an emotion possibly once a year. Nevertheless, the crude passions and sensualities that his good taste forbade him to express in life found an embodiment in his stories, which he was able to read quite safely to the ladies of the court of Napoleon III. And in these, his passions, set as they are in the fine workmanship of his form, he had sharpened and refined until they became very blades of hate and desire.

PHILIP HENDERSON.

PRÉVOST

Born 1st April 1697 at Hesdin, Artois. Educated at local Jesuit School, and in 1713 became a novice of the Order in Paris, pursuing his studies meanwhile at the College of La Flèche. Joins the army at end of 1716, but returns to his convent in 1719. Deserts his convent again shortly afterwards for the army, this time as an officer. Within a year he has travelled in Holland, been deceived by a mistress, renounced the world, and joined the Benedictines at St. Maur. Took his vows at Jumièges in 1721 after a year's novitiate and received in 1726 priest's orders at St. Germer de Flaix. Resides for seven years in various houses of the Order, teaching, praying, studying. In 1728 he was at Abbey of St. Germain-des-Prés, Paris, where he worked on *Gallia Christiana*. Finding this life too rigorous, he applies to the Pope to be transferred to the easier rule of Cluny, but without waiting for brief, left Abbey without leave (1728), and hearing that a *lettre de cachet* had been obtained against him, fled to England. Leaves England for Holland, 1729. *Mémoires et aventures d'un homme de qualité* published (eight vols.) in Paris in 1728–32. *Cleveland, fils naturel de Cromwell*, published (Utrecht, 1730, four vols.). Residing at The Hague, translating the *Historia* of De Thou. Published vols. v, vi, and vii of *Mémoires d'un homme de qualité* at Amsterdam; vol. viii, containing *Les aventres du Chevalier des Grieux et de Manon Lescaut* (1733). Book forbidden in France. Leaves Hague for London (1733), accompanied by a girl who had fallen in love and wished to marry him. As she was a Protestant this could not be. Edited a weekly gazette, modelled on Addison's "Spectator," "Le Pour et contre," which continued till 1740. Returns to France reconciled with Benedictines in 1734. Received into monastery of La Croix-Saint-Lenfroy, dispensed from residence in monastery by becoming almoner to the Prince de Conti (1735). Writes *Doyen de Killerine*. Obtains priory of St. Georges de Sesnes. With the exception of a brief exile in Brussels and Frankfort (1751–2) lived quietly at Chantilly. While walking in the woods near his house was struck down by apoplexy. Peasants carried his body to the village. He returned to consciousness just as a surgeon was opening his body to ascertain the cause of his death—23rd November 1763.

His other works are: *Le Pour et le contre*, Paris, 1733–40, 20 vols. (a great deal of this being the work of Le Fèvre de Saint-Marc); *Histoire de Marguerite d'Anjou, Reine d'Angleterre*, 1740, 2 vols.; *Histoire d'une Greque moderne*, 1741, 2 vols.; *Campagnes philosophiques, ou les mémoires de M. de Montcalm*, 1741, 4 parts; *Mémoires pour servir à l'histoire de Malta*, 1741, 2 vols.; *Histoire de Guillaume le Conquérant*, 1742, 2 vols.; *Mémoires d'un honnête homme*, 1745; *Histoire générale des voyages*, 1745–70, 21 vols., of which Prévost wrote vols. i–xvii; *Manuel lexique ou dictionnaire portatif des mots français*, 1750, 2 vols.; *Le Monde moral*, 1760, 2 vols.; *Mémoires pour servir à l'histoire de la vertu*, 1762; 4 vols.; *Contes, aventures et faits singuliers*, 1764, 2 vols.; *Lettres de mentor à un jeune seigneur*, 1764.

TRANSLATIONS.—*Histoire métallique des Pays-Bas*, de G. van Loon, 1734. With van Effen. *Hist. universelle*, de J. A. de Thou, 1734; *Tout pour l'amour*, of Dryden, 1735; Richardson's *Pamela*, 1742, 4 vols.; *Voyages de Robert Lade*, 1744, 2 vols.; Middleton's *Histoire de Cicéron*, 1744–9, 4 vols.; *Lettres familières de Cicéron*, 1745, 5 vols.; Hume's *Histoire de la Maison de Stuart*, 1760, 3 vols.; Richardson's *Clarissa Harlowe*, 1751, 4 vols., and *Grandisson*, 1775.

Prévost also furnished many articles for the "Journal Etranger" (1755) and the "Journal Encyclopedique" (1756–63).

His collected works were published in fifty-five volumes, 1810–16.

See also Prévost's Life by H. Harrisse, 1896, and G. R. Havens: *The Abbé Prévost and English Literature* and F. H. Wilcox: *Prévost's Translations of Richardson's Novels*, 1947.

MANON LESCAUT

CHAPTER I

Why did he love her?   Curious fool, be still!
Is human love the fruit of human will?

BYRON.

JUST about six months before my departure for Spain, I first met the Chevalier des Grieux. Though I rarely quitted my retreat, still the interest I felt in my child's welfare induced me occasionally to undertake short journeys, which, however, I took good care to abridge as much as possible.

I was one day returning from Rouen, where I had been, at her request, to attend a cause then pending before the Parliament of Normandy, respecting an inheritance to which I had claims derived from my maternal grandfather. Having taken the road by Evreux, where I slept the first night, I on the following day, about dinner-time, reached Passy, a distance of five or six leagues. I was amazed, on entering this quiet town, to see all the inhabitants in commotion. They were pouring from their houses in crowds, towards the gate of a small inn, immediately before which two covered vans were drawn up. Their horses still in harness, and reeking from fatigue and heat, showed that the cortège had only just arrived. I stopped for a moment to learn the cause of the tumult, but could gain little information from the curious mob as they rushed by, heedless of my inquiries, and hastening impatiently towards the inn in the utmost confusion. At length an archer of the civic guard, wearing his bandolier, and carrying a carbine on his shoulder, appeared at the gate; so, beckoning him towards me, I begged to know the cause of the uproar. Nothing, sir, said he, but a dozen of the frail sisterhood, that I and my comrades are conducting to Havre-de-Grace, whence we are to ship them for America. There are one or two of them pretty enough; and it is that, apparently, which attracts the curiosity of these good people.

I should have passed on, satisfied with this explanation, if my attention had not been arrested by the cries of an old woman,

3

who was coming out of the inn with her hands clasped, and exclaiming: A downright barbarity!—A scene to excite horror and compassion! What may this mean? I inquired. Oh! sir; go into the house yourself, said the woman, and see if it is not a sight to rend your heart! Curiosity made me dismount; and leaving my horse to the care of the ostler, I made my way with some difficulty through the crowd, and did indeed behold a scene sufficiently touching.

Among the twelve girls, who were chained together by the waist in two rows, there was one, whose whole air and figure seemed so ill-suited to her present condition, that under other circumstances I should not have hesitated to pronounce her a person of high birth. Her excessive grief, and even the wretched-ness of her attire, detracted so little from her surpassing beauty, that at first sight of her I was inspired with a mingled feeling of respect and pity. She tried, as well as the chain would permit her, to turn herself away, and hide her face from the rude gaze of the spectators. There was something so unaffected in the effort she made to escape observation, that it could but have sprung from natural and innate modesty alone.

As the six men who escorted the unhappy train were together in the room, I took the chief one aside and asked for information respecting this beautiful girl. All that he could supply was of the most vague kind. We brought her, he said, from the Hospital, by order of the lieutenant-general of police. There is no reason to suppose that she was shut up there for good conduct. I have questioned her often upon the road; but she persists in refusing even to answer me. Yet, although I received no orders to make any distinction between her and the others, I cannot help treating her differently, for she seems to me somewhat superior to her companions. Yonder is a young man, continued the archer, who can tell you, better than I can, the cause of her misfortunes. He has followed her from Paris, and has scarcely dried his tears for a single moment. He must be either her brother or her lover.

I turned towards the corner of the room, where this young man was seated. He seemed buried in a profound reverie. Never did I behold a more affecting picture of grief. He was plainly dressed; but one may discover at the first glance a man of birth and education. As I approached him he rose, and there was so refined and noble an expression in his eyes, in his whole countenance, in his every movement, that I felt an involuntary impulse to render him any service in my power. I am unwilling to intrude upon your sorrows, said I, taking a seat beside him, but you will, perhaps, gratify the desire I feel to learn something about that beautiful girl, who seems little formed by nature for the miserable condition in which she is placed.

He answered me candidly, that he could not communicate her history without making himself known, and that he had urgent reasons for preserving his own incognito. I may, however, tell you thus much, for it is no longer a secret to these wretches, he continued, pointing to the guards,—that I adore her with a passion so ardent and absorbing as to render me the most unhappy of human beings. I tried every means at Paris to effect her liberty. Petitions, artifice, force—all failed. Go where she may, I have resolved to follow her,—to the extremity of the world. I shall embark with her and cross to America.

But think of the brutal inhumanity of these cowardly ruffians, he added, speaking of the guards; they will not allow me to approach her! I had planned an open attack upon them some leagues from Paris; having secured, as I thought, the aid of four men, who for a considerable sum hired me their services. The traitors, however, left me to execute my scheme single-handed, and decamped with my money. The impossibility of success made me of course abandon the attempt. I then implored of the guards permission to follow in their train, promising them a recompense. The love of money procured their consent; but as they required payment every time I was allowed to speak to her, my purse was speedily emptied; and now that I am utterly penniless, they are barbarous enough to repulse me brutally, whenever I make the slightest attempt to approach her. It is but a moment since, that venturing to do so, in spite of their threats, one of the fellows raised the butt-end of his musket. I am now driven by their exactions to dispose of the miserable horse that has brought me hither, and am preparing to continue the journey on foot.

Although he seemed to recite this story tranquilly enough, I observed the tears start to his eyes as he concluded. This adventure struck me as being not less singular than it was affecting. I do not press you, said I to him, to make me the confidant of your secrets; but if I can be of use to you in any way, I gladly tender you my services. Alas! replied he, I see not the slightest ray of hope. I must reconcile myself to my destiny in all its rigour. I shall go to America: there, at least, I may be free to live with her I love. I have written to a friend, who will send me money to Havre-de-Grace. My only difficulty is to get so far, and to supply that poor creature, added he, as he cast a look of sorrow at his mistress, with some few comforts upon the way. Well! said I to him, I shall relieve you from that difficulty. Here is some money, of which I entreat your acceptance: I am only sorry that I can be of no greater service to you.

I gave him four louis-d'ors without being perceived by the guards; for I thought that if they knew he had this money, they might have raised the price of their concessions. It occurred to me, even, to come to an understanding with them, in order to secure for the young man the privilege of conversing with his mistress, during the rest of the journey to Havre, without hindrance. I beckoned the chief to approach, and made the proposition to him. It seemed to abash the ruffian, in spite of his habitual effrontery. It is not, sir, said he, in an embarrassed tone, that we refuse to let him speak to the girl, but he wishes to be always near her, which puts us to inconvenience; and it is just that we should be paid for the trouble he occasions. Let us see! said I to him, what would suffice to prevent you from feeling the inconvenience? He had the audacity to demand two louis. I gave them to him on the spot. But have a care, said I to him, that we have no foul play: for I shall give the young man my address, in order that he may write to me on his arrival; and be assured that I am not without the power to punish you. It cost me altogether six louis-d'ors.

The graceful manner and heartfelt gratitude with which the young unknown thanked me, confirmed my notion that he was of good birth, and merited my kindness. I addressed a few words to his mistress before I left the room. She replied to me with a modesty so gentle and so charming that I could not help making, as I went out, a thousand reflections upon the incomprehensible character of women.

Returned to my retreat, I remained in ignorance of the result of this adventure; and ere two years had passed, it was completely blotted from my recollection, when chance brought me an opportunity of learning all the circumstances from beginning to end.

I arrived at Calais, from London, with my pupil, the Marquis of ——. We lodged, if I remember rightly, at the Golden Lion, where, for some reason, we were obliged to spend the following day and night. Walking along the streets in the afternoon, I fancied I saw the same young man whom I had formerly met at Passy. He was miserably dressed, and much paler than when I first saw him. He carried on his arm an old portmanteau, having only just arrived in the town. However, there was an expression in his countenance too amiable not to be easily recognised, and which immediately brought his features to my recollection. Observe that young man, said I to the Marquis; we must accost him.

His joy was beyond expression when, in his turn, he recognised me. Ah, sir! he cried, kissing my hand, I have then once again an opportunity of testifying my eternal gratitude to you! I inquired of him whence he came. He replied, that he had just arrived, by sea, from Havre, where he had lately landed from America. You do not seem to be too well off for money, said I to him; go on to the Golden Lion, where I am lodging; I will join you in a moment.

I returned, in fact, full of impatience to learn the details of his misfortunes, and the circumstances of his voyage to America. I gave him a thousand welcomes, and ordered that they should supply him with everything he wanted. He did not wait to be solicited for the history of his life. Sir, said he to me, your conduct is so generous, that I should consider it base ingratitude to maintain any reserve towards you. You shall learn not only my misfortunes and sufferings, but my faults and most culpable weaknesses. I am sure that, even while you blame me, you will not refuse me your sympathy.

I should here inform the reader that I wrote down the story almost immediately after hearing it; and he may, therefore, be assured of the correctness and fidelity of the narrative. I use the word fidelity with reference to the substance of reflections and sentiments, which the young man conveyed in the most graceful language. Here, then, is his story, which in its progress I shall not encumber with a single observation that was not his own.

CHAPTER II

I loved Ophelia! forty thousand brothers
Could not, with all their quantity of love,
Make up my sum.

SHAKESPEARE.

I WAS seventeen years old, and was finishing my studies at
Amiens, whither my parents, who belonged to one of the first
families in Picardy, had sent me. I led a life so studious and
well regulated, that my masters pointed to me as a model of
conduct for the other scholars. Not that I made any extraordinary efforts to acquire this reputation, but my disposition
was naturally tractable and tranquil; my inclinations led me to
apply to study; and even the natural dislike I felt for vice was
placed to my credit as positive proof of virtue. The successful
progress of my studies, my birth, and some external advantages
of person, made me a general favourite with the inhabitants
of the town.

I completed my public exercises with such general approbation, that the bishop of the diocese, who was present, proposed
to me to enter the church, where I could not fail, he said, to
acquire more distinction than in the Order of Malta, for which
my parents had destined me. I was already decorated with
the Cross, and called the Chevalier des Grieux. The vacation
having arrived, I was preparing to return to my father, who had
promised to send me soon to the Academy.

My only regret on quitting Amiens arose from parting with a
friend, some years older than myself, to whom I had always
been tenderly attached. We had been brought up together;
but from the straitened circumstances of his family, he was
intended to take orders, and was to remain after me at Amiens
to complete the requisite studies for his sacred calling. He
had a thousand good qualities. You will recognise in him the
very best during the course of my history, and above all, a
zeal and fervour of friendship which surpass the most illustrious
examples of antiquity. If I had at that time followed his

8

advice, I should have always continued a discreet and happy man. If I had even taken counsel from his reproaches, when on the brink of that gulf into which my passions afterwards plunged me, I should have been spared the melancholy wreck of both fortune and reputation. But he was doomed to see his friendly admonitions disregarded; nay, even at times repaid by contempt from an ungrateful wretch, who often dared to treat his fraternal conduct as offensive and officious.

I had fixed the day for my departure from Amiens. Alas! that I had not fixed it one day sooner! I should then have carried to my father's house my innocence untarnished.

The very evening before my expected departure, as I was walking with my friend, whose name was Tiberge, we saw the Arras diligence arrive, and sauntered after it to the inn, at which these coaches stop. We had no other motive than curiosity. Some women alighted, and immediately retired into the inn. One remained behind: she was very young, and stood by herself in the court, while a man of advanced age, who appeared to have charge of her, was busy in getting her luggage from the vehicle. She struck me as being so extremely beautiful, that I, who had never before thought of the difference between the sexes, or looked on woman with the slightest attention,—I, whose conduct had been hitherto the theme of universal admiration, felt myself, on the instant, deprived of my reason and self-control. I had been always excessively timid, and easily disconcerted; but now, instead of meeting with any impediment from this weakness, I advanced without the slightest reserve towards her, who had thus become, in a moment, the mistress of my heart.

Although younger than myself, she received my civilities without embarrassment. I asked the cause of her journey to Amiens, and whether she had any acquaintances in the town. She ingenuously told me that she had been sent there by her parents, to commence her novitiate for taking the veil. Love had so quickened my perception, even in the short moment it had been enthroned, that I saw in this announcement a death-blow to my hopes. I spoke to her in a way that made her at once understand what was passing in my mind; for she had more experience than myself. It was against her consent that she was consigned to a convent, doubtless to repress that inclination for pleasure which had already become too manifest, and which caused, in the sequel, all her misfortunes and mine. I combated the cruel intention of her parents with all the arguments that my new-born passion and schoolboy eloquence could suggest. She affected neither austerity nor reserve. She told me, after a moment's silence, that she foresaw, too clearly, what her unhappy fate must be; but that it was, apparently, the will of Heaven, since there were no means left her to avert it. The sweetness of her look, the air of sorrow with which she pronounced these words, or rather perhaps the controlling destiny which led me on to ruin, allowed me not an instant to weigh my answer. I assured her that if she would place reliance on my honour, and on the tender interest with which she had already inspired me, I would sacrifice my life to deliver her from the tyranny of her parents, and to render her happy. I have since been a thousand times astonished in reflecting upon it, to think how I could have expressed myself with so much boldness and facility; but love could never have become a divinity, if he had not often worked miracles.

I made many other pressing and tender speeches; and my unknown fair one was perfectly aware that mine was not the age for deceit. She confessed to me that if I could see but a reasonable hope of being able to effect her enfranchisement, she should deem herself indebted for my kindness in more than life itself could pay. I repeated that I was ready to attempt anything in her behalf; but, not having sufficient experience at once to imagine any reasonable plan of serving her, I did not go beyond this general assurance, from which indeed little good could arise either to her or to myself. Her old guardian having by this time joined us, my hopes would have been blighted, but that she had tact enough to make amends for my stupidity. I was surprised, on his approaching us, to hear her call me her cousin, and say, without being in the slightest degree disconcerted, that as she had been so fortunate as to fall in with me at Amiens, she would not go into the convent until the next morning, in order to have the pleasure of meeting me at supper. Innocent as I was, I at once comprehended the meaning of this ruse; and proposed that she should lodge for the night at the house of an innkeeper, who, after being many years my father's coachman, had lately established himself at Amiens, and who was sincerely attached to me.

I conducted her there myself, at which the old Argus appeared to grumble a little; and my friend Tiberge, who was puzzled by the whole scene, followed, without uttering a word. He had not heard our conversation, having walked up and down the court while I was talking of love to my angelic mistress. As I had some doubts of his discretion, I got rid of him, by begging that he would execute a commission for me. I had thus the happiness, on arriving at the inn, of entertaining alone the sovereign of my heart.

I soon learned that I was less a child than I had before imagined. My heart expanded to a thousand sentiments of pleasure, of which I had not before the remotest idea. A delicious consciousness of enjoyment diffused itself through my whole mind and soul. I sank into a kind of ecstasy, which deprived me for a time of the power of utterance, and which found vent only in a flood of tears.

Manon Lescaut (this she told me was her name) seemed gratified by the visible effect of her own charms. She appeared to me not less excited than myself. She acknowledged that she was greatly pleased with me, and that she should be enchanted to owe to me her freedom and future happiness. She would insist on hearing who I was, and the knowledge only augmented her affection; for, being herself of humble birth, she was flattered by securing for her lover a man of family.

After many reflections, we could discover no other resource than in flight. To effect this it would be requisite to cheat the vigilance of Manon's guardian, who required management, although he was but a servant. We determined, therefore, that, during the night, I should procure a post-chaise, and return with it at break of day to the inn, before he was awake; that we should steal away quietly, and go straight to Paris, where we might be married on our arrival. I had about fifty crowns in my pocket, the fruit of my little savings at school; and she had about twice as much. We imagined, like inexperienced children, that such a sum could never be exhausted, and we counted, with equal confidence, upon the success of our other schemes.

After having supped, with certainly more satisfaction than I had ever before experienced, I retired to prepare for our project. All my arrangements were the more easy, because, for the purpose of returning on the morrow to my father's, my luggage had been already packed. I had, therefore, no difficulty in removing my trunk, and having a chaise prepared for five o'clock in the morning, at which hour the gates of the town would be opened; but I encountered an obstacle which I was little prepared for, and which nearly upset all my plans.

Tiberge, although only three years older than myself, was a youth of unusually strong mind, and of the best regulated conduct. He loved me with singular affection. The sight of so lovely a girl as Manon, my ill-disguised impatience to conduct her to the inn, and the anxiety I betrayed to get rid of him, had excited in his mind some suspicions of my passion. He had not ventured to return to the inn where he had left me, for fear of my being annoyed at his doing so; but went to wait for me at my lodgings, where, although it was ten o'clock at night, I found him on my arrival. His presence annoyed me, and he soon perceived the restraint which it imposed. I am certain, he said to me, without any disguise, that you have some plan in contemplation which you will not confide to me; I see it by your manner. I answered him rather abruptly, that I was not bound to render him an account of all my movements. Certainly not! he replied; but you have always, hitherto, treated me as a friend, and that appellation implies a certain degree of confidence and candour. He pressed me so much and so earnestly to discover my secret, that, having never up to that moment felt the slightest reserve towards him, I confided to him now the whole history of my passion. He heard it with an appearance of disapprobation, which made me tremble; and I immediately repented of my indiscretion, in telling him of my intended elopement. He told me he was too sincerely my friend not to oppose every obstacle in his power to such a scheme; that he would first try all other means of turning me from such a purpose, but that if I refused to renounce so fatal a resolution, he assuredly would inform some persons of my intention, who would be able to defeat it. He held forth upon the subject for a full quarter of an hour, in the most serious tone, and ended by again threatening to inform against me, if I did not pledge him my word that I would return to the paths of discretion and reason.

I was in despair at having so awkwardly betrayed myself. However, love having wonderfully sharpened my intellect during the last two or three hours, I recollected that I had not yet told him of its being my intention to execute my project on the following morning, and I at once determined to deceive him by a little equivocation.

Tiberge, said I to him, up to the present moment I thought you were my friend; and I wished to prove it by the test of confidence. It is true, I am in love; I have not deceived you: but with regard to my flight, that is a project not to be undertaken without deliberation. Call for me to-morrow at nine o'clock: you shall see my mistress, if it be possible, and then judge whether she is not worthy of any risk or sacrifice on my part. He left me, with a thousand protestations of friendship.

I employed the night in preparing for the journey, and on repairing to the inn at early dawn, I found Manon waiting my arrival. She was at her window, which looked upon the street, and perceiving my approach, she came down and opened the door herself. We took our departure silently, and without creating the least alarm. She merely brought away a small portion of her apparel, of which I took charge. The chaise was in readiness, and we were soon at a distance from the town.

You will learn in the sequel what was the conduct of Tiberge when he discovered that I had deceived him; that his zeal to serve me suffered no diminution; and you will observe to what lengths his devotion carried him. How ought I to grieve, when I reflect on the base ingratitude with which his affection was always repaid!

We made such speed on our journey that before night we reached St. Denis. I rode alongside of the chaise, which gave us little opportunity for conversation, except while changing horses; but when we found ourselves so near Paris, and out of the reach of danger, we allowed ourselves time for refreshment, not having tasted food since we quitted Amiens. Passionately in love as I felt with Manon, she knew how to convince me that she was equally so with me. So little did we restrain our fondness, that we had not even patience to reserve our caresses till we were alone. The postilions and innkeepers stared at us with wonder, and I remarked that they appeared surprised at such uncontrollable love in children of our age.

Our project of marriage was forgotten at St. Denis; we defrauded the Church of her rights; and found ourselves united as man and wife without reflecting on the consequences. It is certain that with my easy and constant disposition, I should have been happy for my whole life, if Manon had remained faithful to me. The more I saw of her, the more I discovered in her new perfections. Her mind, her heart, her gentleness and beauty, formed a chain at once so binding and so agreeable, that I could have found perfect happiness in its enduring influence. Terrible fatality! that which has been the source of my despair, might, under a slight change of circumstances, have constituted my happiness. I find myself the most wretched of mankind, by the force of that very constancy from which I might have fairly expected to derive the most serene of human blisses, and the most perfect recompense of love.

We took a furnished apartment at Paris, in the Rue V——, and, as it afterwards turned out, to my sorrow, close to the house of M. de B——, the famous Fermier-général. Three weeks passed, during which I was so absorbed in my passion, that I never gave a thought to my family, nor dreamed of the distress which my father probably felt at my absence. However, as there was yet nothing of profligacy about me, and as Manon conducted herself with the strictest propriety, the tranquil life we led served to restore me by degrees to a sense of duty.

I resolved to effect, if possible, a reconciliation with my parent. My mistress was to me so perfectly lovable, that I could not doubt her power of captivating my father, if I could only find the means of making him acquainted with her good conduct and merit. In a word, I relied on obtaining his consent to our marriage, having given up all idea of accomplishing it without his approval. I mentioned the project to Manon, and explained to her that, besides every motive of filial love and duty, the weightier one of necessity should also have some influence; for our finances were sadly reduced, and I began to see the folly of thinking them, as I once did, inexhaustible.

Manon received the proposition with considerable coldness. However, the difficulties she made, being apparently the suggestions of tenderness alone, or as arising from the natural fear of losing me, if my father, after learning our address, should refuse his assent to our union, I had not the smallest suspicion of the cruel blow she was at the very time preparing to inflict. As to the argument of necessity, she replied that we had still abundant means of living for some weeks longer, and that she would then find a resource in the kindness of some relations in the country, to whom she should write. She tempered her opposition by caresses so tender and impassioned, that I, who lived only for her, and who never had the slightest misgiving as to her love, applauded at once her arguments and her resolutions.

To Manon I had committed the care of our finances, and the household arrangements. In a short time, I observed that our style of living was improved, and that she had treated herself to more expensive dresses. As I calculated that we could hardly have at this period more than fifteen or twenty crowns remaining, I did not conceal my surprise at this mysterious augmentation of our wealth. She begged of me, with a smile, to give myself no trouble on that head. Did I not promise you, said she, that I would find resources? I loved her too purely to experience the slightest suspicion.

One day, having gone out in the afternoon, and told her that I should not be at home so early as usual, I was astonished, on my return, at being detained several minutes at the door. Our only servant was a young girl about our own age. On her letting me in at last, I asked why she had detained me so long? She replied in an embarrassed tone, that she did not hear me knock. I only knocked once, said I; so if you did not hear me, why come to open the door at all? This query disconcerted her so visibly, that losing her presence of mind, she began to cry, assuring me that it was not her fault; and that her mistress had desired her not to open the door until M. de B—— had had time to go down by the back staircase. I was so confounded by this information as to be utterly unable to proceed to our apartment; and was obliged to leave the house, under the pretext of an appointment. I desired the girl, therefore, to let her mistress know that I should return in a few minutes, but on no account to say that she had spoken to me of M. de B——.

My horror was so great, that I shed tears as I went along, hardly knowing from what feeling they flowed. I entered a coffee-house close by, and placing myself at a table, I buried my face between my hands, as though I would turn my eyes inward to ascertain what was passing in my heart. Still, I dared not recall what I had heard the moment before. I strove to look upon it as a dream; and was more than once on the point of returning to my lodgings, determined to attach no importance to what I had heard. It appeared to me so impossible that Manon could have been unfaithful, that I feared even to wrong her by a suspicion. I adored her—that was too certain; I had not on my part given her more proofs of my love than I had received of hers; why then should I charge her with being less sincere and constant than myself? What reason could she have to deceive me? Not three hours before, she had lavished upon me the most tender caresses, and had received mine with transport: I knew her heart as thoroughly as my own. No, no! I said, it is not possible that Manon can have deceived me. She well knows that I live but for her; that I adore her: upon that point I can have no reason to be unhappy.

Notwithstanding these reflections, the visit of M. de B——, and his secret departure, gave me some uneasiness. I remembered, too, the little purchases she had lately made, which seemed beyond our present means. This looked like the liberality of a new lover. And the confidence with which she had foretold resources which were to me unknown? I had some difficulty in solving these mysteries in as favourable a manner as my heart desired.

On the other hand, she had been hardly out of my sight since we entered Paris. However occupied, in our walks, in all our amusements, she was ever at my side. Heavens! even a momentary separation would have been too painful. I could not therefore imagine how Manon could, to any other person, have devoted a single instant.

At last I thought I had discovered a clue to the mystery. M. de B——, said I to myself, is a man extensively engaged in commercial affairs; and Manon's relations have no doubt remitted her money through his house. She has probably already received some from him, and he is come to-day to bring her more. She wishes, perhaps, to derive amusement by and by, from an agreeable surprise, by keeping me at present in the dark. She would doubtless have at once told me all, if I had gone in as usual, instead of coming here to distress myself: at all events, she will not conceal it from me when I broach the subject myself.

I cherished this idea so willingly, that it considerably lightened my grief. I immediately returned to my lodgings, and embraced Manon as tenderly as ever. She received me as usual. At first I was tempted to mention my conjectures, which I now, more than ever, looked upon as certain; but I restrained myself in the hope that she might render it unnecessary by informing me of all that had passed.

Supper was served. Assuming an air of gaiety, I took my seat at table; but by the light of the candles which were between us, I fancied I perceived an air of melancholy about the eyes and countenance of my beloved mistress. The very thought soon damped my gaiety. I remarked that her looks wore an unusual expression, and although nothing could be more soft or languishing, I was at a loss to discover whether they conveyed more of love than of compassion. I gazed at her with equal earnestness, and she perhaps had no less difficulty in comprehending from my countenance what was passing in my heart. We neither spoke nor ate. At length I saw tears starting from her beauteous eyes,—perfidious tears! Oh heavens! I cried, my dearest Manon, why allow your sorrows to afflict you to this degree without imparting their cause to me? She answered me only with sighs, which increased my misery. I arose trembling from my seat: I conjured her, with all the urgent earnestness of love, to let me know the cause of her grief: I wept in endeavouring to soothe her sorrows: I was more dead than alive. A barbarian would have pitied my sufferings as I stood trembling with grief and apprehension.

While my attention was thus confined to her, I heard people coming upstairs. They tapped gently at the door. Manon gave me a kiss, and escaping from my arms, quickly entered the boudoir, turning the key after her. I imagined that, not being dressed to receive strangers, she was unwilling to meet the persons who had knocked; I went to let them in.

I had hardly opened the door, when I found myself seized by three men, whom I recognised as my father's servants. They offered not the least violence, but two of them taking me by the arms, the third examined my pockets, and took out a small knife, the only weapon I had about me. They begged pardon for the necessity they were under of treating me with apparent disrespect; telling me frankly that they were acting by the orders of my father, and that my eldest brother was in a carriage below waiting to receive me. My feelings were so overpowered, that I allowed myself to be led away without making either reply or resistance. I found my brother waiting for me as they had stated. They placed me by his side, and the coachman immediately drove, by his orders, towards St. Denis. My brother embraced me most affectionately, but during our ride he uttered not a word, so that, as I was not inclined for conversation, I had as much leisure as I could desire to reflect upon my misfortunes.

CHAPTER III

That we can call these delicate creatures ours,
And not their appetites.

SHAKESPEARE.

THE whole affair was so involved in obscurity that I could not
see my way even to a reasonable conjecture. I was cruelly
betrayed,—that was certain; but by whom? Tiberge first
occurred to me. Tiberge! said I, it is as much as thy life is
worth, if my suspicions turn out to be well founded. However,
I recollected that he could not by possibility know my abode;
and therefore, he could not have furnished the information.
To accuse Manon was more than my heart was capable of.
The unusual melancholy with which she had lately seemed
weighed down, her tears, the tender kiss she gave me in parting,
made it all as yet a mystery to me. I could only look upon her
recent melancholy as a presentiment of our common misfortune;
and while I was deploring the event which tore me from her,
I was credulous enough to consider her fate as much deserving
of pity as my own.

The result of my reflections was, that I had been seen and
followed in the streets of Paris by some persons of my acquaintance, who had conveyed the information to my father. This
idea comforted me. I made up my mind to encounter some
reproaches, or perhaps harsh treatment, for having outraged
the paternal authority. I resolved, however, to suffer with
patience, and to promise all that might be required of me, in
order to facilitate my speedy return to Paris, that I might
restore life and happiness to my dear Manon.

We soon arrived at St. Denis. My brother, surprised at my
long silence, thought it the effect of fear. He assured me that
I had nothing to apprehend from my father's severity, provided
I showed a disposition to return quietly to the path of duty,
and prove myself worthy of his affection. He made me pass
the night at St. Denis, merely taking the precaution of putting
the three lackeys to sleep in my room. It cost me a pang to
find myself in the same inn where I had stopped with Manon

on our way from Amiens to Paris. The innkeeper and his servants recognised me, and guessed at once the truth of my history. I overheard them say, Ah! that's the handsome young gentleman who travelled this road about a month ago, with the beautiful girl he appeared so much in love with! How pretty she was! The poor young things, how they caressed each other! Pity if they have been separated! I pretended not to hear, and kept as much out of sight as possible.

At St. Denis my brother had a chariot waiting for us, in which we started early the next morning, and arrived at home before night. He saw my father first, in order to make a favourable impression by telling him how quietly I had allowed myself to be brought away, so that his reception of me was less austere than I had expected. He merely rebuked me in general terms for the offence I had committed, by absenting myself without his permission. As for my mistress, he said I richly deserved what had happened to me, for abandoning myself to a person utterly unknown; that he had entertained a better opinion of my discretion; but that he hoped this little adventure would make me wiser. I took the whole lecture only in the sense that accorded with my own notions. I thanked my father for his indulgence, and promised that I would in future observe a better regulated and more obedient course of conduct. I felt that I had secured a triumph; for, from the present aspect of affairs, there was no doubt that I should be free to effect my escape from the house even before the night was over.

We sat down to supper. They rallied me about my Amiens conquest, and my flight with that paragon of fidelity. I took their jokes in good part, glad enough at being permitted to revolve in my mind the plans I had meditated; but some words which fell from my father made me listen with earnest attention. He spoke of perfidy, and the not disinterested kindness he had received at the hands of M. de B——. I was almost paralysed on hearing the name, and begged of my father to explain himself. He turned to my brother, to ask if he had not told me the whole story. My brother answered, that I appeared to him so tranquil upon the road, that he did not suppose I required this remedy to cure me of my folly. I remarked that my father was doubtful whether he should give me the explanation or not. I entreated him so earnestly that he satisfied me, or I should rather say tortured me, with the following most horrible narration.

He began by asking me whether I was really simple enough to believe that I had been really loved by the girl. I told him confidently that I was perfectly sure of it, and that nothing could make me for a moment doubt it. Ha, ha, ha! said he, with a loud laugh; that is excellent! you are a pretty dupe! Admirable idea! 'Twould be a thousand pities, my poor chevalier, to make you a Knight of Malta, with all the requisites you possess for a patient and accommodating husband. He continued in the same tone to ridicule what he was pleased to call my dullness and credulity.

He concluded, while I maintained a profound silence, by saying that, according to the nicest calculation he could make of the time since my departure from Amiens, Manon must have been in love with me about twelve days; for, said he, I know that you left Amiens on the 28th of last month; this is the 29th of the present; it is eleven days since M. de B—— wrote to me; I suppose he required eight days to establish a perfect understanding with your mistress; so that, take eight and eleven from thirty-one days, the time between the 28th of one month and the 29th of the next, there remains twelve, more or less! This joke was followed by shouts of laughter.

I heard it all with a kind of sinking of the heart that I thought I could not bear up against, until he finished. You must know then, continued my father, since you appear as yet ignorant of it, that M. de B—— has won the affections of your idol; for he can't be serious in pretending that it is his disinterested regard for me that has induced him to take her from you. It would be absurd to expect such noble sentiments from a man of his description, and one, besides, who is a perfect stranger to me. He knew that you were my son, and in order to get rid of you, he wrote to inform me of your abode, and of the life you led; saying, at the same time, that strong measures would be necessary to secure you. He offered to procure me the means of laying hold of you; and it was by his direction, as well as that of your mistress herself, that your brother hit upon the moment for catching you unawares. Now, you may congratulate yourself upon the duration of your triumph. You know how to conquer, rapid enough; but you have yet to learn how to secure your conquests.

I could no longer endure these remarks, every one of which struck a dagger to my heart. I arose from the table, and had not advanced four steps towards the door, when I fell upon the floor, perfectly senseless. By prompt applications they soon brought me to myself. My eyes opened only to shed a torrent of tears, and my lips to utter the most sorrowful and heart-rending complaints. My father, who always loved me most affectionately, tried every means to console me. I listened to him, but his words were without effect. I threw myself at his feet, in the attitude of prayer, conjuring him to let me return to Paris, and destroy the monster B——. No! cried I; he has not gained Manon's heart; he may have seduced her by charms, or by drugs; he may have even brutally violated her. Manon loves me. Do I not know that well? He must have terrified her with a poniard, to induce her to abandon me. What must he not have done to have robbed me of my angelic mistress? Oh Heaven! Heaven! can it be possible that Manon deceived me, or that she has ceased to love me!

As I continued to rave about returning at once to Paris, and was perpetually starting up with that purpose, my father clearly saw that while the paroxysm lasted, no arguments could pacify me. He conducted me to one of the upper rooms, and left two servants to keep constant watch over me. I was completely bewildered. I would have given a thousand lives to be but for one quarter of an hour in Paris. I had sense enough, however, to know that having so openly declared my intention, they would not easily allow me to quit my chamber. I looked at the height of the windows. Seeing no possibility of escaping that way, I addressed the servants in the most tranquil tone. I promised, with the most solemn vows, to make at some future day their fortunes, if they would but consent to my escape. I entreated them; I tried caresses, and lastly threats; but all were unavailing. I gave myself up to despair. I resolved to die; and threw myself upon the bed, with a firm determination to quit it only with my life. In this situation I passed the night and the following day. I refused the nourishment that was brought to me next morning.

My father came to see me in the afternoon. He tried, in the most affectionate manner, to soothe my grief. He desired me so urgently to take some refreshment, that, to gratify him, I obeyed his wishes. Several days passed, during which I took nothing but in his presence, and at his special request. He continued to furnish new arguments to restore me to my proper senses, and to inspire me with merited contempt for the faithless Manon. I certainly had lost all esteem for her: how could I esteem the most fickle and perfidious of created beings! But her image—those exquisite features, which were engraven on my heart's core, were still uneffaced. I understood my own feelings: I may die, said I, and I ought to die after so much shame and grief; but I might suffer a thousand deaths without being able to forget the ingrate Manon.

My father was surprised at my still continuing so powerfully affected. He knew that I was imbued with the principles of honour; and not doubting that her infidelity must make me despise her, fancied that my obstinacy proceeded less from this particular passion, than from a general inclination towards the sex. This idea so took possession of his mind, that, prompted only by his affection for me, he came one day to reveal his thoughts. Chevalier, said he to me, it has been hitherto my intention to make you bear the Cross of Malta: I now see that your inclinations do not bend that way. You are an admirer of beauty. I shall be able to find you a wife to your taste. Let me candidly know how you feel upon the subject.

I answered that I could never again see the slightest difference amongst women, and that after the misfortune I had experienced, I detested them all equally. I will find you one, replied my father, smiling, who shall resemble Manon in beauty, but who shall be more faithful. Ah! if you have any mercy, said I, you will restore my Manon to me. Be assured, my dear father, that she has not betrayed me; she is incapable of such base and cruel treachery. It is the perfidious B—— who deceives both her and me. If you could form an idea of her tenderness and her sincerity,—if you only knew her, you yourself would love her! You are absolutely a child, replied my father. How can you so delude yourself, after what I have told you about her? It was she who actually delivered you up to your brother. You ought to obliterate even her name from your memory, and take advantage, if you are wise, of the indulgence I am showing you.

I very clearly perceived that my father was right. It was an involuntary emotion that made me thus take part with the traitor. Alas! replied I, after a moment's silence, it is but too true that I am the unhappy victim of the vilest perfidy. Yes, I continued, while shedding tears of anger, I too clearly perceive that I am indeed but a child. Credulity like mine was easily gulled; but I shall be at no loss to revenge myself. My father inquired of me my intentions: I will go to Paris, I said, set fire to B——'s house, and immolate him and the perfidious Manon together. This burst made my father laugh, and had only the effect of causing me to be more vigilantly watched in my cell.

I thus passed six long months; during the first of which my mind underwent little change. My feelings were in a state of perpetual alternation between hate and love; between hope and despair; according as the tendency of each passing thought brought Manon back to my recollection. At one time, I could see in her the most delightful of women only, and sigh for the pleasure of beholding her once more; at another, I felt she was the most unworthy and perfidious of mistresses, and I would on these occasions swear never again to seek her, but for the purpose of revenge.

I was supplied with books, which served to restore my peace of mind. I read once again all my favourite authors; and I became acquainted with new ones. All my former taste for study was revived. You will see of what use this was to me in the sequel. The light I had already derived from love, enabled me to comprehend many passages in Horace and Virgil which had before appeared obscure. I wrote an amatory commentary upon the fourth book of the Æneid. I intend one day to publish it, and I flatter myself it will be popular.

Alas! I used to exclaim, whilst employed on that work, it was for a heart like mine the faithful Dido sighed, and sighed in vain!

CHAPTER IV

Now, by the strange enchantment that surrounds thee,
There's nothing—nothing thou shalt ask in vain.
ESSEX.

WHILE in my confinement Tiberge came one day to see me.
I was surprised at the affectionate joy with which he saluted
me. I had never, hitherto, observed any peculiar warmth in
his friendship that could lead me to look upon it as anything
more than the partiality common among boys of the same age.
He was so altered, and had grown so manly during the five or
six months since I had last seen him, that his expressive features
and his manner of addressing me inspired me with a feeling of
respect. He spoke more in the character of a mentor than a
schoolfellow, lamented the delusion into which I had fallen,
congratulated me on my reformation, which he believed was now
sincere, and ended by exhorting me to profit by my youthful
error, and open my eyes to the vanity of worldly pleasures.
I looked at him with some astonishment, which he at once
perceived.

My dear chevalier, said he to me, you shall hear nothing but
the strict truth, of which I have assured myself by the most
serious examination. I had, perhaps, as strong an inclination
for pleasure as you, but Heaven had at the same time, in its
mercy, blessed me with a taste for virtue. I exercised my reason
in comparing the consequences of the one with those of the
other, and the divine aid was graciously vouchsafed to my
reflections. I conceived for the world a contempt which nothing
can equal. Can you guess what it is retains me in it now, he
added, and that prevents me from embracing a life of solitude?
Simply the sincere friendship I bear towards you. I know the
excellent qualities of both your heart and head. There is no
good of which you may not render yourself capable. The
blandishments of pleasure have momentarily drawn you aside.
What detriment to the sacred cause of virtue! Your flight from
Amiens gave me such intense sorrow, that I have not since
known a moment's happiness. You may judge of this by the

steps it induced me to take. He then told me how, after discovering that I had deceived him, and gone off with my mistress, he procured horses for the purpose of pursuing me, but having the start of him by four or five hours, he found it impossible to overtake me; that he arrived, however, at St. Denis half an hour after I had left it; that, being very sure that I must have stopped in Paris, he spent six weeks there in a fruitless endeavour to discover me,—visiting every place where he thought he should be likely to meet me, and that one evening he at length recognised my mistress at the play, where she was so gorgeously dressed, that he of course set it down to the account of some new lover; that he had followed her equipage to her house, and had there learned from a servant that she was entertained in this style by M. de B——. I did not stop here, continued he; I returned next day to the house, to learn from her own lips what had become of you. She turned abruptly away when she heard the mention of your name, and I was obliged to return into the country without further information. I there learned the particulars of your adventure, and the extreme annoyance she had caused you; but I was unwilling to visit you until I could have assurance of your being in a more tranquil state.

You have seen Manon then! cried I, sighing. Alas! you are happier than I, who am doomed never again to behold her. He rebuked me for this sigh, which still showed my weakness for the perfidious girl. He flattered me so adroitly upon the goodness of my mind and disposition, that he really inspired me, even on this first visit, with a strong inclination to renounce, as he had done, the pleasures of the world, and enter at once into holy orders.

The idea was so suited to my present frame of mind, that when alone I thought of nothing else. I remembered the words of the Bishop of Amiens, who had given me the same advice, and thought only of the happiness which he predicted would result from my adoption of such a course. Piety itself took part in these suggestions. I shall lead a holy and a Christian life, said I; I shall divide my time between study and religion, which will allow me no leisure for the perilous pleasures of love. I shall despise that which men ordinarily admire; and as I am conscious that my heart will desire nothing but what it can esteem, my cares will not be greater or more numerous than my wants and wishes.

I thereupon pictured to myself in anticipation a course of life peaceful and retired. I fancied a retreat embosomed in a wood, with a limpid stream of running water bounding my garden; a library, comprising the most select works; a limited circle of friends, virtuous and intellectual; a table neatly served, but frugal and temperate. To all these *agrémens* I added a literary correspondence with a friend whose residence should be in Paris, who should give me occasional information upon public affairs, less for the gratification of my curiosity, than to afford a kind of relaxation by hearing of and lamenting the busy follies of men. Shall not I be happy? added I; will not my utmost wishes be thus gratified? This project flattered my inclinations extremely. But after all the details of this most admirable and prudent plan, I felt that my heart still yearned for something; and that in order to leave nothing to desire in this most enchanting retirement, one ought to be able to share it with Manon.

However, Tiberge continuing to pay me frequent visits in order to strengthen me in the purpose with which he had inspired me, I took an opportunity of opening the subject to my father. He declared that his intention ever was to leave his children free to choose a profession, and that in whatever manner I should dispose of myself, all he wished to reserve was the right of aiding me with his counsel. On this occasion he gave me some of the wisest, which tended less to divert me from my project, than to convince me of my good father's sound judgment and discretion.

The recommencement of the scholastic year being at hand, Tiberge and I agreed to enter ourselves together at St. Sulpice, he to pursue his theological studies, and I to begin mine. His merits, which were not unknown to the bishop of the diocese, procured him the promise of a living from that prelate before our departure.

My father, thinking me quite cured of my passion, made no objection to my taking final leave. We arrived at Paris. The Cross of Malta gave place to the ecclesiastical habit, and the designation of the Abbé de Grieux was substituted for that of chevalier. I applied so diligently to study, that in a few months I had made extraordinary progress. I never lost a moment of the day, and employed even part of the night. I soon acquired such a reputation, that I was already congratulated upon the honours which I was sure of obtaining; and, without solicitation on my part, my name was inscribed on the list for a vacant benefice. Piety was by no means neglected, and I entered with ardent devotion into all the exercises of religion. Tiberge was proud of what he considered the work of his own hands, and many a time have I seen him shed tears of delight in noticing what he styled my perfect conversion.

It has never been matter of wonder to me that human resolutions are liable to change; one passion gives them birth, another may destroy them: but when I reflect upon the sacredness of those motives that led me to St. Sulpice, and upon the heartfelt satisfaction I enjoyed while obeying their dictation, I shudder at the facility with which I outraged them all. If it be true that the benign succour afforded by Heaven is at all times equal to the strongest of man's passions, I shall be glad to learn the nature of the deplorable ascendancy which causes us suddenly to swerve from the path of duty, without the power of offering the least resistance, and without even the slightest visitation of remorse.

I now thought myself entirely safe from the dangers of love. I fancied that I could have preferred a single page of St. Augustine, or a quarter of an hour of Christian meditation, to every sensual gratification, not excepting any that I might have derived even from Manon's society. Nevertheless, one unlucky moment plunged me again headlong into the gulf; and my ruin was the more irreparable, because, falling at once to the same depth from whence I had been before rescued, each of the new disorders into which I now lapsed carried me deeper and deeper still down the profound abyss of vice. I had passed nearly a year at Paris without hearing of Manon. It cost me no slight effort to abstain from inquiry; but the unintermitting advice of Tiberge, and my own reflections, secured this victory over my wishes. The last months glided away so tranquilly, that I considered the memory of this charming but treacherous creature about to be consigned to eternal oblivion.

The time arrived when I was to undergo a public examination in the class of theology: I invited several persons of consideration to honour me with their presence on the occasion. My name was mentioned in every quarter of Paris: it even reached the ears of her who had betrayed me. She had some difficulty in recognising it with the prefix of Abbé; but curiosity, or perhaps remorse for having been faithless to me (I could never after ascertain by which of these feelings she was actuated), made her at once take an interest in a name so like mine; and she came with several other women to the Sorbonne, where she was present at my examination, and had doubtless little trouble in recognising my person.

I had not the remotest suspicion of her presence. It is well known that in these places there are private seats for ladies, where they remain screened by a curtain. I returned to St. Sulpice covered with honours and congratulations. It was six in the evening. The moment I returned, a lady was announced, who desired to speak with me. I went to meet her. Heavens! what a surprise! It was Manon. It was she indeed, but more bewitching and brilliant than I had ever beheld her. She was now in her eighteenth year. Her beauty beggars all description. The exquisite grace of her form, the mild sweetness of expression that animated her features, and her engaging air, made her seem the very personification of love. The vision was something too perfect for human beauty.

I stood like one enchanted at beholding her. Unable to divine the object of her visit, I waited trembling and with downcast looks until she explained herself. At first, her embarrassment was equal to mine; but, seeing that I was not disposed to break silence, she raised her hand to her eyes to conceal a starting tear, and then, in a timid tone, said that she well knew she had justly earned my abhorrence by her infidelity; but that if I had ever really felt any love for her, there was not much kindness in allowing two long years to pass without inquiring after her, and as little now in seeing her in the state of mental distress in which she was, without condescending to bestow upon her a single word. I shall not attempt to describe what my feelings were as I listened to this reproof.

She seated herself. I remained standing, with my face half turned aside, for I could not muster courage to meet her look. I several times commenced a reply without power to conclude it. At length I made an effort, and in a tone of poignant grief exclaimed: Perfidious Manon! perfidious, perfidious creature! She had no wish, she repeated with a flood of tears, to attempt to justify her infidelity. What is your wish, then? cried I. I wish to die, she answered, if you will not give me back that heart, without which it is impossible to endure life. Take my life too, then, faithless girl! I exclaimed, in vain endeavouring to restrain my tears; take my life also! it is the sole sacrifice that remains for me to make, for my heart has never ceased to be thine.

I had hardly uttered these words, when she rose in a transport of joy, and approached to embrace me. She loaded me with a thousand caresses. She addressed me by all the endearing appellations with which love supplies his votaries, to enable them to express the most passionate fondness. I still answered with affected coldness; but the sudden transition from a state of quietude, such as that I had up to this moment enjoyed, to the agitation and tumult which were now kindled in my breast and tingled through my veins, thrilled me with a kind of horror, and impressed me with a vague sense that I was about to undergo some great transformation, and to enter upon a new existence.

We sat down close by each other. I took her hand within mine. Ah! Manon, said I, with a look of sorrow, I little thought that love like mine could have been repaid with treachery! It was a poor triumph to betray a heart of which you were the absolute mistress,—whose sole happiness it was to gratify and obey you. Tell me if among others you have found any so affectionate and so devoted? No, no! I believe nature has cast few hearts in the same mould as mine. Tell me at least whether you have ever thought of me with regret! Can I have any reliance on the duration of the feeling that has brought you back to me to-day? I perceive too plainly that you are infinitely lovelier than ever: but I conjure you by all my past sufferings, dearest Manon, to tell me,—can you in future be more faithful?

She gave me in reply such tender assurances of her repentance, and pledged her fidelity with such solemn protestations and vows, that I was inexpressibly affected. Beauteous Manon, said I, with rather a profane mixture of amorous and theological expressions, you are too adorable for a created being. I feel my heart transported with triumphant rapture. It is folly to talk of liberty at St. Sulpice. Fortune and reputation are but slight sacrifices at such a shrine! I plainly foresee it: I can read my destiny in your bright eyes; but what abundant recompense shall I not find in your affections for any loss I may sustain! The favours of fortune have no influence over me:

fame itself appears to me but a mockery; all my projects of a
holy life were wild absurdities: in fact, any joys but those I
may hope for at your side are fit objects of contempt. There
are none that would not vanish into worthlessness before one
single glance of thine!

In promising her, however, a full remission of her past frailties,
I inquired how she permitted herself to be led astray by B——.
She informed me that having seen her at her window, he became
passionately in love with her; that he made his advances in the
true style of a mercantile cit;—that is to say, by giving her to
understand in his letter, that his payments would be proportioned to her favours; that she had admitted his overtures at
first with no other intention than that of getting from him such
a sum as might enable us to live without inconvenience; but
that he had so bewildered her with splendid promises, that she
allowed herself to be misled by degrees. She added, that I
ought to have formed some notion of the remorse she experienced, by her grief on the night of our separation; and
assured me that, in spite of the splendour in which he maintained her, she had never known a moment's happiness with
him, not only, she said, because he was utterly devoid of that
delicacy of sentiment and of those agreeable manners which
I possessed, but because even in the midst of the amusements
which he unceasingly procured her, she could never shake off
the recollection of my love, or her own ingratitude. She then
spoke of Tiberge, and the extreme embarrassment his visit
caused her. A dagger's point, she added, could not have
struck more terror to my heart. I turned from him, unable to
sustain the interview for a moment.

She continued to inform me how she had been apprised of
my residence at Paris, of the change in my condition, and of
her witnessing my examination at the Sorbonne. She told me
how agitated she had been during my intellectual conflict with
the examiner; what difficulty she felt in restraining her tears
as well as her sighs, which were more than once on the point of
spurning all control, and bursting forth; that she was the last
person to leave the hall of examination, for fear of betraying
her distress, and that, following only the instinct of her own
heart, and her ardent desires, she came direct to the seminary,
with the firm resolution of surrendering life itself, if she found
me cruel enough to withhold my forgiveness.

Could any savage remain unmoved by such proofs of cordial repentance as those I had just witnessed? For my part, I felt at the moment that I could gladly have given up all the bishoprics in Christendom for Manon. I asked what course she would recommend in our present emergency. It is requisite, she replied, at all events, to quit the seminary, and settle in some safer place. I consented to everything she proposed. She got into her carriage to go and wait for me at the corner of the street. I escaped the next moment, without attracting the porter's notice. I entered the carriage, and we drove off to a Jew's. I there resumed my lay-dress and sword. Manon furnished the supplies, for I was without a sou, and fearing that I might meet with some new impediment, she would not consent to my returning to my room at St. Sulpice for my purse. My finances were in truth wretchedly low, and hers more than sufficiently enriched by the liberality of M. de B—— to make her think lightly of my loss. We consulted together at the Jew's as to the course we should now adopt.

In order to enhance the sacrifice she had made for me of her late lover, she determined to treat him without the least ceremony. I shall leave him all his furniture, she said; it belongs to him: but I shall assuredly carry off, as I have a right to do, the jewels, and about sixty thousand francs, which I have had from him in the last two years. I have given him no control over me, she added, so that we may remain without apprehension in Paris, taking a convenient house, where we shall live, oh how happily together!

I represented to her that, although there might be no danger for her, there was a great deal for me, who must be sooner or later infallibly recognised, and continually exposed to a repetition of the trials I had before endured. She gave me to understand that she could not quit Paris without regret. I had such a dread of giving her annoyance, that there were no risks I would not have encountered for her sake. However, we compromised matters by resolving to take a house in some village near Paris, from whence it would be easy for us to come into town whenever pleasure or business required it. We fixed on Chaillot, which is at a convenient distance. Manon at once returned to her house, and I went to wait for her at a side-gate of the garden of the Tuileries.

She returned an hour after, in a hired carriage, with a servant-maid, and several trunks, which contained her dresses, and everything she had of value.

We were not long on our way to Chaillot. We lodged the first night at the inn, in order to have time to find a suitable house, or at least a commodious lodging. We found one to our taste the next morning.

My happiness now appeared to be secured beyond the reach of fate. Manon was everything most sweet and amiable. She was so delicate and so unceasing in her attentions to me, that I deemed myself but too bountifully rewarded for all my past troubles. As we had both, by this time, acquired some experience, we discussed rationally the state of our finances. Sixty thousand francs (the amount of our wealth) was not a sum that could be expected to last our whole life; besides, we were neither of us much disposed to control our expenses. Manon's chief virtue assuredly was not economy, any more than it was mine. This was my proposition. Sixty thousand francs, said I, may support us for ten years. Two thousand crowns a year will suffice, if we continue to live at Chaillot. We shall keep up appearances, but live frugally. Our only expense will be occasionally a carriage, and the theatres. We shall do everything in moderation. You like the opera; we shall go twice a week, in the season. As for play, we shall limit ourselves; so that our losses must never exceed three crowns. It is impossible but that in the space of ten years some change must occur in my family: my father is even now of an advanced age; he may die; in which event I must inherit a fortune, and we shall then be above all other fears.

This arrangement would not have been by any means the most silly act of my life, if we had only been prudent enough to persevere in its execution; but our resolutions hardly lasted longer than a month. Manon's passion was for amusement; she was the only object of mine. New temptations to expense constantly presented themselves, and far from regretting the money which she sometimes prodigally lavished, I was the first to procure for her everything likely to afford her pleasure. Our residence at Chaillot began even to appear tiresome.

Winter was approaching, and the whole world returning to town; the country had a deserted look. She proposed to me to take a house in Paris. I did not approve of this; but, in order partly at least to satisfy her, I said that we might hire furnished apartments, and that we might sleep there whenever we were late in quitting the assembly, whither we often went; for the inconvenience of returning so late to Chaillot was her excuse for wishing to leave it. We had thus two dwellings, one in town and the other in the country. This change soon threw our affairs into confusion, and led to two adventures, which eventually caused our ruin.

Manon had a brother in the Guards. He unfortunately lived in the very street in which we had taken lodgings. He one day recognised his sister at the window, and hastened over to us. He was a fellow of the rudest manners, and without the slightest principle of honour. He entered the room swearing in the most horrible way; and as he knew part of his sister's history, he loaded her with abuse and reproaches.

I had gone out the moment before, which was doubtless fortunate for either him or me, for I was little disposed to brook an insult. I only returned to the lodgings after he had left them. The low spirits in which I found Manon convinced me at once that something extraordinary had occurred. She told me of the provoking scene she had just gone through, and of the brutal threats of her brother. I felt such indignation, that I wished to proceed at once to avenge her, when she entreated me with tears to desist.

While we were still talking of the adventure, the guardsman again entered the room in which we sat, without even waiting to be announced. Had I known him, he should not have met from me as civil a reception as he did; but saluting us with a smile upon his countenance, he addressed himself to Manon, and said, he was come to make excuses for his violence; that he had supposed her to be living a life of shame and disgrace, and it was this notion that excited his rage; but having since made inquiry from one of our servants, he had learned such a character of me, that his only wish was now to be on terms with us both.

Although this admission, of having gone for information to one of my own servants, had in it something ludicrous as well as indelicate, I acknowledged his compliments with civility. I thought by doing so to please Manon, and I was not deceived—she was delighted at the reconciliation. We made him stay to dine with us.

In a little time he became so familiar, that hearing us speak of our return to Chaillot, he insisted on accompanying us. We were obliged to give him a seat in our carriage. This was in fact putting him into possession, for he soon began to feel so much pleasure in our company, that he made our house his home, and made himself in some measure master of all that belonged to us. He called me his brother, and, under the semblance of fraternal freedom, he put himself on such a footing as to introduce all his friends without ceremony into our house at Chaillot, and there entertain them at our expense. His magnificent uniforms were procured of my tailor and charged to me, and he even contrived to make Manon and me responsible for all his debts. I pretended to be blind to this system of tyranny, rather than annoy Manon, and even to take no notice of the sums of money which from time to time he received from her. No doubt, as he played very deep, he was honest enough to repay her a part sometimes, when luck turned in his favour; but our finances were utterly inadequate to supply, for any length of time, demands of such magnitude and frequency.

I was on the point of coming to an understanding with him, in order to put an end to the system, when an unfortunate accident saved me that trouble, by involving us in inextricable ruin.

One night we stopped in Paris to sleep, as it had now indeed become our constant habit. The servant-maid who on such occasions remained alone at Chaillot, came early the next morning to inform me that our house had taken fire in the night, and that the flames had been extinguished with great difficulty. I asked whether the furniture had suffered. She answered, that there had been such confusion, owing to the multitude of strangers who came to offer assistance, that she could hardly ascertain what damage had been done. I was principally uneasy about our money, which had been locked up in a little box. I went off in haste to Chaillot. Vain hope! the box had disappeared!

I discovered that one could love money without being a miser. This loss afflicted me to such a degree that I was almost out of my mind. I saw at one glance to what new calamities I should be exposed: poverty was the least of them. I knew Manon thoroughly; I had already had abundant proof that, although faithful and attached to me under happier circumstances, she could not be depended upon in want: pleasure and plenty she loved too well to sacrifice them for my sake. I shall lose her! I cried; miserable chevalier! you are about then to lose all that you love on earth! This thought agitated me to such a degree that I actually for some moments considered whether it would not be best for me to end at once all my miseries by death. I however preserved presence of mind enough to reflect whether I was entirely without resource, and an idea occurred to me which quieted my despair. It would not be impossible, I thought, to conceal our loss from Manon; and I might perhaps discover some ways and means of supplying her, so as to ward off the inconveniences of poverty.

I had calculated, in endeavouring to comfort myself, that twenty thousand crowns would support us for ten years. Suppose that these ten years had now elapsed, and that none of the events which I had looked for in my family had occurred. What then would have been my course? I hardly know; but whatever I should then have done, why may I not do now? How many are there in Paris, who have neither my talents, nor the natural advantages I possess, and who, notwithstanding, owe their support to the exercise of their talents, such as they are.

Has not Providence, I added, while reflecting on the different conditions of life, arranged things wisely? The greater number of the powerful and the rich are fools. No one who knows anything of the world can doubt that. How admirable is the compensating justice thereof! If wealth brought with it talent also, the rich would be too happy, and other men too wretched. To these latter are given personal advantages and genius, to help them out of misery and want. Some of them share the riches of the wealthy by administering to their pleasures, or by making them their dupes; others afford them instruction, and endeavour to make them decent members of society; to be sure, they do not always succeed; but that was probably not the intention of the divine wisdom. In every case they derive a benefit from their labours by living at the expense of their pupils; and, in whatever point of view it is considered, the follies of the rich are a bountiful source of revenue to the humbler classes.

These thoughts restored me a little to my spirits and to my reason. I determined first to consult M. Lescaut, the brother of Manon. He knew Paris perfectly; and I had too many opportunities of learning that it was neither from his own estates, nor from the king's pay, that he derived the principal portion of his income. I had about thirty-three crowns left, which I fortunately happened to have about me. I showed him my purse, and explained to him my misfortune and my fears, and then asked him whether I had any alternative between starvation and blowing out my brains in despair. He coolly replied that suicide was the resource of fools. As to dying of want, there were hundreds of men of genius who found themselves reduced to that state when they would not employ their talents; that it was for myself to discover what I was capable of doing, and he told me to reckon upon his assistance and his advice in any enterprise I might undertake.

Vague enough, M. Lescaut! said I to him: my wants demand a more speedy remedy; for what am I to say to Manon? Apropos of Manon, replied he, what is it that annoys you about her? Cannot you always find in her wherewithal to meet your wants, when you wish it? Such a person ought to support us all, you and me as well as herself. He cut short the answer which I was about to give to such unfeeling and brutal impertinence, by going on to say, that before night he would ensure me a thousand crowns to divide between us, if I would only follow his advice; that he was acquainted with a nobleman, who was so liberal in affairs of the kind, that he was certain he would not hesitate for a moment to give the sum named for the favours of such a girl as Manon.

I stopped him. I had a better opinion of you, said I; I had imagined that your motive for bestowing your friendship upon me was very different indeed from the one you now betray. With the greatest effrontery he acknowledged that he had been always of the same mind, and that his sister having once sacrificed her virtue, though it might be to the man she most loved, he would never have consented to a reconciliation with her, but with the hope of deriving some advantage from her past misconduct.

It was easy to see that we had been hitherto his dupes. Notwithstanding the disgust with which his proposition inspired me, still, as I felt that I had occasion for his services, I said, with apparent complacency, that we ought only to entertain such a plan as a last resource. I begged of him to suggest some other.

He proposed to me to turn my youth and the good looks nature had bestowed upon me to some account, by establishing a liaison with some generous old dame. This was just as little to my taste, for it would necessarily have rendered me unfaithful to Manon.

I mentioned play as the easiest scheme, and the most suitable to my present situation. He admitted that play certainly was a resource, but that it was necessary to consider the point well. Mere play, said he, with its ordinary chances, is the certain road to ruin; and as for attempting, alone and without an ally, to employ the little means an adroit man has for correcting the vagaries of luck, it would be too dangerous an experiment. There was, he stated, a third course, which was to enter into what he called a partnership; but he feared his confederates would consider my youth an objection to my admittance. He, however, promised to use his influence with them; and, what was more than I expected at his hands, he said that he would supply me with a little money whenever I had pressing occasion for any. The only favour I then asked of him was to say nothing to Manon of the loss I had experienced, nor of the subject of our conversation.

I certainly derived little comfort from my visit to Lescaut; I felt even sorry for having confided my secret to him: not a single thing had he done for me that I might not just as well have done for myself, without troubling him; and I could not help dreading that he would violate his promise to keep the secret from Manon. I had also reason to apprehend, from his late avowals, that he might form the design of making use of her for his own vile purposes, or at least of advising her to quit me for some happier and more wealthy lover. This idea brought in its train a thousand reflections, which had no other effect than to torment me, and throw me again into the state of despair in which I had passed the morning. It occurred to me, more than once, to write to my father; and to pretend a new reformation, in order to obtain some pecuniary assistance from him; but I could not forget that, notwithstanding all his natural love and affection for me, he had shut me up for six months in a confined room for my first transgression; and I was certain that, after the scandalous sensation caused by my flight from St. Sulpice, he would be sure to treat me with infinitely more rigour now.

At length, out of this chaos of fancies came an idea that all at once restored ease to my mind, and which I was surprised at not having hit upon sooner: this was, to go again to my friend Tiberge, in whom I might be always sure of finding the same unfailing zeal and friendship. There is nothing more glorious —nothing that does more honour to true virtue, than the confidence with which one approaches a friend of tried integrity; no apprehension, no risk of unkind repulse: if it be not always in his power to afford the required succour, one is sure at least of meeting kindness and compassion. The heart of the poor supplicant, which remains impenetrably closed to the rest of the world, opens in his presence, as a flower expands before the orb of day, from which it instinctively knows it can derive a cheering and benign influence only.

I consider it a blessing to have thought so apropos of Tiberge, and resolved to take measures to find him before evening. I returned at once to my lodgings to write him a line, and fix a convenient place for our meeting. I requested secrecy and discretion, as the most important service he could render me under present circumstances.

The pleasure I derived from the prospect of seeing Tiberge dissipated every trace of melancholy, which Manon would not have failed otherwise to detect in my countenance. I described our misfortune at Chaillot as a trifle which ought not to annoy her; and Paris being the spot she liked best in the world, she was not sorry to hear me say that it would be necessary for us to remain there entirely, until the little damage was repaired which had been caused by the fire at Chaillot.

In an hour I received an answer from Tiberge, who promised to be at the appointed rendezvous. I went there punctually. I certainly felt some shame at encountering a friend whose presence alone ought to be a reproach to my iniquities; but I was supported by the opinion I had of the goodness of his heart, as well as by my anxiety about Manon.

I had begged of him to meet me in the garden of the Palais Royal. He was there before me. He hastened towards me, the moment he saw me approach, and shook me warmly by both hands. I said that I could not help feeling perfectly ashamed to meet him, and that I was weighed down by a sense of my ingratitude; that the first thing I implored of him was to tell me whether I might still consider him my friend, after having so justly incurred the loss of his esteem and affection. He replied, in the kindest possible manner, that it was not in the nature of things to destroy his regard for me; that my misfortunes even, or, if he might so call them, my faults and transgressions, had but increased the interest he felt for me; but that he must confess his affection was not unalloyed by a sentiment of the liveliest sorrow, such as a person may be supposed to feel at seeing a beloved object on the brink of ruin, and beyond the reach of his assistance.

We sat down upon a bench. Alas! said I with a deep sigh, your compassion must be indeed great, my dear Tiberge, if you assure me it is equal to my sufferings. I am almost ashamed to recount them, for I confess they have been brought on by no very creditable course of conduct: the results, however, are so truly melancholy, that a friend even less attached than you would be affected by the recital.

He then begged of me, in proof of friendship, to let him know, without any disguise, all that had occurred to me since my departure from St. Sulpice. I gratified him; and so far from concealing anything, or attempting to extenuate my faults, I spoke of my passion with all the ardour with which it still inspired me. I represented it to him as one of those especial visitations of fate, which draw on the devoted victim to his ruin, and which it is as impossible for virtue itself to resist, as for human wisdom to foresee. I painted to him in the most vivid colours, my excitement, my fears, the state of despair in which I had been two hours before I saw him, and into which I should be again plunged, if I found my friends as relentless as fate had been. I at length made such an impression upon poor Tiberge, that I saw he was as much affected by compassion, as I by the recollection of my sufferings.

He took my hand, and exhorted me to have courage and be comforted; but, as he seemed to consider it settled that Manon and I were to separate, I gave him at once to understand that it was that very separation I considered as the most intolerable of all my misfortunes; and that I was ready to endure not only the last degree of misery, but death itself, of the cruellest kind, rather than seek relief in a remedy worse than the whole accumulation of my woes.

Explain yourself, then, said he to me; what assistance can I afford you, if you reject everything I propose? I had not

courage to tell him that it was from his purse I wanted relief.
He, however, comprehended it in the end; and acknowledging
that he believed he now understood me, he remained for a
moment in an attitude of thought, with the air of a person
revolving something in his mind. Do not imagine, he presently
said, that my hesitation arises from any diminution of my zeal
and friendship; but to what an alternative do you now reduce
me, since I must either refuse you the assistance you ask, or
violate my most sacred duty in affording it! For is it not
participating in your sin to furnish you with the means of
continuing its indulgence?

However, continued he, after a moment's thought, it is perhaps
the excited state into which want has thrown you, that denies
you now the liberty of choosing the proper path. Man's mind
must be at rest, to know the luxury of wisdom and virtue. I
can afford to let you have some money; and permit me, my dear
chevalier, to impose but one condition; that is, that you let me
know the place of your abode, and allow me the opportunity of
using my exertions to reclaim you. I know that there is in
your heart a love of virtue, and that you have been only led
astray by the violence of your passions.

I, of course, agreed to everything he asked, and only begged
of him to deplore the malign destiny which rendered me callous
to the counsels of so virtuous a friend. He then took me to a
banker of his acquaintance, who gave one hundred and seventy
crowns for his note of hand, which was taken as cash. I have
already said that he was not rich. His living was worth about
six thousand francs a year, but as this was the first year since
his induction, he had as yet touched none of the receipts, and
it was out of the future income that he made me this advance.

I felt the full force of his generosity, even to such a degree
as almost to deplore the fatal passion which thus led me to
break through all the restraints of duty. Virtue had for a
moment the ascendancy in my heart, and made me sensible of
my shame and degradation. But this was soon over. For
Manon I could have given up my hopes of heaven, and when
I again found myself at her side, I wondered how I could for
an instant have considered myself degraded by my passion for
this enchanting girl.

Manon was a creature of most extraordinary disposition.
Never had mortal a greater contempt for money, and yet she

was haunted by perpetual dread of wanting it. Her only desire was for pleasure and amusement. She would never have wished to possess a sou, if pleasure could be procured without money. She never even cared what our purse contained, provided she could pass the day agreeably; so that, being neither fond of play nor at all dazzled by the desire of great wealth, nothing was more easy than to satisfy her, by daily finding out amusements suited to her moderate wishes. But it became by habit a thing so absolutely necessary for her to have her mind thus occupied, that, without it, it was impossible to exercise the smallest influence over her temper or inclinations. Although she loved me tenderly, and I was the only person, as she often declared, in whose society she could ever find the pure enjoyments of love, yet I felt thoroughly convinced that her attachment could not withstand certain apprehensions. She would have preferred me, even with a moderate fortune, to the whole world; but I had no kind of doubt that she would, on the other hand, abandon me for some new M. de B——, when I had nothing more to offer her than fidelity and love.

I resolved therefore so to curtail my own individual expenses, as to be able always to meet hers, and rather to deprive myself of a thousand necessaries than even to limit her extravagance. The carriage made me more uneasy than anything else, for I saw no chance of being able to maintain either coachman or horses.

I told M. Lescaut of my difficulties, and did not conceal from him that I had received a thousand francs from a friend. He repeated, that if I wished to try the chances of the gaming-table, he was not without hopes that, by spending a few crowns in entertaining his associates, I might be, on his recommendation, admitted into the association. With all my repugnance to cheating, I yielded to dire necessity.

Lescaut presented me that night as a relation of his own. He added, that I was the more likely to succeed in my new profession, from wanting the favours of fortune. However, to show them that I was not quite reduced to the lowest ebb, he said it was my intention to treat them with a supper. The offer was accepted, and I entertained them *en prince*. They talked a good deal about my fashionable appearance and the apparent amiability of my disposition; they said that the best hopes might be entertained of me, because there was something in my countenance that bespoke the gentleman, and no one therefore could have a suspicion of my honesty: they voted thanks to Lescaut for having introduced so promising a novice, and deputed one of the members to instruct me for some days in the necessary manœuvres.

The principal scene of my exploits was the hotel of Transylvania, where there was a faro table in one room, and other games of cards and dice in the gallery. This *academy* was kept by the Prince of R——, who then lived at Clagny, and most of his officers belonged to our society. Shall I mention it to my shame? I profited quickly by my instructor's tuition. I acquired an amazing facility in sleight of hand tricks, and learned in perfection to *sauter le coup*; with the help of a pair of long ruffles, I shuffled so adroitly as to defy the quickest observer, and I ruined several fair players. My unrivalled skill so quickened the progress of my fortunes, that I found myself master, in a few weeks, of very considerable sums, besides what I divided in good faith with my companions.

I had no longer any fear of communicating to Manon the extent of our loss at Chaillot, and, to console her on the announcement of such disastrous news, I took a furnished house, where we established ourselves in all the pride of opulence and security.

Tiberge was in the habit, at this period, of paying me frequent visits. He was never tired of his moral lectures. Over and over again did he represent to me the injury I was inflicting upon my conscience, my honour, and my fortune. I received all his advice kindly, and although I had not the smallest inclination to adopt it, I had no doubt of its sincerity, for I knew its source. Sometimes I rallied him good-humouredly, and entreated him not to be more tight-laced than some other priests were, and even bishops, who by no means considered a mistress incompatible with a good and holy life. Look, I said, at Manon's eyes, and tell me if there is one in the long catalogue of sins that might not there find a plea of justification. He bore these sallies patiently, and carried his forbearance almost too far: but when he saw my funds increase, and that I had not only returned him the hundred and seventy crowns, but having hired a new house and trebled my expenses, I had plunged deeper than ever into a life of pleasure, he changed his tone and manner towards me. He lamented my obduracy

He warned me against the chastisement of the Divine wrath, and predicted some of the miseries with which indeed I was shortly afterwards visited. It is impossible, he said, that the money which now serves to support your debaucheries can have been acquired honourably. You have come by it unjustly, and in the same way shall it be taken from you. The most awful punishment Heaven could inflict would be to allow you the undisturbed enjoyment of it. All my advice, he added, has been useless; I too plainly perceive that it will shortly become troublesome to you. I now take my leave; you are a weak, as well as an ungrateful friend! May your criminal enjoyments vanish as a shadow! may your ill-gotten wealth leave you without a resource; and may you yourself remain alone and deserted, to learn the vanity of these things, which now divert you from better pursuits! When that time arrives, you will find me disposed to love and to serve you; this day ends our intercourse, and I once for all avow my horror of the life you are leading.

It was in my room and in Manon's presence that he delivered this apostolical harangue. He rose to depart. I was about to detain him; but was prevented by Manon, who said it was better to let the madman go.

What he said, however, did not fail to make some impression upon me. I notice these brief passages of my life when I experienced a returning sentiment of virtue, because it was to those traces, however light, that I was afterwards indebted for whatever of fortitude I displayed under the most trying circumstances.

Manon's caresses soon dissipated the annoyance this scene had caused me. We continued to lead a life entirely devoted to pleasure and love. The increase of our wealth only redoubled our affection. There were none happier among all the devotees of Venus and Fortune. Heavens! why call this a world of misery, when it can furnish a life of such rapturous enjoyment? But alas, it is too soon over! For what ought man to sigh, could such felicity but last for ever? Ours shared the common fate—in being of short duration, and followed by lasting regrets.

I had realised by play such a considerable sum of money, that I thought of investing a portion of it. My servants were not ignorant of my good luck, particularly my valet and Manon's own maid, before whom we often talked without any reserve.

The maid was handsome, and my valet in love with her. They knew they had to deal with a young and inexperienced couple, whom they fancied they could impose upon without much difficulty. They laid a plan, and executed it with so much skill, that they reduced us to a state from which it was never afterwards possible for us to extricate ourselves.

Having supped one evening at Lescaut's, it was about midnight when we returned home. I asked for my valet, and Manon for her maid; neither one nor the other could be found. They had not been seen in the house since eight o'clock, and had gone out, after having some cases carried before them, according to orders which they pretended to have received from me. I at once foresaw a part of the truth, but my suspicions were infinitely surpassed by what presented itself on going into my room. The lock of my closet had been forced, and my cash as well as my best clothes were gone. While I stood stupefied with amazement, Manon came, in the greatest alarm, to inform me that her apartment had been rifled in the same manner.

This blow was so perfectly astounding, so cruel, that it was with difficulty I could refrain from tears. The dread of infecting Manon with my despair made me assume a more contented air. I said, smiling, that I should avenge myself upon some unhappy dupe at the hotel of Transylvania. However, she appeared so sensibly affected, that her grief increased my sorrow infinitely more than my attempt succeeded in supporting her spirits. We are destroyed! said she, with tears in her eyes. I endeavoured, in vain, by my entreaties and caresses, to console her. My own lamentations betrayed my distress and despair. In fact, we were so completely ruined, that we were bereft almost of decent covering.

I determined to send off at once for Lescaut. He advised me to go immediately to the lieutenant of police, and to give information also to the Grand Provost of Paris. I went, but it was to add to my calamities only; for, independently of my visit producing not the smallest good effect, I, by my absence, allowed Lescaut time for discussion with his sister, during which he did not fail to inspire her with the most horrible resolutions. He spoke to her about M. G—— M——, an old voluptuary, who paid prodigally for his pleasures; he so glowingly described the advantages of such a connection, that she entered into all his plans. This discreditable arrangement was all concluded before my return, and the execution of it only postponed till the next morning, after Lescaut should have apprised G—— M——.

I found him, on my return, waiting for me at my house; but Manon had retired to her own apartment, and she had desired the footman to tell me that, having need of repose, she hoped she should not be disturbed that night. Lescaut left me, after offering me a few crowns, which I accepted.

It was nearly four o'clock when I retired to bed; and having revolved in my mind various schemes for retrieving my fortunes, I fell asleep so late that I did not awake till between eleven and twelve o'clock. I rose at once to inquire after Manon's health; they told me that she had gone out an hour before with her brother, who had come for her in a hired carriage. Although there appeared something mysterious in such a proceeding, I endeavoured to check my rising suspicions. I allowed some hours to pass, during which I amused myself with reading. At length, being unable any longer to stifle my uneasiness, I paced up and down the apartments. A sealed letter upon Manon's table at last caught my eye. It was addressed to me, and in her handwriting. I felt my blood freeze as I opened it; it was in these words:

I protest to you, dearest chevalier, that you are the idol of my heart, and that you are the only being on earth whom I can truly love; but do you not see, my own poor dear chevalier, that in the situation to which we are now reduced, fidelity would be worse than madness? Do you think tenderness possibly compatible with starvation? For my part, hunger would be sure to drive me to some fatal end. Heaving some day a sigh for love, I should find it was my last. I adore you, rely upon that; but leave to me, for a short while, the management of our fortunes. God help the man who falls into my hands. My only wish is to render my chevalier rich and happy. My brother will tell you about me; he can vouch for my grief in yielding to the necessity of parting from you.

I remained, after reading this, in a state which it would be difficult to describe; for even now I know not the nature of the feelings which then agitated me. It was one of those unique situations of which others can never have experienced anything even approaching to similarity. It is impossible to explain it, because other persons can have no idea of its nature; and one can hardly even analyse it to oneself. Memory furnishes nothing that will connect it with the past, and therefore ordinary language is inadequate to describe it. Whatever was its nature, however, it is certain that grief, hate, jealousy, and shame entered into its composition. Fortunate would it have proved for me if love also had not been a component part!

That she loves me, I exclaimed, I can believe; but could she, without being a monster, hate me? What right can man ever have to woman's affections which I had not to Manon's? What is left to me, after all the sacrifices I have made for her sake? Yet she abandons me, and the ungrateful creature thinks to screen herself from my reproaches by professions of love! She pretends to dread starvation! God of love, what grossness of sentiment! What an answer to the refinement of my adoration! I had no dread of that kind; I, who have almost sought starvation for her sake, by renouncing fortune and the comforts of my father's house! I, who denied myself actual necessaries, in order to gratify her little whims and caprices! She adores me, she says. If you adored me, ungrateful creature, I well know what course you would have taken; you would never have quitted me, at least without saying adieu. It is only I who can tell the pangs and torments of being separated from all one loves. I must have taken leave of my senses, to have voluntarily brought all this misery upon myself.

My lamentations were interrupted by a visit I little expected; it was from Lescaut. Assassin! cried I, putting my hand upon my sword, where is Manon? what have you done with her? My agitation startled him. He replied, that if this was the reception he was to meet, when he came to offer me the most essential service it was in his power to render me, he should take his leave, and never again cross my threshold. I ran to the door of the apartment, which I shut. Do not imagine, I said, turning towards him, that you can once more make a dupe of me with your lies and inventions. Either defend your life, or tell me where I can find Manon. How impatient you are! replied he; that was in reality the object of my visit. I came to announce a piece of good fortune which you little expected, and for which you will probably feel somewhat grateful. My curiosity was at once excited.

He informed me that Manon, totally unable to endure the dread of want, and, above all, the certainty of being at once obliged to dispense with her equipage, had begged of him to make her acquainted with M. G—— M——, who had a character for liberality. He carefully avoided telling me that this was the result of his own advice, and that he had prepared the way before he introduced his sister. I took her there this morning, said he, and the fellow was so enchanted with her looks that he at once invited her to accompany him to his country seat, where he is gone to pass some days. As I plainly perceived, said Lescaut, the advantage it may be to you, I took care to let him know that she had lately experienced very considerable losses; and I so piqued his generosity that he began by giving her four hundred crowns. I told him that was well enough for a commencement, but that my sister would have, for the future, many demands for money; that she had the charge of a young brother, who had been thrown upon her hands since the death of our parents; and that, if he wished to prove himself worthy of her affections, he would not allow her to suffer uneasiness upon account of this child, whom she regarded as part of herself. This speech produced its effect; he at once promised to take a house for you and Manon, for you must know that you are the poor little orphan. He undertook to set you up in furniture, and to give you four hundred livres a month, which if I calculate rightly, will amount to four thousand eight hundred per annum. He left orders with his steward to look out for a house, and to have it in readiness by the time he returned. You will soon, therefore, again see Manon, who begged of me to give you a thousand tender messages, and to assure you that she loves you more dearly than ever.

CHAPTER V

Infected with that leprosy of lust,
Which taints the hoariest years of vicious men;
Making them ransack to the very last
The dregs of pleasure for their vanish'd joys.

BYRON.

ON sitting down to reflect upon this strange turn of fate, I found myself so perplexed, and consequently so incapable of arriving at any rational conclusion, that I allowed Lescaut to put repeated questions to me without in the slightest degree attending to their purport. It was then that honour and virtue made me feel the most poignant remorse, and that I recalled with bitterness Amiens, my father's house, St. Sulpice, and every spot where I had ever lived in happy innocence. By what a terrific interval was I now separated from that blessed state! I beheld it no longer but as a dim shadow in the distance, still attracting my regrets and desires, but without the power of rousing me to exertion. By what fatality, said I, have I become thus degraded? Love is not a guilty passion! why then has it been to me the source of profligacy and distress? Who prevented me from leading a virtuous and tranquil life with Manon? Why did I not marry her before I obtained any concession from her love? Would not my father, who had the tenderest regard for me, have given his consent, if I had taken the fair and candid course of soliciting him? Yes, my father would himself have cherished her as one far too good to be his son's wife! I should have been happy in the love of Manon, in the affection of my father, in the esteem of the world, with a moderate portion of the good things of life, and above all with the consciousness of virtue. Disastrous change! Into what an infamous character is it here proposed that I should sink? To share—— But can I hesitate, if Manon herself suggests it, and if I am to lose her except upon such conditions? Lescaut, said I, putting my hands to my eyes as if to shut out such a horrifying vision, if your intention was to render me a service,

49

I give you thanks. You might perhaps have struck out a more reputable course, but it is so settled, is it not? Let us then only think of profiting by your labour, and fulfilling your engagements.

Lescaut, who had been considerably embarrassed, not only by my fury, but by the long silence which followed it, was too happy to see me now take a course so different from what he had anticipated. He had not a particle of courage, of which indeed I have, in the sequel of my story, abundant proof. Yes, yes, he quickly answered, it is good service I have rendered you, and you will find that we shall derive infinitely more advantage from it than you now expect. We consulted then as to the best mode of preventing the suspicions which G—— M—— might entertain of our relationship, when he found me older and of riper manhood than he probably imagined. The only plan we could hit upon was to assume in his presence an innocent and provincial air, and to persuade him that it was my intention to enter the Church, and that with that view I was obliged to go every day to the college. We also determined that I should appear as awkward as I possibly could the first time I was admitted to the honour of an introduction.

He returned to town three or four days after, and at once conducted Manon to the house which his steward had in the meantime prepared. She immediately apprised Lescaut of her return, and he having informed me, we went together to her new abode. The old lover had already gone out.

In spite of the submission with which I had resigned myself to her wishes, I could not, at our meeting, repress the compunctious visitings of my conscience. I appeared before her grieved and dejected. The joy I felt at seeing her once more could not altogether dispel my sorrow for her infidelity: she, on the contrary, appeared transported with the pleasure of seeing me. She accused me of coldness. I could not help muttering the words perfidious and unfaithful, though they were profusely mixed with sighs.

At first she laughed at me for my simplicity; but when she found that I continued to look at her with an unchanging expression of melancholy, and that I could not bring myself to enter with alacrity into a scene so repugnant to all my feelings, she went alone into her boudoir. I very soon followed her, and then I found her in a flood of tears. I asked the cause of her sorrow.

You can easily understand it, said she; how can you wish me to live, if my presence can no longer have any other effect than to give you an air of sadness and chagrin? Not one kiss have you given me during the long hour you have been in the house, while you have received my caresses with the dignified indifference of a Grand Turk, receiving the forced homage of the Sultanas of his harem.

Hearken to me, Manon, said I, embracing her; I cannot conceal from you that my heart is bitterly afflicted. I do not now allude to the uneasiness your sudden flight caused me, nor to the unkindness of quitting me without a word of consolation, after having passed the night away from me. The pleasure of seeing you again would more than compensate for all; but do you imagine that I can reflect without sighs and tears upon the degrading and unhappy life which you now wish me to lead in this house? Say nothing of my birth, or of my feelings of honour; love like mine derives no aid from arguments of that feeble nature; but do you imagine that I can without emotion see my love so badly recompensed, or rather so cruelly treated, by an ungrateful and unfeeling mistress?

She interrupted me. Stop, chevalier, said she, it is useless to torture me with reproaches, which, coming from you, always pierce my heart. I see what annoys you. I had hoped that you would have agreed to the project which I had devised for mending our shattered fortunes, and it was from a feeling of delicacy to you that I began the execution of it without your assistance; but I give it up since it does not meet your approbation. She added that she would now merely request a little patient forbearance during the remainder of the day; that she had already received five hundred crowns from the old gentleman, and that he had promised to bring her that evening a magnificent pearl necklace with other jewels, and, in advance, half of the yearly pension he had engaged to allow her. Leave me only time enough, said she to me, to get possession of these presents; I promise you that he will have little to boast of from his connection with me, for in the country I repulsed all his advances, putting him off till our return to town. It is true that he has kissed my hand a thousand times over, and it is but just that he should pay for even this amusement: I am sure that, considering his riches as well as his age, five or six thousand francs is not an unreasonable price!

Her determination was of more value in my eyes than twenty thousand crowns. I could feel that I was not yet bereft of every sentiment of honour, by the satisfaction I experienced at escaping thus from infamy. But I was born for brief joys, and miseries of long duration. Fate never rescued me from one precipice, but to lead me to another. When I had expressed my delight to Manon at this change in her intentions, I told her she had better inform Lescaut of it, in order that we might take our measures in concert. At first he murmured, but the money in hand induced him to enter into our views. It was then determined that we should all meet at G—— M——'s supper table, and that, for two reasons: first, for the amusement of passing me off as a schoolboy, and brother to Manon; and secondly, to prevent the old profligate from taking any liberties with his mistress, on the strength of his liberal payments in advance. Lescaut and I were to retire, when he went to the room where he expected to pass the night; and Manon, instead of following him, promised to come out, and join us. Lescaut undertook to have a coach waiting at the door.

The supper hour having arrived, M. G—— M—— made his appearance. Already Lescaut was with his sister in the supper room. The moment the lover entered, he presented his fair one with a complete set of pearls, necklaces, ear-rings, and bracelets, which must have cost at least a thousand crowns. He then placed on the table before her, in louis d'or, two thousand four hundred francs, the half of her year's allowance. He seasoned his present with many pretty speeches in the true style of the old court. Manon could not refuse him a few kisses: it was sealing her right to the money which he had just handed to her. I was at the door, and waiting for Lescaut's signal to enter the room.

He approached to take me by the hand, while Manon was securing the money and jewels, and leading me towards M. G—— M——, he desired me to make my bow. I made two or three most profound ones. Pray excuse him, sir, said Lescaut, he is a mere child. He has not yet acquired much of the *ton* of Paris; but no doubt with a little trouble we shall improve him. You will often have the honour of seeing that gentleman, here, said he, turning towards me: take advantage of it, and endeavour to imitate so good a model.

The old libertine appeared to be pleased with me. He patted

me on the cheek, saying that I was a fine boy, but that I should
be on my guard in Paris, where young men were easily debauched.
Lescaut assured him that I was naturally of so grave a character
that I thought of nothing but becoming a clergyman, and that,
even as a child, my favourite amusement was building little
chapels. I fancy a likeness to Manon, said the old gentleman,
putting his hand under my chin. I answered him, with the
most simple air,—Sir, the fact is, that we are very closely
connected, and I love my sister as another portion of myself.
Do you hear that, said he to Lescaut; he is indeed a clever boy!
It is a pity he should not see something of the world. Oh, sir,
I replied, I have seen a great deal of it at home, attending church,
and I believe I might find in Paris some greater fools than myself.
Listen! said he; it is positively wonderful in a boy from the
country.

The whole conversation during supper was of the same kind.
Manon, with her usual gaiety, was several times on the point
of spoiling the joke by her bursts of laughter. I contrived,
while eating, to recount his own identical history, and to paint
even the fate that awaited him. Lescaut and Manon were in
an agony of fear during my recital, especially while I was drawing his portrait to the life: but his own vanity prevented him
from recognising it, and I did it so well that he was the first to
pronounce it extremely laughable. You will allow that I had
reason for dwelling on this ridiculous scene.

At length it was time to retire. He hinted at the impatience
of love. Lescaut and I took our departure. G—— M—— went
to his room, and Manon, making some excuse for her absence,
came to join us at the gate. The coach, that was waiting for
us a few doors off, drove up towards us, and we were out of the
street in an instant.

Although I must confess that this proceeding appeared to me
little short of actual robbery, it was not the most dishonest
one with which I thought I had to reproach myself. I had more
scruples about the money which I had won at play. However,
we derived as little advantage from one as from the other; and
Heaven sometimes ordains that the lightest fault shall meet
the severest punishment.

M. G—— M—— was not long in finding out that he had been
duped. I am not sure whether he took any steps that night
to discover us, but he had influence enough to ensure an effectual

pursuit, and we were sufficiently imprudent to rely upon the extent of Paris and the distance between our residence and his. Not only did he discover our abode and our circumstances, but also who I was—the life that I had led in Paris—Manon's former connection with B——,—the manner in which she had deceived him: in a word, all the scandalous facts of our history. He therefore resolved to have us apprehended, and treated less as criminals than as vagabonds. An officer came abruptly one morning into our bedroom, with half a dozen archers of the guard. They first took possession of our money, or I should rather say, of G—— M——'s. They made us quickly get up, and conducted us to the door, where we found two coaches, into one of which they forced poor Manon, without any explanation, and I was taken in the other to St. Lazare.

One must have experienced this kind of reverse, to understand the despair that is caused by it. The police were savage enough to deny me the consolation of embracing Manon, or of bidding her farewell. I remained for a long time ignorant of her fate. It was perhaps fortunate for me that I was kept in a state of ignorance, for had I known what she suffered, I should have lost my senses, probably my life.

My unhappy mistress was dragged then from my presence, and taken to a place the very name of which fills me with horror to remember. This to be the lot of a creature the most perfect, who must have shared the most splendid throne on earth, if other men had only seen and felt as I did! She was not treated harshly there, but was shut up in a narrow prison, and obliged, in solitary confinement, to perform a certain quantity of work each day, as a necessary condition for obtaining the most unpalatable food. I did not learn this till a long time after, when I had myself endured some months of rough and cruel treatment.

My guards not having told me where it was that they had been ordered to conduct me, it was only on my arrival at St. Lazare that I learned my destination. I would have preferred death, at that moment, to the state into which I believed myself about to be thrown. I had the utmost terror of this place. My misery was increased by the guards on my entrance, examining once more my pockets, to ascertain whether I had about me any arms or weapons of defence.

The governor appeared. He had been informed of my

apprehension. He saluted me with great mildness. Do not, my good sir, said I to him, allow me to be treated with indignity. I would suffer a hundred deaths rather than quietly submit to degrading treatment. No, no, he replied, you will act quietly and prudently, and we shall be mutually content with each other. He begged of me to ascend to one of the highest rooms; I followed him without a murmur. The archers accompanied us to the door, and the governor, entering the room, made a sign for them to depart. I am your prisoner, I suppose? said I; well, what do you intend to do with me? He said, he was delighted to see me adopt so reasonable a tone; that it would be his duty to endeavour to inspire me with a taste for virtue and religion, and mine to profit by his exhortations and advice: that lightly as I might be disposed to rate his attentions to me, I should find nothing but enjoyment in my solitude. Ah, enjoyment, indeed! replied I; you do not know, my good sir, the only thing on earth that could afford me enjoyment. I know it, said he, but I trust your inclinations will change. His answer showed that he had heard of my adventures, and perhaps of my name. I begged to know if such were the fact. He told me candidly that they had informed him of every particular.

This blow was the severest of any I had yet experienced. I literally shed a torrent of tears, in all the bitterness of unmixed despair; I could not reconcile myself to the humiliation which would make me a proverb to all my acquaintances, and the disgrace of my family. I passed a week in the most profound dejection, without being capable of gaining any information, or of occupying myself with anything but my own degradation. The remembrance even of Manon added nothing to my grief; it only occurred to me as a circumstance that had preceded my new sorrow; and the sense of shame and confusion was at present the all-absorbing passion.

There are few persons who have experienced the force of these special workings of the mind. The generality of men are only sensible of five or six passions, in the limited round of which they pass their lives, and within which all their agitations are confined. Remove them from the influence of love and hate, pleasure and pain, hope and fear, and they have no further feeling. But persons of a finer cast can be affected in a thousand different ways; it would almost seem that they had more than five senses, and that they are accessible to ideas and sensations which far exceed the ordinary faculties of human nature; and, conscious that they possess a capacity which raises them above the common herd, there is nothing of which they are more jealous. Hence springs their impatience under contempt and ridicule; and hence it is that a sense of debasement is perhaps the most violent of all their emotions.

I had this melancholy advantage at St. Lazare. My grief appeared to the governor so excessive, that, dreading the consequences, he thought he was bound to treat me with more mildness and indulgence. He visited me two or three times a day; he often made me take a turn with him in the garden, and showed his interest for me in his exhortations and good advice. I listened always attentively; and warmly expressed my sense of his kindness, from which he derived hopes of my ultimate conversion.

You appear to me, said he one day, of a disposition so mild and tractable, that I cannot comprehend the excesses into which you have fallen. Two things astonish me: one is, how, with your good qualities, you could have ever abandoned yourself to vice; and the other, which amazes me still more, is, how you can receive with such perfect temper my advice and instructions, after having lived so long in a course of debauchery. If it be sincere repentance, you present a singular example of the benign mercy of Heaven; if it proceed from the natural goodness of your disposition, then you certainly have that within you which warrants the hope that a protracted residence in this place will not be required to bring you back to a regular and respectable life.

I was delighted to find that he had such an opinion of me. I resolved to strengthen it by a continuance of good conduct, convinced that it was the surest means of abridging the term of my confinement. I begged of him to furnish me with books. He was agreeably surprised to find that when he requested me to say what I should prefer, I mentioned only some religious and instructive works. I pretended to devote myself assiduously to study, and I thus gave him convincing proof of the moral reformation he was so anxious to bring about. It was nothing, however, but rank hypocrisy—I blush to confess it. Instead of studying, when alone I did nothing but curse my destiny. I lavished the bitterest execrations on my prison, and the tyrants who detained me there. If I ceased for a moment from these lamentations, it was only to relapse into the tormenting remembrance of my fatal and unhappy love. Manon's absence,—the mystery in which her fate was veiled,—the dread of never again beholding her; these formed the subject of my melancholy thoughts. I fancied her in the arms of G—— M——. Far from imagining that he could have been brute enough to subject her to the same treatment to which I was condemned, I felt persuaded that he had only procured my removal, in order that he might possess her in undisturbed enjoyment.

Oh! how miserable were the days and nights I thus passed! They seemed to be of endless duration. My only hope of escape now, was in hypocrisy; I scrutinised the countenance, and carefully marked every observation that fell from the governor, in order to ascertain what he really thought of me; and looking on him as the sole arbiter of my future fate, I made it my study to win, if possible, his favour. I soon had the satisfaction to find that I was firmly established in his good graces, and no longer doubted his disposition to befriend me.

I, one day, ventured to ask him whether my liberation depended on him. He replied that it was not altogether in his hands, but that he had no doubt that on his representation M. G—— M——, at whose instance the lieutenant-general of police had ordered me to be confined, would consent to my being set at liberty. May I flatter myself, rejoined I, in the mildest tone, that he will consider two months, which I have now spent in this prison, as a sufficient atonement? He offered to speak to him, if I wished it. I implored him without delay to do me that favour.

He told me two days afterwards that G—— M—— was so sensibly affected by what he had heard, that he not only was ready to consent to my liberation, but that he had even expressed a strong desire to become better acquainted with me, and that he himself purposed to pay me a visit in prison. Although his presence could not afford me much pleasure, I looked upon it as a certain prelude to my liberation.

He accordingly came to St. Lazare. I met him with an air more grave and certainly less silly than I had exhibited at his house with Manon. He spoke reasonably enough of my former bad conduct. He added, as if to excuse his own delinquencies, that it was graciously permitted to the weakness of man to indulge in certain pleasures, almost, indeed, prompted by nature, but that dishonesty and such shameful practices ought to be, and always would be, inexorably punished.

I listened to all he said with an air of submission, which quite charmed him. I betrayed no symptoms of annoyance even at some jokes in which he indulged about my relationship with Manon and Lescaut, and about the little chapels of which he supposed I must have had time to erect a great many in St. Lazare, as I was so fond of that occupation. But he happened, unluckily both for me and for himself, to add, that he hoped Manon had also employed herself in the same edifying manner at the Magdalen. Notwithstanding the thrill of horror I felt at the sound of the name, I had still presence of mind enough to beg, in the gentlest manner, that he would explain himself. Oh! yes, he replied, she has been these last two months at the Magdalen learning to be prudent, and I trust she has improved herself as much there, as you have done at St. Lazare!

If an eternal imprisonment, or death itself, had been presented to my view, I could not have restrained the excitement into which this afflicting announcement threw me. I flung myself upon him in so violent a rage that half my strength was exhausted by the effort. I had, however, more than enough left to drag him to the ground, and grasp him by the throat. I should infallibly have strangled him, if his fall, and the half-stifled cries which he had still the power to utter, had not attracted the governor and several of the priests to my room. They rescued him from my fury.

I was, myself, breathless and almost impotent from rage. Oh God! I cried—Heavenly justice! Must I survive this infamy? I tried again to seize the barbarian who had thus roused my indignation—they prevented me. My despair,—my cries,—my tears, exceeded all belief: I raved in so incoherent a manner that all the bystanders, who were ignorant of the cause, looked at each other with as much dread as surprise.

G—— M—— in the meantime adjusted his wig and cravat, and in his anger at having been so ill-treated, ordered me to be kept under more severe restraint than before, and to be punished in the manner usual with offenders in St. Lazare. No, sir! said the governor, it is not with a person of his birth that we are in the habit of using such means of coercion; besides, he is habitually so mild and well-conducted, that I cannot but think you must have given provocation for such excessive violence. This reply disconcerted G—— M—— beyond measure and he went away, declaring that he knew how to be revenged on the governor, as well as on me, and every one else who dared to thwart him.

The Superior, having ordered some of the brotherhood to escort him out of the prison, remained alone with me. He conjured me to tell him at once what was the cause of the fracas.—Oh, my good sir! said I to him, continuing to cry like a child, imagine the most horrible cruelty, figure to yourself the most inhuman of atrocities—that is what G—— M—— has had the cowardly baseness to perpetrate: he has pierced my heart. Never shall I recover from this blow! I would gladly tell you the whole circumstance, added I, sobbing with grief; you are kind-hearted, and cannot fail to pity me.

I gave him, as briefly as I could, a history of my long-standing and insurmountable passion for Manon, of the flourishing condition of our fortunes previous to the robbery committed by our servants, of the offers which G—— M—— had made to my mistress, of the understanding they had come to, and the manner in which it had been defeated. To be sure, I represented things to him in as favourable a light for us as possible. Now you can comprehend, continued I, the source of M. G—— M——'s holy zeal for my conversion. He has had influence enough to have me shut up here, out of mere revenge. That I can pardon; but, my good sir, that is not all. He has taken from me my heart's blood: he has had Manon shamefully incarcerated in the Magdalen; and had the effrontery to announce it to me this day with his own lips. In the Magdalen, good sir! Oh heavens! my adorable mistress, my beloved Manon, a degraded inmate of the Hospital! How shall I command strength of mind enough to survive this grief and shame!

The good Father, seeing me in such affliction, endeavoured to console me. He told me that he had never understood my history, as I just now related it; he had of course known that I led a dissolute life, but he had imagined that M. G—— M——'s interest about me was the result of his esteem and friendship for my family; that it was in this sense he had explained the matter to him; that what I had now told him should assuredly produce a change in my treatment, and that he had no doubt but the accurate detail which he should immediately transmit to the lieutenant-general of police would bring about my liberation.

He then inquired why I had never thought of informing my family of what had taken place, since they had not been instrumental to my incarceration. I satisfactorily answered this by stating my unwillingness to cause my father pain, or to bring upon myself the humiliation of such an exposure. In the end, he promised to go directly to the lieutenant-general of police; if it were only, said he, to be beforehand with M. G—— M——, who went off in such a rage, and who had sufficient influence to make himself formidable.

I looked for the good Father's return with all the suspense of a man expecting sentence of death. It was torture to me to think of Manon at the Magdalen. Besides the infamy of such a prison, I knew not how she might be treated there; and the recollection of some particulars I had formerly heard of this horrible place, incessantly renewed my misery. Cost what it might, I was so bent upon relieving her by some means or other, that I should assuredly have set fire to St. Lazare, if no other mode of escape had presented itself.

I considered what chances would remain to me if the lieutenant-general still kept me in confinement. I taxed my ingenuity: I scanned every imaginable gleam of hope—I could discover nothing that gave me any prospect of escape, and I feared that I should experience only more rigid confinement, if I made an unsuccessful attempt. I thought of some friends from whom I might hope for aid, but then, how was I to make them aware of my situation? At length I fancied that I had hit upon a plan so ingenious, as to offer a fair probability of success. I postponed the details of its arrangement until after the Superior's return, in case of his having failed in the object of his visit.

He soon arrived: I did not observe upon his countenance any of those marks of joy that indicate good news. I have spoken, said he, to the lieutenant-general of police, but I was too late. M. G—— M—— went straight to him after quitting us, and so prejudiced him against you, that he was on the point of sending me fresh instructions to subject you to closer confinement.

However, when I let him know the truth of your story, he reconsidered the matter, and, smiling at the incontinence of old

G—— M——, he said it would be necessary to keep you here for six months longer, in order to pacify him; the less to be lamented, he added, because your morals would be sure to benefit by your residence here. He desired that I would show you every kindness and attention, and I need not assure you that you shall have no reason to complain of your treatment.

This speech of the Superior's was long enough to afford me time to form a prudent resolution. I saw that by betraying too strong an impatience for my liberty, I should probably be upsetting all my projects. I acknowledged to him, that, as it was necessary for me to remain, it was an infinite comfort to know that I possessed a place in his esteem. I then requested, and with unaffected sincerity, a favour, which could be of no consequence to others, and which would contribute much to my peace of mind; it was to inform a friend of mine, a devout clergyman, who lived at St. Sulpice, that I was at St. Lazare, and to permit me occasionally to receive his visits.

This was of course my friend Tiberge; not that I could hope from him the assistance necessary for effecting my liberty; but I wished to make him the unconscious instrument of my designs. In a word, this was my project: I wished to write to Lescaut, and to charge him and our common friends with the task of my deliverance. The first difficulty was to have my letter conveyed to him: this should be Tiberge's office. However, as he knew him to be Manon's brother, I doubted whether he would take charge of this commission. My plan was to enclose my letter to Lescaut in another to some respectable man of my acquaintance, begging of him to transmit the first to its address without delay; and as it was necessary that I should have personal communication with Lescaut, in order to arrange our proceedings, I told him to call on me at St. Lazare, and assume the name of my eldest brother, as if he had come to Paris expressly to see me. I postponed till our meeting all mention of the safest and most expeditious course I intended to suggest for our future conduct. The governor informed Tiberge of my wish to see him. This ever-faithful friend had not so entirely lost sight of me as to be ignorant of my present abode, and it is probable that, in his heart, he did not regret the circumstance, from an idea that it might furnish the means of my moral regeneration. He lost no time in paying me the desired visit.

CHAPTER VI

It is a strange thing to note the excess of this passion; and how it braves the nature and value of things, by this—that the speaking in a perpetual hyperbole is comely in nothing but in love.—BACON.

My interview with Tiberge was of the most friendly description. I saw that his object was to discover the present temper of my mind. I opened my heart to him without any reserve, except as to the mere point of my intention of escaping. It is not from such a friend as you, said I, that I can ever wish to dissemble my real feelings. If you flattered yourself with a hope that you were at last about to find me grown prudent and regular in my conduct, a libertine reclaimed by the chastisements of fortune, released alike from the trammels of love, and the dominion that Manon wields over me, I must in candour say, that you deceive yourself. You still behold me, as you left me four months ago, the slave,—if you will, the unhappy slave,—of a passion, from which I now hope, as fervently and as confidently as I ever did, to derive eventually solid comfort.

He answered, that such an acknowledgment rendered me utterly inexcusable; that it was no uncommon case to meet sinners who allowed themselves to be so dazzled with the glare of vice as to prefer it openly to the true splendour of virtue; they were at least deluded by the false image of happiness, the poor dupes of an empty shadow; but to know and feel as I did, that the object of my attachment was only calculated to render me culpable and unhappy, and to continue thus voluntarily in a career of misery and crime, involved a contradiction of ideas and of conduct little creditable to my reason.

Tiberge, replied I, it is easy to triumph when your arguments are unopposed. Allow me to reason for a few moments in my turn. Can you pretend that what you call the happiness of virtue is exempt from troubles, and crosses, and cares? By what name will you designate the dungeon, the rack, the inflictions and tortures of tyrants? Will you say with the

Mystics [1] that the soul derives pleasure from the torments of the body? You are not bold enough to hold such a doctrine—a paradox not to be maintained. This happiness, then, that you prize so much, has a thousand drawbacks, or is, more properly speaking, but a tissue of sufferings through which one hopes to attain felicity. If by the power of imagination one can even derive pleasure from these sufferings, hoping that they may lead to a happy end, why, let me ask, do you deem my conduct senseless, when it is directed by precisely the same principle? I love Manon: I wade through sorrow and suffering in order to attain happiness with her. My path is one indeed of difficulties, but the mere hope of reaching the desired goal makes it easy and delightful; and I shall think myself but too bountifully repaid by one moment of her society, for all the troubles I encounter in my course. There appears therefore no difference between us, or, if there be any, it is assuredly in my favour; for the bliss I hope for is near and tangible, yours is far distant, and purely speculative. Mine is of the same kind as my sufferings, that is to say, evident to my senses; yours is of an incomprehensible nature, and only discernible through the dim medium of faith.

Tiberge appeared shocked by my remarks. He retired two or three paces from me, while he said, in the most serious tone, that my argument was not only a violation of good sense, but that it was the miserable sophistry of irreligion; for the comparison, he added, of the pitiful reward of your sufferings with that held out to us by the divine revelation, is the essence of impiety and absurdity combined.

I acknowledge, said I, that the comparison is not a just one, but my argument does not at all depend upon it. I was about to explain what you consider a contradiction,—the persevering in a painful pursuit; and I think I have satisfactorily proved, that if there be any contradiction in that, we shall be both equally obnoxious to the charge. It was in this light, only, that I could observe no difference in our cases, and I cannot as yet perceive any.

You may probably answer, that the proposed end, the

[1] A favourite tenet of the Mystics, advocated by Madame de Guyon, and adopted by the amiable and eloquent Fénelon, was, that the love of the Supreme Being must be pure and disinterested; that is, exempt from all views of interest, and all hope of reward. See the controversy between Bossuet and Fénelon.

promised reward, of virtue, is infinitely superior to that of love? No one disputes it, but that is not the question—we are only discussing the relative aid they both afford in the endurance of affliction. Judge of that by the practical effect: are there not multitudes who abandon a life of strict virtue? how few give up the pursuits of love!

Again, you will reply that if there be difficulties in the exercise of virtue, they are by no means universal and sure; that the good man does not necessarily meet tyrants and tortures, and that, on the contrary, a life of virtue is perfectly compatible with repose and enjoyment. I can say with equal truth, that love is often accompanied by content and happiness; and what makes another distinction of infinite advantage to my argument, I may add that love, though it often deludes, never holds out other than hopes of bliss and joy, whilst religion exacts from her votaries mortification and sorrow.

Do not be alarmed, said I, perceiving that I had almost offended his zealous feelings of devotion. I only wish to say, that there is no more unsuccessful method of weaning man's heart from love, than by endeavouring to decry its enjoyments, and by promising him more pleasure from the exercise of virtue. It is an inherent principle in our nature, that our felicity consists only in pleasure. I defy you to conceive any other notion of it; and it requires little time to arrive at the conviction, that, of all pleasures, those of love are immeasurably the most enchanting. A man quickly discerns the delusion, when he hears the promise made of livelier enjoyment, and the effect of such misrepresentation is only to make him doubt the truth of a more solid promise.

Let the preacher who seeks the reformation of a sinner tell me that virtue is indispensably necessary, but not disguise its difficulty and its attendant denials. Say that the enjoyments of love are fleeting, if you will, that they are rigidly forbidden, that they lead with certainty to eternal suffering; and, what would assuredly make a deeper impression upon me than any other argument, say that the more sweet and delectable they are, the brighter will be the reward of Heaven for giving them up in sacrifice; but do in the name of justice admit, that, constituted as the heart of man is, they form here, on earth, our most perfect happiness.

My last sentence restored to Tiberge his good humour. He

allowed that my ideas were not altogether so unreasonable.
The only point he made, was in asking me why I did not carry
my own principle into operation, by sacrificing my passion to
the hope of that remuneration of which I had drawn so brilliant
a picture. Oh! my dear friend, replied I; that it is which
makes me conscious of my own misery and weakness: true,
alas! it is indeed my duty to act according to my argument;
but have I the power of governing my own actions? What
aid will enable me to forget Manon's charms? God forgive me,
said Tiberge, I can almost fancy you a Jansenist.[1] I know not
of what sect I am, replied I, nor do I indeed very clearly see
to which I ought to belong; but I cannot help feeling the truth
of this at least of their tenets.

One effect of our conversation was to revive my friend's pity
for me in all its force. He perceived that there was in my
errors more of weakness than of vice; and he was the more
disposed in the end to give me assistance; without which I
should infallibly have perished from distress of mind. However,
I carefully concealed from him my intention of escaping from
St. Lazare. I merely begged of him to take charge of my
letter; I had it ready before he came, and I soon found an
excuse for the necessity of writing. He faithfully transmitted
it, and Lescaut received before evening the one I had enclosed
for him.

He came to see me next morning, and fortunately was
admitted under my brother's name. I was overjoyed at finding
him in my room. I carefully closed the door. Let us lose no
time, I said. First tell me about Manon, and then advise me
how I am to shake off these fetters. He assured me that he
had not seen his sister since the day before my arrest, and that
it was only by repeated inquiries, and after much trouble, that
he had at length been able to discover her fate as well as mine;
and that he had two or three times presented himself at the
Magdalen, and been refused admittance. Wretch! muttered
I to myself, dearly shall G—— M—— pay for this!

As to your escape, continued Lescaut, it will not be so easy
as you imagine. Last evening, I and a couple of friends walked

[1] The first proposition of the Jansenists was, that there are divine
precepts which good men, notwithstanding their desire to observe them,
are nevertheless absolutely unable to obey: God not having given them
such a measure of grace as is essentially necessary to render them capable
of obedience.—Mosheim's *Eccles. Hist.*, ii. 397.

round this establishment to reconnoitre it; and we agreed that, as your windows looked into a court surrounded by buildings, as you yourself mentioned in your letter, there would be vast difficulty in getting you out. Besides, you are on the third story, and it would be impossible to introduce ropes or ladders through the window. I therefore see no means from without—in the house itself we must hit upon some scheme.

No, replied I; I have examined everything minutely, particularly since, through the governor's indulgence, my confinement has been less rigorous. I am no longer locked into my room; I have liberty to walk in the gallery; but there is, upon every landing, a strong door kept closed night and day, so that it is impossible that ingenuity alone, unaided by some violent efforts, can rescue me.

Wait, said I, after turning in my mind for a moment an idea that struck me as excellent; could you bring me a pistol? Softly, said Lescaut to me, you don't think of committing murder? I assured him that I had so little intention of shooting any one, that it would not be even necessary to have the pistol loaded. Bring it to me to-morrow, I added, and do not fail to be exactly opposite the great entrance with two or three of your friends at eleven to-morrow night; I think I shall be able to join you there. He in vain requested me to explain my plan. I told him that such an attempt as I contemplated could only appear rational after it had succeeded. I begged of him to shorten his visit, in order that he might with the less difficulty be admitted next morning. He was accordingly admitted as readily as on his first visit. He had put on so serious an air, moreover, that a stranger would have taken him for a respectable person.

When I found in my hand the instrument of my liberty, I no longer doubted my success. It was certainly a strange and a bold project; but of what was I not capable, with the motives that inspired me? I had, since I was allowed permission to walk in the galleries, found opportunities of observing that every night the porter brought the keys of all the doors to the governor, and subsequently there always reigned a profound silence in the house, which showed that the inmates had retired to rest. There was an open communication between my room and that of the Superior. My resolution was, if he refused quietly to surrender the keys, to force him, by fear of the pistol,

to deliver them up, and then by their help to gain the street.
I impatiently awaited the moment for executing my purpose.
The porter arrived at his usual time, that is to say, soon after
nine o'clock. I allowed an hour to elapse, in order that the
priests as well as the servants might be all asleep. I at length
proceeded with my pistol and a lighted candle. I first gave a
gentle tap at the governor's door to awaken without alarming
him. I knocked a second time before he heard me; and supposing of course that it was one of the priests who was taken ill
and wanted assistance, he got out of bed, dressed himself, and
came to the door. He had, however, the precaution to ask
first who it was, and what was wanted? I was obliged to
mention my name, but I assumed a plaintive tone, to make
him believe that I was indisposed. Ah! it is you, my dear boy,
said he on opening the door; what can bring you here at this
hour? I stepped inside the door, and leading him to the
opposite side of the room, I declared to him that it was absolutely
impossible for me to remain longer at St. Lazare; that the night
was the most favourable time for going out unobserved, and
that I confidently expected, from his tried friendship, that he
would consent to open the gates for me, or entrust me with
the keys to let myself out.

This compliment to his friendship seemed to surprise him.
He stood for a few moments looking at me without making
any reply. Finding that I had no time to lose, I just begged
to assure him that I had the most lively sense of all his kind-
nesses, but that freedom was dearer to man than every other
consideration, especially so to me, who had been cruelly and
unjustly deprived of it; that I was resolved this night to recover it, cost what it would, and fearing lest he might raise his
voice and call for assistance, I let him see the powerful incentive
to silence which I had kept concealed in my bosom. A pistol!
cried he. What! my son? will you take away my life in return
for the attentions I have shown you? God forbid, replied I;
you are too reasonable to drive me to that horrible extremity:
but I am determined to be free, and so firmly determined, that
if you defeat my project, I will put an end to your existence.
But, my dear son! said he, pale and frightened, what have I
done to you? What reason have you for taking my life?
No! replied I, impatiently, I have no design upon your life, if
you, yourself, wish to live; open but the doors for me, and you

will find me the most attached of friends. I perceived the keys upon the table. I requested he would take them in his hand and walk before me, making as little noise as he possibly could.

He saw the necessity of consenting. We proceeded, and as he opened each door, he repeated, always with a sigh, Ah! my son, who could have believed it?—No noise, good Father, no noise, I as often answered in my turn. At length we reached a kind of barrier, just inside the great entrance. I already fancied myself free, and kept close behind the governor, with my candle in one hand, and my pistol in the other.

While he was endeavouring to open the heavy gate, one of the servants, who slept in an adjoining room, hearing the noise of the bolts, jumped out of bed, and peeped forth to see what was passing. The good Father apparently thought him strong enough to overpower me. He commanded him, most imprudently, to come to his assistance. He was a powerful ruffian, and threw himself upon me without an instant's hesitation. There was no time for parleying—I levelled my pistol and lodged the contents in his breast! See, Father, of what mischief you have been the cause, said I to my guide; but that must not prevent us from finishing our work, I added, pushing him on towards the last door. He did not dare refuse to open it. I made my exit in perfect safety, and, a few paces off, found Lescaut with two friends waiting for me, according to his promise.

We removed at once to a distance. Lescaut inquired whether he had not heard the report of a pistol? You are to blame, said I, why did you bring it charged? I, however, could not help thanking him for having taken this precaution, without which I doubtless must have continued much longer at St. Lazare. We went to pass the night at a tavern, where I made up, in some degree, for the miserable fare which had been doled out to me for nearly three months. I was very far, however, from tasting perfect enjoyment; Manon's sufferings were mine. She must be released, said I to my companions: this was my sole object in desiring my own liberty. I rely on your aiding me with all your ingenuity; as for myself, my life shall be devoted to the purpose.

Lescaut, who was not deficient in tact, and still less in that better part of valour called discretion, dwelt upon the necessity of acting with extreme caution: he said that my escape from

St. Lazare, and the accident that happened on my leaving it, would assuredly create a sensation; that the lieutenant-general of police would cause a strict search to be made for me, and it would be difficult to evade him; in fine, that, unless disposed to encounter something worse, perhaps, than St. Lazare, it would be requisite for me to remain concealed for a few days, in order to give the enemy's zeal time to cool. No doubt this was wise counsel; but, one should have been wise oneself to have followed it. Such calculating slowness little suited my passion. The utmost I could bring myself to promise was, that I would sleep through the whole of the next day. He locked me in my bedroom, where I remained patiently until night.

I employed great part of the time in devising schemes for relieving Manon. I felt persuaded that her prison was even more inaccessible than mine had been. Force was out of the question. Artifice was the only resource; but the goddess of invention herself could not have told me how to begin. I felt the impossibility of working in the dark, and therefore postponed the further consideration of my schemes until I could acquire some knowledge of the internal arrangements of the Hospital, in which she was confined.

As soon as night restored to me my liberty, I begged of Lescaut to accompany me. We were not long in drawing one of the porters into conversation; he appeared a reasonable man. I passed for a stranger who had often with admiration heard talk of the Hospital, and of the order that reigned within it. I inquired into the most minute details; and, proceeding from one subject to another, we at length spoke of the managers, and of these I begged to know the names and the respective characters. He gave me such information upon the latter point as at once suggested an idea which flattered my hopes, and I immediately set about carrying it into execution. I asked him (this being a matter essential to my plan) whether any of the gentlemen had children. He said he could not answer me with certainty as to all, but as for M. de T——, one of the principal directors, he knew that he had a son old enough to be married, and who had come several times to the Hospital with his father. This was enough for my purpose.

I immediately put an end to our interview, and, in returning, I told Lescaut of the plan I had formed. I have taken it, said

I, into my head, that M. de T——, the son, who is rich and of good family, must have the same taste for pleasure that other young men of his age generally have. He could hardly be so bad a friend to the fair sex, nor so absurd as to refuse his services in an affair of love. I have arranged a plan for interesting him in favour of Manon. If he is a man of feeling and of right mind, he will give us his assistance from generosity. If he is not to be touched by a motive of this kind, he will at least do something for a handsome girl, if it were only with the hope of hereafter sharing her favours. I will not defer seeing him, added I, beyond to-morrow. I really feel so elated by this project, that I derive from it a good omen.

Lescaut himself allowed that the idea was not unreasonable, and that we might fairly entertain a hope of turning it to account. I passed the night less sorrowfully.

Next morning I dressed as well as, in my present state of indigence, I could possibly contrive to do; and went in a hackney coach to the residence of M. de T——. He was surprised at receiving a visit from a perfect stranger. I augured favourably from his countenance and the civility of his manner. I explained my object in the most candid way; and, to excite his feelings as much as possible, I spoke of my ardent passion and of Manon's merit, as of two things that were unequalled, except by each other. He told me, that although he had never seen Manon, he had heard of her; at least, if the person I was talking of was the same who had been the mistress of old G——M——. I conjectured that he must have heard of the part I had acted in that transaction, and in order to conciliate him more and more by treating him with confidence, I told him everything that had occurred to Manon and myself. You see, sir, said I, that all that can interest me in life, all that can command my affections, is in your hands. I have no reserve with you, because I have been informed of your generous and noble character; and, being of the same age, I trust I shall find some resemblance in our dispositions.

He seemed flattered by this mark of candour and confidence. He replied in a manner that became a man of the world, and a man of feeling also, for they are not always synonymous terms. He told me that he appreciated my visit as a piece of good fortune; that he considered my friendship as a valuable acquisition, and that he would endeavour to prove himself worthy of it, by the sincerity of his services. He could not absolutely promise to restore Manon to my arms, because, as he said, he himself had very little influence; but he offered to procure me the pleasure of seeing her, and to do everything in his power to effect her release. I was the more satisfied with this frank avowal as to his want of influence, than I should have been by an unqualified promise of fulfilling all my wishes. I found in his moderation a pledge of his sincerity: in a word, I no longer doubted my entire success. The promise alone of enabling me to see Manon filled me with gratitude, and I testified it in so earnest a manner, as to give him a favourable opinion of my heart and disposition; we shook hands warmly, and parted sworn friends, merely from mutual regard, and that natural feeling which prompts a man of kind and generous sentiments to esteem another of congenial mind.

He, indeed, exceeded me in the proofs of his esteem; for, inferring from my adventures, and especially my late escape from St. Lazare, that I might be in want of money, he offered me his purse, and pressed me to accept it. I refused, but said to him, You are too kind, my dear sir! If in addition to such proofs of kindness and friendship, you enable me to see Manon again, rely on my eternal regard and gratitude. If you succeed in restoring altogether this dear creature to my arms, I should think myself happy in spilling the last drop of my blood in your service.

Before we parted, we agreed as to the time and place for our meeting. He was so considerate as to appoint the afternoon of the same day.

I waited for him at a café, where he joined me about four o'clock, and we went together towards the Magdalen; my knees trembled under me as I crossed the courts. Ye heavenly powers! said I, then I shall once more behold the idol of my heart —the dear object of so many sighs and lamentations! All I now ask of Providence is, to vouchsafe me strength enough to reach her presence, and after that, to dispose as it pleaseth of my future fate, and of my life itself. Beyond this, I have no prayer to utter.

M. de T—— spoke to some of the porters of the establishment, who appeared all anxious to please him. The quarter in which Manon's room lay was pointed out to us, and our guide carried in his hand the key of her chamber: it was of frightful size. I asked the man who conducted us, and whose duty it was to attend to Manon, how she passed her time? He said, that she had a temper of the most angelic sweetness; that even he, disagreeable as his official duties must render him, had never heard from her a single syllable in the nature of rebuke or harshness; that her tears had never ceased to flow during the first six weeks after her arrival, but that latterly she seemed to bear her misfortunes with more resignation, and that she employed herself from morning till night with her needle, excepting some hours that she, each day, devoted to reading. I asked whether she had been decently provided for. He assured me that at least she had never felt the want of necessaries.

We now approached her door. My heart beat almost audibly in my bosom. I said to M. de T——, Go in alone, and prepare her for my visit; I fear that she may be overcome by seeing me unexpectedly. The door was opened. I remained in the passage, and listened to the conversation. He said that he came to bring her consolation; that he was a friend of mine, and felt deeply interested for the happiness of us both. She asked with the tenderest anxiety, whether he could tell her what had become of me. He promised that she should soon see me at her feet, as affectionate and as faithful as ever. When? she asked. This very day, said he; the happy moment shall not be long delayed; nay, this very instant even, if you wish it. She at once understood that I was at the door; as she was rushing towards it, I entered. We embraced each other with that abounding and impassioned tenderness, which an absence of many months makes so delicious to those who truly love. Our sighs, our broken exclamations, the thousand endearing appellations of love, exchanged in languishing rapture, astonished M. de T——, and affected him even to tears.

I cannot help envying you, said he, as he begged us to be seated; there is no lot, however glorious, that I would hold as comparable to the possession of a mistress at once so tender and impassioned. Nor would I, I replied, give up her love for universal empire!

The remainder of an interview which had been so long and so ardently desired by me, was of course as tender as the commencement. Poor Manon related all her adventures, and I told her mine: we bitterly wept over each other's story. M. de T—— consoled us by his renewed promises to exert himself in our service. He advised us not to make this, our first inter-

view, of too long duration, that he might have the less difficulty
in procuring us the same enjoyment again. He at length
induced us to follow his advice. Manon especially could not
reconcile herself to the separation: she made me a hundred
times resume my seat. At one time she held me by my hands,
at another by my coat. Alas! she said, in what an abode do
you leave me! Who will answer for my ever seeing you again?
M. de T—— promised her that he would often come and see her
with me. As to the abode, he said, it must no longer be called
the Magdalen; it is Versailles! now that it contains a person
who deserves the empire of all hearts.

I made the man who attended a present as I went out, in
order to quicken his zeal and attentions. This fellow had a
mind less rough and vulgar than the generality of his class.
He had witnessed our interview, and was affected by it. The
interest he felt was doubtless increased by the louis d'or I
gave him. He took me aside as we went down into the court-
yard. Sir, said he, if you will only take me into your service,
or indemnify me in any way for the loss of the situation which I
fill here, I think I should not have much difficulty in liberating
the beauteous Manon.

I caught readily at the suggestion, and, although at the
moment I was almost in a state of destitution, I gave him
promises far beyond his desires. I considered that it would
be at all times easy to recompense a man of his description.
Be assured, my friend, said I to him, that there is nothing I
will not be ready to do for you, and that your fortune is just as
certain as my own. I inquired what means he intended to
employ. None other, said he, than merely to open the door of
her cell for her at night, and to conduct her to the street door,
where you, of course, will be to receive her. I asked whether
there was no danger of her being recognised as she traversed
the long galleries and the courts. He admitted that there was
danger, but that nothing could be done without some slight risk.

Although I was delighted to find him so determined, I called
M. de T——, and informed him of the project, and of the only
difficulty in the way. He thought it not so easy of execution.
He allowed the possibility of escaping thus: But if she be
recognised, continued he, if she be stopped in the attempt, all
hope will be over with her, perhaps for ever. Besides, you
would be obliged to quit Paris instantly, for you could never

F 834

evade the search that would be made for you: they would
redouble their efforts as much on your own account as hers
A single man may easily escape detection, but in company with
a handsome woman, it would be utterly impossible to remain
undiscovered.

However sound this reasoning, it could not, in my mind
outweigh the immediate prospect of restoring Manon to liberty
I said as much to M. de T——, and trusted that he would
excuse my imprudence and rashness, on the ground of love
I added that it was already my intention to quit Paris for
some neighbouring village, as I had once before done. We then
settled with the servant that he should carry his project into
execution the following day, and to render our success as certain
as he could, we resolved to carry into the prison men's clothes
in order to facilitate her escape. There was a difficulty to be
surmounted in carrying them in, but I had ingenuity enough to
meet it. I begged of M. de T—— only to put on two light
waistcoats the next morning, and I undertook to arrange
the rest.

We returned the following day to the Hospital. I took with
me linen, stockings, etc. for Manon, and over my body-coat
a surtout, which concealed the bulk I carried in my pockets
We remained but a moment in her room. M. de T—— left her
one of his waistcoats; I gave her my short coat, the surtout
being sufficient for me. She found nothing wanting for her
complete equipment but a pair of pantaloons, which in my
hurry I had forgotten.

The want of so necessary an article might have amused us
if the embarrassment it caused had been of a less serious kind
I was in despair at having our whole scheme foiled by a trifling
omission of this nature. However, I soon hit on a remedy
and determined to make my own exit *sans-culotte*, leaving that
portion of my dress with Manon. My surtout was long, and I
contrived by the help of a few pins to put myself in a decent
condition for passing the gate.

The remainder of the day appeared to me of endless length
When at last night came, we went in a coach to within a few
yards of the Hospital. We were not long waiting, when we saw
Manon make her appearance with her guide. The door of the
coach being opened, they both stepped in without delay. I
opened my arms to receive my adored mistress; she trembled

ike an aspen leaf. The coachman asked where he was to drive? To the end of the world! I exclaimed; to some place where I can never again be separated from Manon.

This burst, which I could not control, was near bringing me into fresh trouble. The coachman reflected upon what I said, and when I afterwards told him the name of the street to which I wished him to drive, he answered that he feared I was about to implicate him in some bad business; that he saw plainly enough that the good-looking young man whom I called Manon was a girl eloping from the Hospital, and that he was little disposed indeed to ruin himself for love of me.

Extortion was the source of this scoundrel's delicacy. We were still too near the Hospital to make any noise. Silence! said I to him, you shall have a louis d'or for the job:—for less than that he would have helped me to burn the Hospital.

We arrived at Lescaut's house. As it was late, M. de T—— left us on the way, promising to visit us the next morning. The servant alone remained.

I held Manon in such close embrace in my arms, that we occupied but one place in the coach. She cried for joy, and I could feel her tears trickling down my cheeks.

When we were about getting out at Lescaut's, I had a new difficulty with the coachman, which was attended with the most unfortunate results. I repented of having promised the fellow a louis d'or, not only because it was extravagant folly, but for another stronger reason, that it was at the moment out of my power to pay him. I called for Lescaut, and he came down to the door. I whispered to him the cause of my present embarrassment. Being naturally rough, and not at all in the habit of treating hackney-coachmen with respect, he answered that I could not be serious. A louis! said he; twenty blows of a cane would be the right payment for that rascal! I entreated him not to destroy us; when he snatched my cane from my hand, and was about to lay it on the coachman. The fellow had probably before experienced the weight of a guardsman's arm, and instantly drove off, crying out, that I had cheated him, and should hear of him again. I in vain endeavoured to stop him.

His flight caused me, of course, the greatest alarm. I had no doubt that he would immediately give information to the police. You have ruined me, said I to Lescaut; I shall be no longer safe at your house; we must go hence at once. I gave Manon my arm, and as quickly as possible got out of the dangerous neighbourhood. Lescaut accompanied us.

The Chevalier des Grieux having occupied more than an hour with his story, I begged him to give himself a little rest, and meanwhile to share our supper. He saw, by the attention we paid him, that we were amused, and promised that we should hear something of perhaps greater interest in the sequel. When we had finished supper, he continued in the following words.

CHAPTER VII

> . . . How chances mock,
> And changes fill the cup of alteration
> With divers liquors.
>
> SHAKESPEARE.

How inscrutably does Providence connect events! We had hardly proceeded for five minutes on our way, when a man, whose face I could not see, recognised Lescaut. He had no doubt been watching for him near his home, with the horrible intention which he now unhappily executed. It *is* Lescaut! said he, snapping a pistol at his head; he shall sup to-night with the angels! He then instantly disappeared. Lescaut fell, without the least sign of life. I pressed Manon to fly, for we could be of no use to a dead man, and I feared being arrested by the police, who would certainly be soon upon the spot. I turned down the first narrow street with her and the servant: she was so overpowered by the scene she had just witnessed, that I could hardly support her. At last, at the end of the street, I perceived a hackney-coach; we got into it, but when the coachman asked whither he should drive, I was scarcely able to answer him. I had no certain asylum—no confidential friend to whom I could have recourse. I was almost destitute of money, having but one dollar left in my purse. Fright and fatigue had so unnerved Manon, that she was almost fainting at my side. My imagination too was full of the murder of Lescaut, and I was not without strong apprehensions of the patrol. What was to be done? I luckily remembered the inn at Chaillot, where we first went to reside in that village. I hoped to be not only secure, but to continue there for some time without being pressed for payment. Take us to Chaillot, said I to the coachman. He refused to drive us so far at that late hour for less than twelve francs. A new embarrassment! At last we agreed for half that sum—all that my purse contained.

I tried to console Manon as we went along, but despair was rankling in my own heart. I should have destroyed myself

77

a thousand times over, if I had not felt that I held in my arms all that could attach me to life: this reflection reconciled me. I possess her at least, said I; she loves me! she is mine! Vainly does Tiberge call this a mere phantom of happiness. I could without feeling interest or emotion, see the whole world besides perish around me. Why? Because I have in it no object of affection beyond her.

This sentiment was true; however, while I so lightly esteemed the good things of the world, I felt that there was no doing without some little portion of them, were it only to inspire a more thorough contempt for the remainder. Love is more powerful than wealth—more attractive than grandeur or fame, but, alas! it cannot exist without certain artificial aids; and there is nothing more humiliating to the feelings of a sensitive lover, than to find himself, by want of means, reduced to the level of the most vulgar minds.

It was eleven o'clock when we arrived at Chaillot. They received us at the inn as old acquaintances, and expressed no sort of surprise at seeing Manon in male attire, for it was the custom in Paris and the environs to adopt all disguises. I took care to have her served with as much attention as if I had been in prosperous circumstances. She was ignorant of my poverty, and I carefully kept her so, being resolved to return alone the following day to Paris, to seek some cure for this vexatious kind of malady.

At supper she appeared pale and thin; I had not observed this at the Hospital, as the room in which I saw her was badly lighted. I asked her if the excessive paleness were not caused by the shock of witnessing her brother's death? She assured me that, horrified as she naturally was at the event, her paleness was purely the effect of a three months' absence from me. You do love me then devotedly? I exclaimed.

A thousand times more than I can tell! was her reply.

You will never leave me again? I added.

No! never, never! answered she.

This assurance was confirmed by so many caresses and vows, that it appeared impossible she could, to the end of time, forget them. I have never doubted that she was at that moment sincere. What motive could she have had for dissembling to such a degree? But she became afterwards still more volatile than ever, or rather she was no longer anything, and entirely forgot herself, when, in poverty and want, she saw other women living in abundance. I was now on the point of receiving a new proof of her inconstancy, which threw all that had passed into the shade, and which led to the strangest adventure that ever happened to a man of my birth and prospects.

As I knew her disposition, I hastened the next day to Paris. The death of her brother, and the necessity of getting linen and clothes for her, were such good reasons, that I had no occasion for any further pretext. I left the inn, with the intention, as I told Manon and the landlord, of going in a hired carriage, but this was a mere flourish; necessity obliged me to travel on foot: I walked very fast as far as Cours-la-Reine, where I intended to rest. A moment of solitude and tranquillity was requisite to compose myself, and to consider what was to be done in Paris.

I sat down upon the grass. I plunged into a sea of thoughts and considerations, which at length resolved themselves into three principal heads. I had pressing want of an infinite number of absolute necessaries; I had to seek some mode of at least raising a hope for the future; and, though last, not least in importance, I had to gain information, and adopt measures, to secure Manon's safety and my own. After having exhausted myself in devising projects upon these three chief points, I was obliged to put out of view for the moment the two last. We were not ill sheltered from observation in the inn at Chaillot; and as to future wants, I thought it would be time enough to think about them when those of the moment were satisfied.

The main object now was to replenish my purse. M. de T—— had once offered me his, but I had an extreme repugnance to mention the subject to him again. What a degradation to expose one's misery to a stranger, and to ask for charity: it must be either a man of low mind who would thus demean himself, and that from a baseness which must render him insensible to the degradation, or a humble Christian, from a consciousness of generosity in himself, which must put him above the sense of shame. I would have sacrificed half my life to be spared the humiliation.

Tiberge, said I, kind Tiberge, will he refuse me what he has it in his power to grant? No, he will assuredly sympathise in my misery; but he will also torture me with his lectures! One must endure his reproaches, his exhortations, his threats: I shall have to purchase his assistance so dearly, that I would rather make any sacrifice than encounter this distressing scene, which cannot fail to leave me full of sorrow and remorse. Well, thought I again, all hope must be relinquished, since no other course presents itself: so far am I from adopting either of these, that I would sooner shed half my blood than face one of these evils, or the last drop rather than encounter both. Yes, the very last drop, I repeated after a moment's reflection, I would sacrifice willingly rather than submit to such base supplication!

But it is not in reality a question of my existence! Manon's life and maintenance, her love and her fidelity, are at stake! What consideration can outweigh that? In her are centred all my glory, happiness, and future fortune! There are doubtless many things that I would gladly give up my life to obtain, or to avoid; but to estimate a thing merely beyond the value of my own life, is not putting it on a par with that of Manon. This idea soon decided me: I went on my way, resolved to go first to Tiberge, and afterwards to M. de T——.

On entering Paris I took a hackney-coach, though I had not wherewithal to pay for it; I calculated on the loan I was going to solicit. I drove to the Luxembourg, whence I sent word to Tiberge that I was waiting for him. I had not to stay many minutes. I told him without hesitation the extremity of my wants. He asked if the fifty pounds which I had returned to him would suffice, and he at once went to fetch it with that generous air, that pleasure in bestowing which "blesseth him that gives, and him that takes," and which can only be known to love or to true friendship.

Although I had never entertained a doubt of Tiberge's readiness to grant my request, yet I was surprised at having obtained it on such easy terms, that is to say, without a word of reprimand for my impenitence; but I was premature in fancying myself safe from his reproaches, for when he had counted out the money, and I was on the point of going away, he begged of me to take a walk with him in the garden. I had not mentioned Manon's name; he knew nothing of her escape; so that his lecture was merely upon my own rash flight from St. Lazare, and upon his apprehensions lest, instead of profiting by the lessons of morality which I had received there, I should again relapse into dissipation.

He told me, that having gone to pay me a visit at St. Lazare, the day after my escape, he had been astonished beyond expression at hearing the mode in which I had effected it; that he had afterwards a conversation with the Superior; that the good Father had not quite recovered the shock; that he had, however, the generosity to conceal the real circumstances from the lieutenant-general of police, and that he had prevented the death of the porter from becoming known outside the walls; that I had, therefore, upon that score, no ground for alarm, but that, if I retained one grain of prudence, I should profit by this happy turn which Providence had given to my affairs, and begin by writing to my father, and reconciling myself to his favour; and finally that, if I would be guided by his advice, I should at once quit Paris, and return to the bosom of my family.

I listened to him attentively till he had finished. There was much in what he said to gratify me. In the first place, I was delighted to learn that I had nothing to fear on account of St. Lazare—the streets of Paris at least were again open to me. Then I rejoiced to find that Tiberge had no suspicion of Manon's escape, and her return to my arms. I even remarked that he had not mentioned her name, probably from the idea that, by my seeming indifference to her, she had become less dear to my heart. I resolved, if not to return home, at least to write to my father, as he advised me, and to assure him that I was disposed to return to my duty, and consult his wishes. My intention was to urge him to send me money for the purpose of pursuing my ordinary studies at the University, for I should have found it difficult to persuade him that I had any inclination to resume my ecclesiastical habit. I was in truth not at all averse to what I was now going to promise him. On the contrary, I was ready to apply myself to some creditable and rational pursuit, so far as the occupation would be compatible with my love. I reckoned upon being able to live with my mistress, and at the same time continuing my studies. I saw no inconsistency in this plan.

These thoughts were so satisfactory to my mind, that I promised Tiberge to dispatch a letter by that day's post to my father: in fact, on leaving him, I went into a scrivener's, and wrote in such a submissive and dutiful tone, that, on reading over my own letter, I anticipated the triumph I was going to achieve over my father's heart.

Although I had money enough to pay for a hackney-coach

after my interview with Tiberge, I felt a pleasure in walking independently through the streets to M. de T——'s house. There was great comfort in this unaccustomed exercise of my liberty, as to which my friend had assured me I had nothing now to apprehend. However, it suddenly occurred to me, that he had been only referring to St. Lazare, and that I had the other affair of the Hospital on my hands; being implicated, if not as an accomplice, at all events as a witness. This thought alarmed me so much, that I slipped down the first narrow street, and called a coach. I went at once to M. de T——'s, and he laughed at my apprehensions. I myself thought them ridiculous enough, when he informed me that there was no more danger from Lescaut's affray, than from the Hospital adventure. He told me that, from the fear of their suspecting that he had a hand in Manon's escape, he had gone that morning to the Hospital and asked to see her, pretending not to know anything of what had happened; that they were so far from entertaining the least suspicion of either of us, that they lost no time in relating the adventure as a piece of news to him; and that they wondered how so pretty a girl as Manon Lescaut could have thought of eloping with a servant: that he replied with seeming indifference, that it by no means astonished him, for people would do anything for the sake of liberty.

He continued to tell me how he then went to Lescaut's apartments, in the hope of finding me there with my dear mistress; that the master of the house, who was a coachmaker, protested he had seen neither me nor Manon; but that it was no wonder that we had not appeared there, if our object was to see Lescaut, for that we must have doubtless heard of his having been assassinated about the very same time; upon which, he related all that he knew of the cause and circumstances of the murder.

About two hours previously, a guardsman of Lescaut's acquaintance had come to see him, and proposed play. Lescaut had such a rapid and extravagant run of luck, that in an hour the young man was minus twelve hundred francs,—all the money he had. Finding himself without a sou, he begged of Lescaut to lend him half the sum he had lost; and there being some difficulty on this point, an angry quarrel arose between them. Lescaut had refused to give him the required satisfaction, and the other swore, on quitting him, that he would take his life; a threat which he carried into execution the same night. M. de T—— was kind enough to add, that he had felt the utmost anxiety on our account, and that, such as they were, he should gladly continue to us his services. I at once told him the place of our retreat. He begged of me to allow him to sup with us.

As I had nothing more to do than to procure the linen and clothes for Manon, I told him that we might start almost immediately, if he would be so good as to wait for me a moment while I went into one or two shops. I know not whether he suspected that I made this proposition with the view of calling his generosity into play, or whether it was by the mere impulse of a kind heart; but, having consented to start immediately, he took me to a shopkeeper, who had lately furnished his house. He there made me select several articles of a much higher price than I had proposed to myself; and when I was about paying the bill, he desired the man not to take a sou from me. This he did so gracefully, that I felt no shame in accepting his present. We then took the road to Chaillot together, where I arrived much more easy in mind than when I had left it that morning.

My return and the polite attentions of M. de T—— dispelled all Manon's melancholy. Let us forget our past annoyances, my dear soul, said I to her, and endeavour to live a still happier life than before. After all, there are worse masters than love: fate cannot subject us to as much sorrow as love enables us to taste of happiness. Our supper was a true scene of joy.

In possession of Manon and of twelve hundred and fifty francs, I was prouder and more contented than the richest voluptuary of Paris with untold treasures. Wealth should be measured by the means it affords us of satisfying our desires. There did not remain to me at this moment a single wish unaccomplished. Even the future gave me little concern. I felt a hope, amounting almost to certainty, that my father would allow me the means of living respectably in Paris, because I had become entitled, on entering upon my twentieth year, to a share of my mother's fortune. I did not conceal from Manon what was the extent of my present wealth; but I added, that it might suffice to support us until our fortune was bettered, either by the inheritance I have just alluded to, or by the resources of the hazard-table.

CHAPTER VIII

This Passion hath its floods in the very times of weakness, which are great prosperity, and great adversity; both which times kindle Love, and make it more fervent.—BACON.

FOR several weeks I thus continued to think only of enjoying the full luxury of my situation; and being restrained, by a sense of honour, as well as a lurking apprehension of the police, from renewing my intimacy with my former companions at the hotel of Transylvania, I began to play in certain coteries less notorious, where my good luck rendered it unnecessary for me to have recourse to my former accomplishments. I passed a part of the afternoon in town, and returned always to supper at Chaillot, accompanied very often by M. de T——, whose intimacy and friendship for us daily increased.

Manon soon found resources against ennui. She became acquainted with some young ladies, whom the spring brought into the neighbourhood. They occupied their leisure hours in walking, and the customary amusements of persons of their sex and age. Their little gains at cards (always within innocent limits) were laid out in defraying the expense of a coach, in which they took an airing occasionally in the Bois de Boulogne; and each night when I returned, I was sure of finding Manon more beautiful—more contented—more affectionate than ever.

There arose, however, certain clouds, which seemed to threaten the continuance of this blissful tranquillity, but they were soon dispelled; and Manon's sprightliness made the affair so excessively comical in its termination, that it is even now pleasing to recur to it, as a proof of the tenderness as well as the cheerfulness of her disposition.

The only servant we had came to me one day, with great embarrassment, and taking me aside, told me that he had a secret of the utmost importance to communicate to me. I urged him to explain himself without reserve. After some hesitation, he gave me to understand that a foreigner of high rank had apparently fallen in love with Manon. I felt my blood boil at the announcement. Has she shown any penchant for him? I inquired, interrupting my informant with more impatience than was requisite, if I desired to have a full explanation.

He was alarmed at my excitement; and replied in an undecided tone, that he had not made sufficiently minute observation to satisfy me; but that, having noticed for several days together the regular arrival of the stranger at the Bois de Boulogne, where, quitting his carriage, he walked by himself in the cross-avenues, appearing to seek opportunities of meeting Manon, it had occurred to him to form an acquaintance with the servants, in order to discover the name of their master; that they spoke of him as an Italian prince, and that they also suspected he was upon some adventure of gallantry. He had not been able to learn anything further, he added, trembling as he spoke, because the prince, then on the point of leaving the wood, had approached him, and with the most condescending familiarity asked his name; upon which, as if he at once knew that he was in our service, he congratulated him on having, for his mistress, the most enchanting person upon earth.

I listened to this recital with the greatest impatience. He ended with the most awkward excuses, which I attributed to the premature and imprudent display of my own agitation. In vain I implored him to continue his history. He protested that he knew nothing more, and that what he had previously told me, having only happened the preceding day, he had not had a second opportunity of seeing the prince's servants. I encouraged him, not only with praises, but with a substantial recompense; and without betraying the slightest distrust of Manon, I requested him, in the mildest manner, to keep strict watch upon all the foreigner's movements.

In truth, the effect of his fright was to leave me in a state of the cruellest suspense. It was possible that she had ordered him to suppress part of the truth. However, after a little reflection, I recovered sufficiently from my fears to see the manner in which I had exposed my weaknesses. I could hardly consider it a crime in Manon to be loved. Judging from appearances, it was probable that she was not even aware of her conquest. And what kind of life shall I in future lead, thought I, if I am capable of letting jealousy so easily take possession of my mind?

I returned on the following day to Paris, with no other

intention than to hasten the improvement of my fortune, by playing deeper than ever, in order to be in a condition to quit Chaillot on the first real occasion for uneasiness. That night I learned nothing at all calculated to trouble my repose. The foreigner had, as usual, made his appearance in the Bois de Boulogne; and venturing, from what had passed the preceding day, to accost my servant more familiarly, he spoke to him openly of his passion, but in such terms as not to lead to the slightest suspicion of Manon's being aware of it. He put a thousand questions to him, and at last tried to bribe him with large promises; and taking a letter from his pocket, he in vain entreated him, with the promise of some louis d'ors, to convey it to her.

Two days passed without anything more occurring: the third was of a different character. I learned on my arrival, later than usual, from Paris, that Manon, while in the wood, had left her companions for a moment, and that the foreigner, who had followed her at a short distance, approached, upon her making him a sign, and that she handed him a letter, which he took with a transport of joy. He had only time to express his delight by kissing the *billet-doux*, for she was out of sight in an instant. But she appeared in unusually high spirits the remainder of the day; and even after her return to our lodgings, her gaiety continued. I trembled at every word.

Are you perfectly sure, said I, in an agony of fear, to my servant, that your eyes have not deceived you? He called Heaven to witness the truth of what he had told me.

I know not to what excess the torments of my mind would have driven me, if Manon, who heard me come in, had not met me with an air of impatience, and complained of my delay. Before I had time to reply, she loaded me with caresses; and when she found we were alone, she reproached me warmly with the habit I was contracting of staying out so late. My silence gave her an opportunity of continuing; and she then said that for the last three weeks I had never spent one entire day in her society; that she could not endure such prolonged absence; that she should at least expect me to give up a day to her from time to time, and that she particularly wished me to be with her on the following day from morning till night.

You may be very certain I shall do that, said I, in rather a sharp tone. She did not appear to notice my annoyance; she seemed to me to have more than her usual cheerfulness; and she described, with infinite pleasantry, the manner in which she had spent the day.

Incomprehensible girl! said I to myself; what am I to expect after such a prelude? The adventures of my first separation occurred to me; nevertheless, I fancied I saw in her cheerfulness, and the affectionate reception she gave me, an air of truth that perfectly accorded with her professions.

It was an easy matter at supper to account for the low spirits which I could not conceal, by attributing them to a loss I had that day sustained at the gaming-table. I considered it most fortunate that the idea of my remaining all the next day at Chaillot was suggested by herself: I should thus have ample time for deliberation. My presence would prevent any fears for at least the next day; and if nothing should occur to compel me to disclose the discovery I had already made, I was determined on the following day to move my establishment into town, and fix myself in a quarter where I should have nothing to apprehend from the interference of princes. This arrangement made me pass the night more tranquilly, but it by no means put an end to the alarm I felt at the prospect of a new infidelity.

When I awoke in the morning, Manon said to me, that although we were to pass the day at home, she did not at all wish that I should be less carefully dressed than on other occasions; and that she had a particular fancy for doing the duties of my toilette that morning with her own hands. It was an amusement she often indulged in: but she appeared to take more pains on this occasion than I had ever observed before. To gratify her, I was obliged to sit at her toilette table, and try all the different modes she imagined for dressing my hair. In the course of the operation, she made me often turn my head round towards her, and putting both hands upon my shoulders, she would examine me with most anxious curiosity: then, showing her approbation by one or two kisses, she would make me resume my position before the glass, in order to continue her occupation.

This amatory trifling engaged us till dinner-time. The pleasure she seemed to derive from it, and her more than usual gaiety, appeared to me so thoroughly natural, that I found it impossible any longer to suspect the treason I had previously conjured up; and I was several times on the point of candidly opening my mind to her, and throwing off a load that had begun to weigh heavily upon my heart: but I flattered myself with the hope that the explanation would every moment come from herself, and I anticipated the delicious triumph this would afford me.

We returned to her boudoir. She began again to put my hair in order, and I humoured all her whims; when they came to say that the Prince of —— was below, and wished to see her. The name alone almost threw me into a rage.

What then, exclaimed I, as I indignantly pushed her from me, who?—what prince?

She made no answer to my inquiries.

Show him upstairs, said she coolly to the servant; and then turning towards me, Dearest love! you whom I so fervently adore, she added in the most bewitching tone, I only ask of you one moment's patience; one moment, one single moment! I will love you ten thousand times more than ever: your compliance now shall never, during my life, be forgotten.

Indignation and astonishment deprived me of the power of utterance. She renewed her entreaties, and I could not find adequate expressions to convey my feelings of anger and contempt. But hearing the door of the antechamber open, she grasped with one hand my locks, which were floating over my shoulders, while she took her toilette mirror in the other, and with all her strength led me in this manner to the door of the boudoir, which she opened with her knee, and presented to the foreigner, who had been prevented by the noise he heard inside from advancing beyond the middle of the antechamber, a spectacle that must have indeed amazed him. I saw a man extremely well dressed, but with a particularly ill-favoured countenance.

Notwithstanding his embarrassment, he made her a profound bow. Manon gave him no time for speech-making; she held up the mirror before him: Look, sir, said she to him, observe yourself minutely, and I only ask you then to do me justice. You wish me to love you: this is the man whom I love, and whom I have sworn to love during my whole life: make the comparison yourself. If you think you can rival him in my affections, tell me at least upon what pretensions; for I solemnly declare to you, that, in the estimation of your most obedient humble servant, all the princes in Italy are not worth a single one of the hairs I now hold in my hand.

During this whimsical harangue, which she had apparently prepared beforehand, I tried in vain to disengage myself, and feeling compassion for a person of such consideration, I was desirous, by my politeness at least, of making some reparation for this little outrage. But recovering his self-possession with the ease of a man accustomed to the world, he put an end to my feelings of pity by his reply, which was, in my opinion, rude enough.

Young lady! young lady! said he to her, with a sardonic smile, my eyes in truth are opened, and I perceive that you are much less of a novice than I had pictured to myself.

He immediately retired without looking at her again, muttering to himself that the French women were quite as bad as those of Italy. I felt little desire, on this occasion, to change his opinion of the fair sex.

Manon let go my hand, threw herself into an arm-chair, and made the room resound with her shouts of laughter. I candidly confess that I was touched most sensibly by this unexpected proof of her affection, and by the sacrifice of her own interest which I had just witnessed, and which she could only have been induced to make by her excessive love for me. Still, however, I could not help thinking she had gone rather too far. I reproached her with what I called her indiscretion. She told me that my rival, after having besieged her for several days in the Bois de Boulogne, and having made her comprehend his object by signs and grimaces, had actually made an open declaration of love; informing her at the same time of his name and all his titles, by means of a letter, which he had sent through the hands of the coachman who drove her and her companions; that he had promised her, on the other side of the Alps, a brilliant fortune and eternal adoration; that she returned to Chaillot, with the intention of relating to me the whole adventure, but that, fancying it might be made a source of amusement to us, she could not help gratifying her whim; that she accordingly invited the Italian prince, by a flattering note, to pay her a visit; and that it had afforded her equal delight to make me an accomplice, without giving me the least suspicion of her plan. I said not a word of the information I had received through another channel; and the intoxication of triumphant love made me applaud all she had done.

CHAPTER IX

'Twas ever thus;—from childhood's hour
I've seen my fondest hopes decay;—
I never loved a tree or flower,
But it was sure to fade away;
I never nursed a dear Gazelle,
To glad me with its dark-blue eye,
But, when it came to know me well,
And love me, it was sure to die.

MOORE.

DURING my life I have remarked that fate has invariably chosen for the time of its severest visitations, those moments when my fortune seemed established on the firmest basis. In the friendship of M. de T——, and the tender affections of Manon, I imagined myself so thoroughly happy, that I could not harbour the slightest apprehension of any new misfortune: there was one nevertheless, at this very period impending, which reduced me to the state in which you beheld me at Passy, and which eventually brought in its train miseries of so deplorable a nature, that you will have difficulty in believing the simple recital that follows.

One evening, when M. de T—— remained to sup with us, we heard the sound of a carriage stopping at the door of the inn Curiosity tempted us to see who it was that arrived at this hour. They told us it was young G—— M——, the son of our most vindictive enemy, of that debauched old sinner who had incarcerated me in St. Lazare, and Manon in the Hospital His name made the blood mount to my cheeks.—It is Providence that has led him here, said I to M. de T——, that I may punish him for the cowardly baseness of his father. He shall not escape without our measuring swords at least. M. de T——, who knew him, and was even one of his most intimate friends, tried to moderate my feelings of anger towards him. He assured me that he was a most amiable young man, and so little capable of countenancing his father's conduct, that I could not be many minutes in his society without feeling esteem and affection for him. After saying many more things in his praise, he begged my permission to invite him to come and sit in our apartment

90

as well as to share the remainder of our supper. As to the objection of Manon being exposed by this proceeding to any danger, he pledged his honour and good faith, that when once the young man became acquainted with us, we should find in him a most zealous defender. After such an assurance, I could offer no further opposition.

M. de T—— did not introduce him without delaying a few moments outside, to let him know who we were. He certainly came in with an air that prepossessed us in his favour: he shook hands with me; we sat down; he admired Manon; he appeared pleased with me, and with everything that belonged to us; and he ate with an appetite that did abundant honour to our hospitality.

When the table was cleared, our conversation became more serious. He hung down his head while he spoke of his father's conduct towards us. He made, on his own part, the most submissive excuses.—I say the less upon the subject, said he, because I do not wish to recall a circumstance that fills me with grief and shame. If he were sincere in the beginning, he became much more so in the end, for the conversation had not lasted half an hour, when I perceived that Manon's charms had made a visible impression upon him. His looks and his manner became by degrees more tender. He, however, allowed no expression to escape him; but, without even the aid of jealousy, I had had experience enough in love affairs to discern what was passing.

He remained with us till a late hour in the night, and before he took his leave, congratulated himself on having made our acquaintance, and begged permission to call and renew the offer of his services. He went off next morning with M. de T——, who accepted the offer of a seat in his carriage.

I felt, as I before said, not the slightest symptom of jealousy: I had a more foolish confidence than ever in Manon's vows. This dear creature had so absolute a dominion over my whole soul and affections, that I could give place to no other sentiment towards her than that of admiration and love. Far from considering it a crime that she should have pleased young G—— M——, I was gratified by the effect of her charms, and experienced only a feeling of pride in being loved by a girl whom the whole world found so enchanting. I did not even deem it worth while to mention my suspicions to her. We were for some days occupied in arranging her new wardrobe, and in considering whether we might venture to the theatre without the risk of being recognised. M. de T—— came again to see us before the end of the week, and we consulted him upon this point. He saw clearly that the way to please Manon was to say yes: we resolved to go all together that same evening.

We were not able, however, to carry this intention into effect; for, having taken me aside:—I have been in the greatest embarrassment, said he to me, since I saw you, and that is the cause of my visiting you to-day. G—— M—— is in love with your mistress: he told me so in confidence; I am his intimate friend, and disposed to do him any service in my power; but I am not less devoted to you; his designs appeared to me unjustifiable, and I expressed my disapprobation of them; I should not have divulged his secret, if he had only intended to use fair and ordinary means for gaining Manon's affections; but he is aware of her capricious disposition; he has learned, God knows how, that her ruling passion is for affluence and pleasure; and, as he is already in possession of a considerable fortune, he declared his intention of tempting her at once with a present of great value, and the offer of an annuity of six thousand francs; if I had in all other points considered you both in an equal light, I should have had perhaps to do more violence to my feelings in betraying him: but a sense of justice as well as of friendship was on your side, and the more so from having been myself the imprudent, though unconscious, cause of his passion in introducing him here. I feel it my duty therefore to avert any evil consequences from the mischief I have inadvertently caused.

I thanked M. de T—— for rendering me so important a service, and confessed to him, in a like spirit of confidence, that Manon's disposition was precisely what G—— M—— had imagined; that is to say, that she was incapable of enduring even the thought of poverty.—However, said I to him, when it is a mere question of more or less, I do not believe that she would give me up for any other person; I can afford to let her want for nothing, and I have from day to day reason to hope that my fortune will improve; I only dread one thing, continued I, which is, that G—— M—— may take unfair advantage of the knowledge he has of our place of residence, and bring us into trouble by disclosing it.

M. de T—— assured me that I might be perfectly easy upon

that head; that G—— M—— might be capable of a silly passion, but not of an act of baseness; that if he ever could be villain enough for such a thing, he, de T——, would be the first to punish him, and by that means make reparation for the mischief he had occasioned.—I feel grateful for what you say, said I, but the mischief will have been all done, and the remedy even seems doubtful; the wisest plan therefore will be to quit Chaillot, and go to reside elsewhere.—Very true, said M. de T——, but you will not be able to do it quickly enough, for G—— M—— is to be here at noon; he told me so yesterday, and it was that intelligence that made me come so early this morning to inform you of his intentions. You may expect him every moment.

The urgency of the occasion made me view this matter in a more serious light. As it seemed to me impossible to escape the visit of G—— M——, and perhaps equally so to prevent him from making his declaration to Manon, I resolved to tell her beforehand of the designs of my new rival. I fancied that when she knew I was aware of the offers that would be made to her, and made probably in my presence, she would be the more likely to reject them. I told M. de T—— of my intention, and he observed that he thought it a matter of extreme delicacy. —I admit it, said I, but no man ever had more reason for confiding in a mistress, than I have for relying on the affection of mine. The only thing that could possibly for a moment blind her, is the splendour of his offers; no doubt she loves her ease, but she loves me also; and in my present circumstances, I cannot believe that she would abandon me for the son of the man who had incarcerated her in the Magdalen. In fine, I persisted in my intentions, and taking Manon aside, I candidly told her what I had learned.

She thanked me for the good opinion I entertained of her, and promised to receive G—— M——'s offers in a way that should prevent a repetition of them.—No, said I, you must not irritate him by incivility: he has it in his power to injure us. But you know well enough, you little rogue, continued I, smiling, how to rid yourself of a disagreeable or useless lover! After a moment's pause she said: I have just thought of an admirable plan, and I certainly have a fertile invention. G—— M—— is the son of our bitterest enemy: we must avenge ourselves on the father, not through the son's person, but through his purse. My plan is to listen to his proposals, accept his presents, and then laugh at him.

The project is not a bad one, said I to her; but you forget my dear child, that it is precisely the same course that conducted us formerly to the penitentiary. I represented to her the danger of such an enterprise; she replied, that the only thing necessary was to take our measures with caution, and she found an answer to every objection I started. Show me the lover who does not blindly humour every whim of an adored mistress, and I will then allow that I was wrong in yielding so easily on this occasion. The resolution was taken to make a dupe of G—— M——, and by an unforeseen and unlucky turn of fortune, I became the victim myself.

About eleven o'clock his carriage drove up to the door. He made the most complaisant and refined speeches upon the liberty he had taken of coming to dine with us uninvited. He was not surprised at meeting M. de T——, who had the night before promised to meet him there, and who had, under some pretext or other, refused a seat in his carriage. Although there was not a single person in the party who was not at heart meditating treachery, we all sat down with an air of mutual confidence and friendship. G—— M—— easily found an opportunity of declaring his sentiments to Manon. I did not wish to annoy him by appearing vigilant, so I left the room purposely for several minutes.

I perceived on my return that he had not had to encounter any very discouraging austerity on Manon's part, for he was in the best possible spirits. I affected good humour also. He was laughing in his mind at my simplicity, while I was not less diverted by his own. During the whole evening we were thus supplying to each other an inexhaustible fund of amusement. I contrived, before his departure, to let him have Manon for another moment to himself; so that he had reason to applaud my complaisance, as well as the hospitable reception I had given him.

As soon as he got into his carriage with M. de T——, Manon ran towards me with extended arms, and embraced me; laughing all the while immoderately. She repeated all his speeches and proposals, without altering a word. This was the substance:— He of course adored her; and wished to share with her a large fortune of which he was already in possession, without counting what he was to inherit at his father's death. She should be sole

mistress of his heart and fortune; and as an immediate token
of his liberality, he was ready at once to supply her with an
equipage, a furnished house, a lady's maid, three footmen, and
a man-cook.

There is indeed a son, said I, very different from his father!
But tell me truly, now, does not such an offer tempt you?—

Me! she replied, adapting to the idea two verses from Racine,—

> Moi! vous me soupçonnez de cette perfidie?
> Moi! je pourrais souffrir un visage odieux,
> Qui rappelle toujours l'Hôpital à mes yeux?

No! replied I, continuing the parody,—

> J'aurais peine à penser que l'Hôpital, madame,
> Fût un trait dont l'amour l'eût gravé dans votre âme.

But it assuredly is a temptation—a furnished house, a lady's
maid, a cook, a carriage, and three servants—gallantry can offer
but few more seductive temptations.

She protested that her heart was entirely mine, and that it
was for the future only open to the impressions I chose to make
upon it.—I look upon his promises, said she, as an instrument
for revenge, rather than as a mark of love. I asked her if she
thought of accepting the hotel and the carriage. She replied
that his money was all she wanted.

The difficulty was, how to obtain the one without the other;
we resolved to wait for a detailed explanation of the whole
project in a letter which G—— M—— promised to write to
her, and which in fact she received next morning by a servant
out of livery, who, very cleverly, contrived an opportunity
of speaking to her alone. She told him to wait for an answer,
and immediately brought the letter to me: we opened it together.

Passing over the usual commonplace expressions of tenderness, it gave a particular detail of my rival's promises. There
were no limits to the expense. He engaged to pay her down
ten thousand francs on her taking possession of the hotel, and
to supply her expenditure in such a way as that she should
never have less than that sum at her command. The appointed
day for her entering into possession was close at hand. He
only required two days for all his preparations, and he mentioned
the name of the street and the hotel, where he promised to be
in waiting for her in the afternoon of the second day, if she
could manage to escape my vigilance. That was the only point

upon which he begged of her to relieve his uneasiness; he seemed to be quite satisfied upon every other: but he added that, if she apprehended any difficulty in escaping from me, he could find sure means for facilitating her flight.

G—— M—— the younger was more cunning than the old gentleman. He wanted to secure his prey before he counted out the cash. We considered what course Manon should adopt. I made another effort to induce her to give up the scheme, and strongly represented all its dangers; nothing, however, could shake her determination.

Her answer to G—— M—— was brief, merely assuring him that she could be, without the least difficulty, in Paris on the appointed day, and that he might expect her with certainty.

We then resolved, that I should instantly hire lodgings in some village on the other side of Paris, and that I should take our luggage with me; that in the afternoon of the following day, which was the time appointed, she should go to Paris; that, after receiving G—— M——'s presents, she should earnestly entreat him to take her to the theatre; that she should carry with her as large a portion of the money as she could, and charge my servant with the remainder, for it was agreed that he was to accompany her. He was the man who had rescued her from the Magdalen, and he was devotedly attached to us. I was to be with a hackney-coach at the end of the street of St. André-des-arcs, and to leave it there about seven o'clock, while I stole, under cover of the twilight, to the door of the theatre. Manon promised to make some excuse for quitting her box for a moment, when she would come down and join me. The rest could be easily done. We were then to return to my hackney-coach, and quit Paris by the Faubourg St. Antoine, which was the road to our new residence.

This plan, extravagant as it was, appeared to us satisfactorily arranged. But our greatest folly was in imagining that, succeed as we might in its execution, it would be possible for us to escape the consequences. Nevertheless, we exposed ourselves to all risk with the blindest confidence. Manon took her departure with Marcel,—so was the servant called. I could not help feeling a pang as she took leave of me.—Manon, said I, do not deceive me; will you be faithful to me? She complained, in the tenderest tone, of my want of confidence, and renewed all her protestations of eternal love.

She was to be in Paris at three o'clock. I went some time after. I spent the remainder of the afternoon moping in the Café de Fère, near the Pont St. Michel. I remained there till nightfall. I then hired a hackney-coach, which I placed, according to our plan, at the end of the street of St. André-des-arcs, and went on foot to the door of the theatre. I was surprised at not seeing Marcel, who was to have been there waiting for me. I waited patiently for a full hour, standing among a crowd of lackeys, and gazing at every person that passed. At length, seven o'clock having struck, without my being able to discover anything or any person connected with our project, I procured a pit ticket, in order to ascertain if Manon and G—— M—— were in the boxes. Neither one nor the other could I find. I returned to the door, where I again stopped for a quarter of an hour, in an agony of impatience and uneasiness. No person appeared, and I went back to the coach, without knowing what to conjecture. The coachman, seeing me, advanced a few paces towards me, and said, with a mysterious air, that a very handsome young person had been waiting more than an hour for me in the coach; that she described me so exactly that he could not be mistaken, and having learned that I intended to return, she said she would enter the coach and wait with patience.

I felt confident that it was Manon. I approached. I beheld a very pretty face, certainly, but alas, not hers. The lady asked, in a voice that I had never before heard, whether she had the honour of speaking to the Chevalier des Grieux? I answered, That is my name.—I have a letter for you, said she, which will tell you what has brought me here, and by what means I learned your name. I begged she would allow me a few moments to read it in an adjoining café. She proposed to follow me, and advised me to ask for a private room, to which I consented.—Who is the writer of this letter? I inquired. She referred me to the letter itself.

I recognised Manon's hand. This is nearly the substance of the letter: G—— M—— had received her with a politeness and magnificence beyond anything she had previously conceived. He had loaded her with the most gorgeous presents. She had the prospect of almost imperial splendour. She assured me, however, that she could not forget me amidst all this magnificence; but that, not being able to prevail on G—— M—— to

take her that evening to the play, she was obliged to defer the
pleasure of seeing me; and that, as a slight consolation for the
disappointment which she feared this might cause me, she had
found a messenger in one of the loveliest girls in all Paris. She
signed herself, Your loving and constant, MANON LESCAUT.

There was something so cruel and so insulting in the letter,
that, what between indignation and grief, I resolutely determined
to forget eternally my ungrateful and perjured mistress. I
looked at the young woman who stood before me: she was
exceedingly pretty, and I could have wished that she had been
sufficiently so to render me inconstant in my turn. But there
were wanting those lovely and languishing eyes, that divine
gracefulness, that exquisite complexion, in fine, those innumer-
able charms which nature had so profusely lavished upon the
perfidious Manon.—No, no, said I, turning away from her;
the ungrateful wretch who sent you knew in her heart that
she was sending you on a useless errand. Return to her;
and tell her from me, to triumph in her crime, and enjoy it, if
she can, without remorse. I abandon her in despair, and, at
the same time, renounce all women, who, without her fascina-
tion, are no doubt her equals in baseness and infidelity.

I was then on the point of going away, determined never to
bestow another thought on Manon: the mortal jealousy that
was racking my heart lay concealed under a dark and sullen
melancholy, and I fancied, because I felt none of those violent
emotions which I had experienced upon former occasions, that
I had shaken off my thraldom. Alas! I was even at that
moment infinitely more the dupe of love, than of G—— M——
and Manon.

The girl who had brought the letter, seeing me about to
depart, asked me what I wished her to say to M. G—— M——,
and to the lady who was with him? At this question, I stepped
back again into the room, and by one of those unaccountable
transitions that are only known to the victims of violent passion,
I passed in an instant from the state of subdued tranquillity
which I have just described, into an ungovernable fury.—
Away! said I to her; tell the traitor G—— M—— and his
abandoned mistress the state of despair into which your accursed
mission has cast me; but warn them that it shall not be long a
source of amusement to them, and that my own hands shall
be warmed with the heart's blood of both! I sank back upon

a chair; my hat fell on one side, and my cane upon the other: torrents of bitter tears rolled down my cheeks. The paroxysm of rage changed into a profound and silent grief: I did nothing but weep and sigh.—Approach, my child, approach, said I to the young girl; approach, since it is you they have sent to bring me comfort; tell me whether you have any balm to administer for the pangs of despair and rage—any argument to offer against the crime of self-destruction, which I have resolved upon, after ridding the world of two perfidious monsters. Yes, approach, continued I, perceiving that she advanced with timid and doubtful steps; come and dry my sorrows; come and restore peace to my mind; come and tell me that at least you love me: you are handsome,—I may perhaps love you in return. The poor child, who was only sixteen or seventeen years of age, and who appeared more modest than girls of her class generally are, was thunderstruck at this unusual scene. She however gently approached to caress me, when with uplifted hands I rudely repulsed her.—What do you wish with me? exclaimed I to her.—Ah! you are a woman, and of a sex I abhor, and can no longer tolerate; the very gentleness of your look threatens me with some new treason. Go, leave me here alone! She made me a curtsy without uttering a word, and turned to go out. I called to her to stop:—Tell me at least, said I, where-fore,—how,—with what design they sent you here? how did you discover my name, or the place where you could find me?

She told me that she had long known M. G—— M——; that he had sent for her that evening about five o'clock; and that, having followed the servant who had been dispatched to her, she was shown into a large house, where she found him playing at picquet with a beautiful young woman; and that they both charged her to deliver the letter into my hands, after telling her that she would find me in a hackney-coach at the bottom of the street of St. André. I asked if they had said nothing more. She blushed while she replied, that they had certainly made her believe that I should be glad of her society.—They have deceived you too, said I, my poor girl,—they have deceived you; you are a woman, and probably wish for a lover; but you must find one who is rich and happy, and it is not here you will find him. Return, return to M. G—— M——; he possesses everything requisite to make a man beloved. He has furnished houses and equipages to bestow, while I, who have nothing but constancy of love to offer, am despised for my poverty, and laughed at for my simplicity.

I continued in a tone of sorrow or violence, as these feelings alternately took possession of my mind. However, by the very excess of my agitation, I became gradually so subdued as to be able calmly to reflect upon the situation of affairs. I compared this new misfortune with those which I had already experienced of the same kind, and I could not perceive that there was any more reason for despair now, than upon former occasions. I knew Manon: why then distress myself on account of a calamity which I could not but have plainly foreseen? Why not rather think of seeking a remedy? there was yet time; I at least ought not to spare my own exertions, if I wished to avoid the bitter reproach of having contributed, by my own indolence, to my misery. I thereupon set about considering every means of raising a gleam of hope.

To attempt to take her by main force from the hands of G—— M—— was too desperate a project, calculated only to ruin me, and without the slightest probability of succeeding. But it seemed to me that if I could ensure a moment's interview with her, I could not fail to regain my influence over her affections. I so well knew how to excite her sensibilities! I was so confident of her love for me! The very whim even of sending me a pretty woman by way of consoling me, I would stake my existence, was her idea, and that it was the suggestion of her own sincere sympathy for my sufferings.

I resolved to exert every nerve to procure an interview. After a multitude of plans which I canvassed one after another, I fixed upon the following:—M. de T—— had shown so much sincerity in the services he had rendered me, that I could not entertain a doubt of his zeal and good faith. I proposed to call upon him at once, and make him send for G—— M——, under pretence of some important business. Half an hour would suffice to enable me to see Manon. I thought it would not be difficult to get introduced into her apartment during G—— M——'s absence.

This determination pacified me, and I gave a liberal present to the girl, who was still with me; and in order to prevent her from returning to those who had sent her, I took down her address, and half promised to call upon her at a later hour. I then got into the hackney - coach, and drove quickly to

M. de T——'s. I was fortunate enough to find him at home.
I had been apprehensive upon this point as I went along. A
single sentence put him in possession of the whole case, as well
of my sufferings, as of the friendly service I had come to
supplicate at his hands.

He was so astonished to learn that G—— M—— had been
able to seduce Manon from me, that, not being aware that I
had myself lent a hand to my own misfortune, he generously
offered to assemble his friends, and evoke their aid for the
deliverance of my mistress. I told him that such a proceeding
might by its publicity be attended with danger to Manon and
to me.—Let us risk our lives, said I, only as a last resource.
My plan is of a more peaceful nature, and promising at least
equal success. He entered without a murmur into all that I
proposed; so again stating that all I required was, that he should
send for G—— M——, and contrive to keep him an hour or two
from home, we at once set about our operations.

We first of all considered what expedient we could make use
of for keeping him out so long a time. I proposed that he should
write a note dated from a café, begging of him to come there as
soon as possible upon an affair of too urgent importance to admit
of delay. I will watch, added I, the moment he quits the house,
and introduce myself without any difficulty, being only known
to Manon, and my servant Marcel. You can at the same time
tell G—— M——, that the important affair upon which you
wished to see him was the immediate want of a sum of money;
that you had just emptied your purse at play, and that you had
played on, with continued bad luck, upon credit. He will
require some time to take you to his father's house, where he
keeps his money, and I shall have quite sufficient for the
execution of my plan.

M. de T—— minutely adhered to these directions. I left him
in a café, where he at once wrote his letter. I took my station
close by Manon's house. I saw de T——'s messenger arrive, and
G—— M—— come out the next moment, followed by a servant.
Allowing him barely time to get out of the street, I advanced to
my deceiver's door, and notwithstanding the anger I felt, I
knocked with as much respect as at the portal of a church.
Fortunately it was Marcel who opened for me. Although I
had nothing to apprehend from the other servants, I asked him
in a low voice if he could conduct me unseen into the room in

which Manon was. He said that was easily done, by merely ascending the great staircase. Come then at once, said I to him, and endeavour to prevent anyone from coming up while I am there. I reached the apartment without any difficulty.

Manon was reading. I had there an opportunity of admiring the singular character of this girl. Instead of being nervous or alarmed at my appearance, she scarcely betrayed a symptom of surprise, which few persons, however indifferent, could restrain, on seeing one whom they imagined to be far distant. —Ah! it is you, my dear love, said she, approaching to embrace me with her usual tenderness. Good heavens, how venturesome and foolhardy you are! Who could have expected to see you in this place! Instead of embracing her in return, I repulsed her with indignation, and retreated two or three paces from her. This evidently disconcerted her. She remained immovable, and fixed her eyes on me, while she changed colour.

I was in reality so delighted to behold her once more, that, with so much real cause for anger, I could hardly bring my lips to upbraid her. My heart, however, felt the cruel outrage she had inflicted upon me. I endeavoured to revive the recollection of it in my own mind, in order to excite my feelings, and put on a look of stern indignation. I remained silent for a few moments, when I remarked that she observed my agitation, and trembled: apparently the effect of her fears.

I could no longer endure this spectacle.—Ah! Manon, said I to her in the mildest tone, faithless and perjured Manon! How am I to complain of your conduct? I see you pale and trembling, and I am still so much alive to your slightest sufferings, that I am unwilling to add to them by my reproaches. But, Manon, I tell you that my heart is pierced with sorrow at your treatment of me,—treatment that is seldom inflicted but with the purpose of destroying one's life. This is the third time, Manon; I have kept a correct account; it is impossible to forget that. It is now for you to consider what course you will adopt; for my afflicted heart is no longer capable of sustaining such shocks. I know and feel that it must give way, and it is at this moment ready to burst with grief. I can say no more, added I, throwing myself into a chair; I have hardly strength to speak, or to support myself.

She made me no reply; but when I was seated, she sank down upon her knees, and rested her head upon my lap, covering her face with her hands. I perceived in a moment that she was shedding floods of tears. Heavens! with what conflicting sensations was I at that instant agitated! Ah! Manon, Manon, said I, sighing, it is too late to give me tears after the death-blow you have inflicted. You affect a sorrow which you cannot feel. The greatest of your misfortunes is no doubt my presence, which has been always an obstacle to your happiness. Open your eyes; look up and see who it is that is here; you will not throw away tears of tenderness upon an unhappy wretch whom you have betrayed and abandoned.

She kissed my hands without changing her position. Inconstant Manon, said I again, ungrateful and faithless girl, where now are all your promises and your vows? Capricious and cruel that you are! what has now become of the love that you protested for me this very day? Just Heavens, added I, is it thus you permit a traitor to mock you, after having called you so solemnly to witness her vows! Recompense and reward then are for the perjured! Despair and neglect are the lot of fidelity and truth!

These words conveyed even to my own mind a sentiment so bitterly severe, that, in spite of myself, some tears escaped from me. Manon perceived this by the change in my voice. She at length spoke. I must have indeed done something most culpable, said she, sobbing with grief, to have excited and annoyed you to this degree; but, I call Heaven to attest my utter unconsciousness of crime, and my innocence of all criminal intention!

This speech struck me as so devoid of reason and of truth, that I could not restrain a lively feeling of anger. Horrible hypocrisy! cried I; I see more plainly than ever that you are dishonest and treacherous. Now at length I learn your wretched disposition. Adieu, base creature, said I, rising from my seat; I would prefer death a thousand times rather than continue to hold the slightest communication with you. May Heaven punish me, if I ever again waste upon you the smallest regard! Live on with your new lover,—renounce all feelings of honour, —detest me,—your love is now a matter to me of utter insignificance!

Manon was so terrified by the violence of my anger, that, remaining on her knees by the chair from which I had just before risen, breathless and trembling, she fixed her eyes upon me. I advanced a little farther towards the door, but, unless I had lost the last spark of humanity, I could not continue longer unmoved by such a spectacle.

So far, indeed, was I from this kind of stoical indifference, that, rushing at once into the very opposite extreme, I returned, or rather flew back to her without an instant's reflection. I lifted her in my arms; I gave her a thousand tender kisses; I implored her to pardon my ungovernable temper; I confessed that I was an absolute brute, and unworthy of being loved by such an angel.

I made her sit down, and throwing myself, in my turn, upon my knees, I conjured her to listen to me in that attitude. Then I briefly expressed all that a submissive and impassioned lover could say most tender and respectful. I supplicated her pardon. She let her arms fall over my neck, as she said that it was she who stood in need of forgiveness, and begged of me in mercy to forget all the annoyances she had caused me, and that she began, with reason, to fear that I should not approve of what she had to say in her justification. Me! said I, interrupting her impatiently; I require no justification; I approve of all you have done. It is not for me to demand excuses for anything you do; I am but too happy, too contented, if my dear Manon will only leave me master of her affections! But, continued I, remembering that it was the crisis of my fate,—may I not, Manon, all-powerful Manon, you who wield at your pleasure my joys and sorrows, may I not be permitted, after having conciliated you by my submission and all the signs of repentance, to speak to you now of my misery and distress? May I now learn from your own lips what my destiny is to be, and whether you are resolved to sign my death-warrant, by spending even a single night with my rival?

She considered a moment before she replied. My good chevalier, said she, resuming the most tranquil tone, if you had only at first explained yourself thus distinctly, you would have spared yourself a world of trouble, and prevented a scene that has really annoyed me. Since your distress is the result of jealousy, I could at first have cured that by offering to accompany you where you pleased. But I imagined it was caused by the letter which I was obliged to write in the presence of G—— M——, and of the girl whom we sent with it. I thought you might have construed that letter into a mockery; and have fancied that, by sending such a messenger, I meant to announce my abandonment of you for the sake of G—— M——. It was this idea that at once overwhelmed me with grief; for, innocent as I knew myself to be, I could not but allow that appearances were against me. However, continued she, I will leave you to judge of my conduct, after I shall have explained the whole truth.

She then told me all that had occurred to her after joining G—— M——, whom she found punctually awaiting her arrival. He had in fact received her in the most princely style. He showed her through all the apartments, which were fitted up in the neatest and most correct taste. He had counted out to her in her boudoir ten thousand francs, as well as a quantity of jewels, amongst which were the identical pearl necklace and bracelets which she had once before received as a present from his father. He then led her into a splendid room, which she had not before seen, and in which an exquisite collation was served; she was waited upon by the new servants, whom he had hired purposely for her, and whom he now desired to consider themselves as exclusively her attendants; the carriage and the horses were afterwards paraded, and he then proposed a game of cards, until supper should be announced.

I acknowledge, continued Manon, that I was dazzled by all this magnificence. It struck me that it would be madness to sacrifice at once so many good things for the mere sake of carrying off the money and the jewels already in my possession; that it was a certain fortune made for both you and me, and that we might pass the remainder of our lives most agreeably and comfortably at the expense of G—— M——.

Instead of proposing the theatre, I thought it more prudent to sound his feelings with regard to you, in order to ascertain what facilities we should have for meeting in future, on the supposition that I could carry my project into effect. I found him of a most tractable disposition. He asked me how I felt towards you, and if I had not experienced some compunction at quitting you. I told him that you were so truly amiable, and had ever treated me with such undeviating kindness, that it was impossible I could hate you. He admitted that you were a man of merit, and expressed an ardent desire to gain your friendship.

He was anxious to know how I thought you would take my elopement, particularly when you should learn that I was in his hands. I answered, that our love was of such long standing as to have had time to moderate a little; that, besides, you were not in very easy circumstances, and would probably not consider my departure as any severe misfortune, inasmuch as it would relieve you from a burden of no very insignificant nature. I added that, being perfectly convinced you would take the whole matter rationally, I had not hesitated to tell you that I had some business in Paris; that you had at once consented, and that having accompanied me yourself, you did not seem very uneasy when we separated.

If I thought, said he to me, that he could bring himself to live on good terms with me, I should be too happy to make him a tender of my services and attentions. I assured him that, from what I knew of your disposition, I had no doubt you would acknowledge his kindness in a congenial spirit: especially, I added, if he could assist you in your affairs, which had become embarrassed since your disagreement with your family. He interrupted me by declaring, that he would gladly render you any service in his power, and that if you were disposed to form a new attachment, he would introduce you to an extremely pretty woman, whom he had just given up for me.

I approved of all he said, she added, for fear of exciting any suspicions; and being more and more satisfied of the feasibility of my scheme, I only longed for an opportunity of letting you into it, lest you should be alarmed at my not keeping my appointment. With this view I suggested the idea of sending this young lady to you, in order to have an opportunity of writing; I was obliged to have recourse to this plan, because I could not see a chance of his leaving me to myself for a moment.

He was greatly amused with my proposition; he called his valet, and asking him whether he could immediately find his late mistress, he dispatched him at once in search of her. He imagined that she would have to go to Chaillot to meet you, but I told him that, when we parted, I promised to meet you again at the theatre, or that, if anything should prevent me from going there, you were to wait for me in a coach at the end of the street of St. André; that consequently it would be best to send your new love there, if it were only to save you from the misery of suspense during the whole night. I said it would be also necessary to write you a line of explanation, without which you would probably be puzzled by the whole transaction. He consented; but I was obliged to write in his presence; and I took especial care not to explain matters too palpably in my letter.

This is the history, said Manon, of the entire affair. I conceal nothing from you, of either my conduct or my intentions. The girl arrived; I thought her handsome; and as I doubted not that you would be mortified by my absence, I did most sincerely hope that she would be able to dissipate something of your ennui: for it is the fidelity of the heart alone that I value. I should have been too delighted to have sent Marcel, but I could not for a single instant find an opportunity of telling him what I wished to communicate to you. She finished her story by describing the embarrassment into which M. de T——'s letter had thrown G—— M——; he hesitated, said she, about leaving, and assured me that he should not be long absent; and it is on this account that I am uneasy at seeing you here, and that I betrayed, at your appearance, some slight feeling of surprise.

I listened to her with great patience. There were certainly parts of her recital sufficiently cruel and mortifying; for the intention, at least, of the infidelity was so obvious, that she had not even taken the trouble to disguise it. She could never have imagined that G—— M—— meant to venerate her as a vestal. She must therefore clearly have made up her mind to pass at least one night with him. What an avowal for a lover's ears! However, I considered myself as partly the cause of her guilt, by having been the first to let her know G—— M——'s sentiments towards her, and by the silly readiness with which I entered into this rash project. Besides, by a natural bent of my mind, peculiar I believe to myself, I was duped by the ingenuousness of her story,—by that open and winning manner with which she related even the circumstances most calculated to annoy me. There is nothing of wanton vice, said I to myself, in her transgressions; she is volatile and imprudent, but she is sincere and affectionate. My love alone rendered me blind to all her faults. I was enchanted at the prospect of rescuing her that very night from my rival. I said to her: With whom do you mean to pass the night? She was evidently disconcerted by the question, and answered me in an embarrassed manner with *buts* and *ifs*.

I felt for her, and interrupted her by saying that I at once expected her to accompany me.

Nothing can give me more pleasure, said she; but you don't approve then of my project?

Is it not enough, replied I, that I approve of all that you have, up to this moment, done?

What, said she, are we not even to take the ten thousand francs with us? Why, he gave me the money; it is mine.

I advised her to leave everything, and let us think only of escaping; for although I had been hardly half an hour with her, I began to dread the return of G—— M——. However, she so earnestly urged me to consent to our going out with something in our pockets, that I thought myself bound to make her, on my part, some concession, in return for all she yielded to me.

While we were getting ready for our departure, I heard some-one knock at the street door. I felt convinced that it must be G—— M——; and in the heat of the moment, I told Manon, that as sure as he appeared I would take his life. In truth, I felt that I was not sufficiently recovered from my late excitement to be able to restrain my fury if I met him. Marcel put an end to my uneasiness, by handing me a letter which he had received for me at the door; it was from M. de T——.

He told me that, as G—— M—— had gone to his father's house for the money which he wanted, he had taken advantage of his absence to communicate to me an amusing idea that had just come into his head;—that it appeared to him, I could not possibly take a more agreeable revenge upon my rival, than by eating his supper, and spending the night in the very bed which he had hoped to share with my mistress; all this seemed to him easy enough, if I could only find two or three men upon whom I could depend, of courage sufficient to stop him in the street, and detain him in custody until next morning;—that he would undertake to keep him occupied for another hour at least, under some pretext, which he could devise before G—— M——'s return.

I showed the note to Manon; I told her at the same time of the manner in which I had procured the interview with her. My scheme, as well as the new one of M. de T——'s, delighted her: we laughed heartily at it for some minutes; but when I treated it as a mere joke, I was surprised at her insisting seriously upon it, as a thing perfectly practicable, and too delightful to be neglected. In vain I inquired where she thought I could possibly find, on a sudden, men fit for such an adventure? and on whom I could rely for keeping G—— M—— in strict custody? She said that I should at least try, as M. de T—— ensured us yet a full hour; and as to my other objections, she said that I was playing the tyrant, and did not show the slightest indulgence to her fancies. She said that it was impossible there could be a more enchanting project. You will have his place at supper; you will sleep in his bed; and to-morrow, as early as you like, you can walk off with both his mistress and his money. You may thus, at one blow, be amply revenged upon father and son.

I yielded to her entreaties, in spite of the secret misgivings of my own mind, which seemed to forebode the unhappy catastrophe that afterwards befell me. I went out with the intention of asking two or three guardsmen, with whom Lescaut had made me acquainted, to undertake the arrest of G—— M——. I found only one of them at home, but he was a fellow ripe for any adventure; and he no sooner heard our plan, than he assured me of certain success: all he required was six pistoles, to reward the three private soldiers whom he determined to employ in the business. I begged of him to lose no time. He got them together in less than a quarter of an hour. I waited at his lodgings till he returned with them, and then conducted him to the corner of a street through which I knew G—— M—— must pass on going back to Manon's house. I requested him not to treat G—— M—— roughly, but to keep him confined, and so strictly watched, until seven o'clock next morning, that I might be free from all apprehension of his escape. He told me his intention was to bring him a prisoner to his own room, and make him undress and sleep in his bed, while he and his gallant comrades should spend the night in drinking and playing.

I remained with them until we saw G—— M—— returning homewards; and I then withdrew a few steps into a dark recess in the street, to enjoy so entertaining and extraordinary a scene. The officer challenged him with a pistol to his breast, and then told him, in a civil tone, that he did not want either his money or his life; but that if he hesitated to follow him, or if he gave the slightest alarm, he would blow his brains out. G—— M——, seeing that his assailant was supported by three soldiers, and perhaps not uninfluenced by a dread of the pistol, yielded without further resistance. I saw him led away like a lamb.

CHAPTER X

What lost a world, and bade a hero fly?
The timid tear in Cleopatra's eye.
Yet be the soft triumvir's fault forgiven,
By this, how many lose—not earth—but heaven!
Consign their souls to man's eternal foe,
And seal their own, to spare some wanton's, woe!

BYRON.

I SOON returned to Manon; and to prevent the servants from having any suspicion, I told her in their hearing, that she need not expect M. G—— M—— to supper; that he was most reluctantly occupied with business which detained him, and that he had commissioned me to come and make his excuses, and to fill his place at the supper table; which, in the company of so beautiful a lady, I could not but consider a very high honour. She seconded me with her usual adroitness. We sat down to supper. I put on the most serious air I could assume, while the servants were in the room, and at length having got rid of them, we passed, beyond all comparison, the most agreeable evening of my life. I gave Marcel orders to find a hackney-coach, and engage it to be at the gate on the following morning a little before six o'clock. I pretended to take leave of Manon about midnight, but easily gaining admission again, through Marcel, I proceeded to occupy G—— M——'s bed, as I had filled his place at the supper table.

In the meantime our evil genius was at work for our destruction. We were like children enjoying the success of our silly scheme, while the sword hung suspended over our heads. The thread which upheld it was just about to break; but the better to understand all the circumstances of our ruin, it is necessary to know the immediate cause.

G—— M—— was followed by a servant, when he was stopped by my friend the guardsman. Alarmed by what he saw, this fellow retraced his steps, and the first thing he did was to go and inform old G—— M—— of what had just happened.

Such a piece of news, of course, excited him greatly. This

was his only son; and considering the old gentleman's advanced
age, he was extremely active and ardent. He first inquired of
the servant what his son had been doing that afternoon; whether
he had had any quarrel on his own account, or interfered in any
other; whether he had been in any suspicious house. The
lackey, who fancied his master in imminent danger, and thought
he ought not to have any reserve in such an emergency, dis-
closed at once all that he knew of his connection with Manon,
and of the expense he had gone to on her account; the manner
in which he had passed the afternoon with her until about
nine o'clock, the circumstance of his leaving her, and the outrage he encountered on his return. This was enough to convince
him that his son's affair was a love quarrel. Although it was
then at least half-past ten at night, he determined at once to
call on the lieutenant of police. He begged of him to issue
immediate orders to all the detachments that were out on duty,
and he himself, taking some men with him, hastened to the
street where his son had been stopped: he visited every place
where he thought he might have a chance of finding him; and
not being able to discover the slightest trace of him, he went off
to the house of his mistress, to which he thought he probably
might by this time have returned.

I was stepping into bed when he arrived. The door of the
chamber being closed, I did not hear the knock at the gate,
but he rushed into the house, accompanied by two archers of
the guard, and after fruitless inquiries of the servants about his
son, he resolved to try whether he could get any information
from their mistress. He came up to the apartment, still
accompanied by the guard. We were just on the point of lying
down when he burst open the door, and electrified us by his
appearance. Heavens! said I to Manon, it is old G—— M——.
I attempted to get possession of my sword; but it was fortunately entangled in my belt. The archers, who saw my object,
advanced to lay hold of me. Stript to my shirt, I could, of
course, offer no resistance, and they speedily deprived me of all
means of defence.

G—— M——, although a good deal embarrassed by the whole
scene, soon recognised me; and Manon still more easily. Is
this a dream? said he, in the most serious tone—do I not see
before me the Chevalier des Grieux and Manon Lescaut? I
was so overcome with shame and disappointment, that I could

make him no reply. He appeared for some minutes revolving different thoughts in his mind; and as if they had suddenly excited his anger, he exclaimed, addressing himself to me: Wretch! I am confident that you have murdered my son!

I felt indignant at so insulting a charge. You hoary and lecherous villain! I exclaimed, if I had been inclined to kill any of your worthless family, it is with you I should most assuredly have commenced.

Hold him fast, cried he to the archers; he must give me some tidings of my son; I shall have him hanged to-morrow, if he does not presently let me know how he has disposed of him.

You will have me hanged, said I, will you? Infamous scoundrel! it is for such as you that the gibbet is erected. Know that the blood which flows in my veins is noble, and purer in every sense than yours. Yes, I added, I do know what has happened to your son; and if you irritate me further, I will have him strangled before morning; and I promise you the consolation of meeting in your own person the same fate, after he is disposed of.

I was imprudent in acknowledging that I knew where his son was, but excess of anger made me commit this indiscretion. He immediately called in five or six other archers, who were waiting at the gate, and ordered them to take all the servants into custody. Ah! ah! Chevalier, said he, in a tone of sardonic raillery,—so you do know where my son is, and you will have him strangled, you say? We will try to set that matter to rights.

I now saw the folly I had committed.

He approached Manon, who was sitting upon the bed, bathed in a flood of tears. He said something, with the most cruel irony, of the despotic power she wielded over old and young, father and son,—her edifying dominion over her empire. This superannuated monster of incontinence actually attempted to take liberties with her.

Take care, exclaimed I, how you lay a finger upon her!— neither divine nor human law will be able, should your folly arouse it, to shield you from my vengeance!

He quitted the room, desiring the archers to make us dress as quickly as possible.

I know not what were his intentions at that moment with regard to us: we might perhaps have regained our liberty if

we had told him where his son was. As I dressed, I considered
whether this would not be the wisest course. But if, on quitting
the room, such had been the disposition of his mind, it was
very different when he returned. He had first gone to question
Manon's servants, who were in the custody of the guard. From
those who had been expressly hired for her service by his son,
he could learn nothing; but when he found that Marcel had
been previously our servant, he determined to extract some
information from him, by means of intimidation, threats, or
bribes.

This lad was faithful, but weak and unsophisticated. The
remembrance of what he had done at the penitentiary for
Manon's release, joined to the terror with which G—— M——
now inspired him, so subdued his mind, that he thought they
were about leading him to the gallows, or the rack. He promised
that, if they would spare his life, he would disclose everything
he knew. This speech made G—— M—— imagine that there
was something more serious in the affair than he had before
supposed; he not only gave Marcel a promise of his life, but a
handsome reward in hand for his intended confession.

The booby then told him the leading features of our plot, of
which we had made no secret before him, as he was himself to
have borne a part in it. True, he knew nothing of the alterations
we had made at Paris in our original design; but he had been
informed, before quitting Chaillot, of our projected adventure,
and of the part he was to perform. He therefore told him
that the object was to make a dupe of his son; and that Manon
was to receive, if she had not already received, ten thousand
francs, which, according to our project, would be effectually
lost to G—— M——, his heirs and assigns for ever.

Having acquired this information, the old gentleman hastened
back in a rage to the apartment. Without uttering a word,
he passed into the boudoir, where he easily put his hand upon
the money and the jewels. He then accosted us, bursting with
rage; and holding up what he was pleased to call our plunder,
he loaded us with the most indignant reproaches. He placed
close to Manon's eye the pearl necklace and bracelets. Do you
recognise them? said he, in a tone of mockery; it is not, perhaps,
the first time you may have seen them. The identical pearls,
by my faith! They were selected by your own exquisite taste!
The poor innocents! added he; they really are most amiable

creatures, both one and the other; but they are perhaps a little too much inclined to roguery.

I could hardly contain my indignation at this speech. I would have given for one moment's liberty—Heavens! what would I not have given? At length, I suppressed my feelings sufficiently to say in a tone of moderation, which was but the refinement of rage: Put an end, sir, to this insolent mockery! What is your object? What do you purpose doing with us?

M. Chevalier, he answered, my object is to see you quietly lodged in the prison of Le Châtelet. To-morrow will bring daylight with it, and we shall then be able to take a clearer view of matters; and I hope you will at last do me the favour to let me know where my son is.

It did not require much consideration to feel convinced that our incarceration in Le Châtelet would be a serious calamity. I foresaw all the dangers that would ensue. In spite of my pride, I plainly saw the necessity of bending before my fate, and conciliating my most implacable enemy by submission. I begged of him, in the quietest manner, to listen to me.—I wish to do myself but common justice, sir, said I to him; I admit that my youth has led me into egregious follies; and that you have had fair reason to complain: but if you have ever felt the resistless power of love, if you can enter into the sufferings of an unhappy young man, from whom all that he most loved was ravished, you may think me perhaps not so culpable in seeking the gratification of an innocent revenge; or at least, you may consider me sufficiently punished, by the exposure and degradation I have just now endured. Neither pains nor imprisonment will be requisite to make me tell you where your son now is. He is in perfect safety. It was never my intention to injure him, nor to give you just cause for offence. I am ready to let you know the place where he is safely passing the night, if, in return, you will set us at liberty.

The old tiger, far from being softened by my prayer, turned his back upon me and laughed. A few words escaped him, which showed that he perfectly well knew our whole plan from the commencement. As for his son, the brute said that he would easily find him, since I had not assassinated him. Conduct them to the Petit-Châtelet, said he to the archers; and take especial care that the chevalier does not escape you: he is a scamp that once before escaped from St. Lazare.

He went out, and left me in a condition that you may picture to yourself. O Heavens! cried I to myself, I receive with humble submission all your visitations; but that a wretched scoundrel should thus have the power to tyrannise over me! this it is that plunges me into the depths of despair! The archers begged that we would not detain them any longer. They had a coach at the door.—Come, my dear angel, said I to Manon, as we went down, come, let us submit to our destiny in all its rigour: it may one day please Heaven to render us more happy.

We went in the same coach. I supported her in my arms. I had not heard her utter a single word since G—— M——'s first appearance: but now, finding herself alone with me, she addressed me in the tenderest manner, and accused herself of being the cause of all my troubles. I assured her that I never could complain, while she continued to love me. It is not I that have reason to complain, I added; imprisonment for a few months has no terrors for me, and I would infinitely prefer Le Châtelet to St. Lazare; but it is for you, my dearest soul, that my heart bleeds. What a lot for such an angel! How can you, gracious Heaven! subject to such rigour the most perfect work of your own hands? Why are we not both of us born with qualities conformable to our wretched condition? We are endowed with spirit, with taste, with feeling; while the vilest of God's creatures,—brutes, alone worthy of our unhappy fate, are revelling in all the favours of fortune.

These feelings filled me with grief; but it was bliss compared with my prospects for the future. My fear, on account of Manon, knew no bounds. She had already been an inmate of the Magdalen; and even if she had left it by fair means, I knew that a relapse of this nature would be attended with disastrous consequences. I wished to let her know my fears: I was apprehensive of exciting hers. I trembled for her, without daring to put her on her guard against the danger; and I embraced her tenderly, to satisfy her, at least, of my love, which was almost the only sentiment to which I dared to give expression.—Manon, said I, tell me sincerely, will you ever cease to love me?

She answered, that it made her unhappy to think that I could doubt it.

Very well, replied I, I do so no longer; and with this

conviction, I may well defy all my enemies. Through the influence of my family, I can ensure my own liberation from the Châtelet; and my life will be of little use, and of short duration, if I do not succeed in rescuing you.

We arrived at the prison, where they put us into separate cells. This blow was the less severe, because I was prepared for it. I recommended Manon to the attention of the porter, telling him that I was a person of some distinction, and promising him a considerable recompense. I embraced my dearest mistress before we parted; I implored her not to distress herself too much, and to fear nothing while I lived. I had money with me: I gave her some; and I paid the porter, out of what remained, the amount of a month's expenses for both of us in advance. This had an excellent effect, for I found myself placed in an apartment comfortably furnished, and they assured me that Manon was in one equally good.

I immediately set about devising the means of procuring my liberty. There certainly had been nothing actually criminal in my conduct; and supposing even that our felonious intention was established by the evidence of Marcel, I knew that criminal intentions alone were not punishable. I resolved to write immediately to my father, and beg of him to come himself to Paris. I felt much less humiliation, as I have already said, in being in Le Châtelet than in St. Lazare. Besides, although I preserved all proper respect for the paternal authority, age and experience had considerably lessened my timidity. I wrote, and they made no difficulty in the prison about forwarding my letter; but it was a trouble I should have spared myself, had I known that my father was about to arrive on the following day in Paris. He had received the letter I had written to him a week before; it gave him extreme delight; but, notwithstanding the flattering hopes I had held out of my conversion, he could not implicitly rely on my statements. He determined therefore to satisfy himself of my reformation by the evidence of his own senses, and to regulate his conduct towards me according to his conviction of my sincerity. He arrived the day after my imprisonment.

His first visit was to Tiberge, to whose care I begged that he would address his answer. He could not learn from him either my present abode or condition: Tiberge merely told him of my principal adventures since I had escaped from St. Lazare.

Tiberge spoke warmly of the disposition to virtue which I had evinced at our last interview. He added, that he considered me as having quite got rid of Manon; but that he was nevertheless surprised at my not having given him any intelligence about myself for a week. My father was not to be duped. He fully comprehended that there was something in the silence of which Tiberge complained, which had escaped my poor friend's penetration; and he took such pains to find me out, that in two days after his arrival he learned that I was in Le Châtelet.

Before I received this visit, which I little expected so soon, I had the honour of one from the lieutenant-general of police, or, to call things by their right names, I was subjected to an official examination. He upbraided me certainly, but not in any harsh or annoying manner. He told me, in the kindest tone, that he bitterly lamented my bad conduct; that I had committed a gross indiscretion in making an enemy of such a man as M. G—— M——; that in truth it was easy to see that there was, in the affair, more of imprudence and folly than of malice; but that still it was the second time I had been brought as a culprit under his cognisance; and that he had hoped I should have become more sedate, after the experience of two or three months in St. Lazare.

Delighted at finding that I had a rational judge to deal with, I explained the affair to him in a manner at once so respectful and so moderate, that he seemed exceedingly satisfied with my answers to all the queries he put. He desired me not to abandon myself to grief, and assured me that he felt every disposition to serve me, as well on account of my birth as my inexperience. I ventured to bespeak his attentions in favour of Manon, and I dwelt upon her gentle and excellent disposition. He replied, with a smile, that he had not yet seen her, but that she had been represented to him as a most dangerous person. This expression so excited my sympathy, that I urged a thousand anxious arguments in favour of my poor mistress, and I could not restrain even from shedding tears. He desired them to conduct me back to my chamber. Love! love! cried this grave magistrate as I went out, thou art never to be reconciled with discretion!

I had been occupied with the most melancholy reflections, and was thinking of the conversation I had had with the lieutenant-general of police, when I heard my door open. It was my father. Although I ought to have been half prepared for seeing him, and had reasons to expect his arrival within a day or two, yet I was so thunderstruck, that I could willingly have sunk into the earth, if it had been open at my feet. I embraced him in the greatest possible state of confusion. He took a seat, without either one or other of us having uttered a word.

As I remained standing, with my head uncovered, and my eyes cast on the ground, Be seated, sir, said he in a solemn voice; be seated. I have to thank the notoriety of your debaucheries for learning the place of your abode. It is the privilege of such fame as yours, that it cannot lie concealed. You are acquiring celebrity by an unerring path. Doubtless it will lead you to the Grève,[1] and you will then have the unfading glory of being held up to the admiration of the world.

I made no reply. He continued: What an unhappy lot is that of a father, who having tenderly loved a child, and strained every nerve to bring him up a virtuous and respectable man, finds him turn out in the end a worthless profligate, who dishonours him. To an ordinary reverse of fortune one may be reconciled; time softens the affliction, and even the indulgence of sorrow itself is not unavailing; but what remedy is there for an evil that is perpetually augmenting, such as the profligacy of a vicious son, who has deserted every principle of honour, and is ever plunging from deep into deeper vice? You are silent, added he: look at this counterfeit modesty, this hypocritical air of gentleness!—might he not pass for the most respectable member of his family?

Although I could not but feel that I deserved, in some degree, these reproaches, yet he appeared to me to carry them beyond all reason. I thought I might be permitted to explain my feelings.

I assure you, sir, said I to him, that the modesty which you ridicule is by no means affected; it is the natural feeling of a son who entertains sincere respect for his father, and above all, a father irritated as you justly are by his faults. Neither have I, sir, the slightest wish to pass for the most respectable

---

[1] Who has e'er been at Paris must needs know the Grève,
The fatal retreat of th' unfortunate brave,
Where honour and justice most oddly contribute,
To ease heroes' pains by the halter and gibbet.—PRIOR,

member of my family. I know that I have merited your reproaches, but I conjure you to temper them with mercy, and not to look upon me as the most infamous of mankind. I do not deserve such harsh names. It is love, you know it, that has caused all my errors. Fatal passion! Have you yourself never felt its force? Is it possible that you, with the same blood in your veins that flows in mine, should have passed through life unscathed by the same excitements? Love has rendered me perhaps foolishly tender,—too easily excited,—too impassioned,—too faithful, and probably too indulgent to the desires and caprices, or, if you will, the faults of an adored mistress. These are my crimes; are they such as to reflect dishonour upon you? Come, my dear father, said I tenderly, show some pity for a son, who has never ceased to feel respect and affection for you,—who has not renounced, as you say, all feelings of honour and of duty, and who is himself a thousand times more an object of pity than you imagine. I could not help shedding a tear as I concluded this appeal.

A father's heart is a chef-d'œuvre of creation. There nature rules in undisturbed dominion, and regulates at will its most secret springs. He was a man of high feeling and good taste, and was so sensibly affected by the turn I had given to my defence, that he could no longer hide from me the change I had wrought.

Come to me, my poor chevalier, said he; come and embrace me. I do pity you!

I embraced him: he pressed me to him in such a manner, that I guessed what was passing in his heart.

But how are we, said he, to extricate you from this place? Explain to me the real situation of your affairs.

As there really was not anything in my conduct so grossly improper as to reflect dishonour upon me; at least, in comparison with the conduct of other young men of a certain station in the world; and as a mistress is not considered a disgrace, any more than a little dexterity in drawing some advantage from play, I gave my father a candid detail of the life I had been leading. As I recounted each transgression, I took care to cite some illustrious example in my justification, in order to palliate my own faults.

I lived, said I, with a mistress without the solemnity of marriage. The Duke of —— keeps two before the eyes of all

Paris. M—— D—— has had one now for ten years, and loves her with a fidelity which he has never shown to his wife. Two-thirds of the men of fashion in Paris keep mistresses.

I certainly have on one or two occasions cheated at play. Well, the Marquis of —— and the Count —— have no other source of revenue. The Prince of —— and the Duke of —— are at the head of a gang of the same industrious order. As for the designs I had upon the pockets of the two G—— M——s, I might just as easily have proved that I had abundant models for that also; but I had too much pride to plead guilty to this charge, and rest on the justification of example; so that I begged of my father to ascribe my weakness on this occasion to the violence of the two passions which agitated me—Revenge and Love.

He asked me whether I could suggest any means of obtaining my liberty, and in such a way as to avoid publicity as much as possible. I told him of the kind feelings which the lieutenant-general of police had expressed towards me. If you encounter any obstacles, said I, they will be offered only by the two G—— M——s; so that I think it would be advisable to call upon them. He promised to do so.

I did not dare ask him to solicit Manon's liberation; this was not from want of courage, but from the apprehension of exasperating him by such a proposition, and perhaps driving him to form some design fatal to the future happiness of us both. It remains to this hour a problem whether this fear on my part was not the immediate cause of all my most terrible misfortunes, by preventing me from ascertaining my father's disposition, and endeavouring to inspire him with favourable feelings towards my poor mistress: I might have perhaps once more succeeded in exciting his commiseration; I might have put him on his guard against the impression which he was sure of receiving from a visit to old G—— M——. But how can I tell what the consequences would have been! My unhappy fate would have most probably counteracted all my efforts; but it would have been a consolation to have had nothing else but that, and the cruelty of my enemies, to blame for my afflictions.

On quitting me, my father went to pay a visit to M. G—— M——. He found him with his son, whom the guardsman had safely restored to liberty. I never learned the particulars of their conversation; but I could easily infer them from the

disastrous results. They went together (the two old gentlemen) to the lieutenant-general of police, from whom they
requested one favour each: the first was to have me at once
liberated from Le Châtelet; the second to condemn Manon to
perpetual imprisonment, or to transport her for life to America.
They happened, at that very period, to be sending out a number
of convicts to the Mississippi. The lieutenant-general promised
to have her embarked on board the first vessel that sailed.

M. G—— M—— and my father came together to bring me
the news of my liberation. M. G—— M—— said something
civil with reference to what had passed; and having congratulated me upon my happiness in having such a father, he
exhorted me to profit henceforward by his instruction and
example. My father desired me to express my sorrow for the
injustice I had even contemplated against his family, and my
gratitude for his having assisted in procuring my liberation.

We all left the prison together, without the mention of Manon's
name. I dared not in their presence speak of her to the turn-
keys. Alas! all my entreaties in her favour would have been
useless. The cruel sentence upon Manon had arrived at the
same time as the warrant for my discharge. The unfortunate
girl was conducted in an hour after to the Hospital, to be there
classed with some other wretched women, who had been
condemned to the same punishment.

My father having forced me to accompany him to the house
where he was residing, it was near six o'clock before I had an
opportunity of escaping his vigilance. In returning to Le
Châtelet, my only wish was to convey some refreshments to
Manon, and to recommend her to the attention of the porter;
for I had no hope of being permitted to see her; nor had I, as
yet, had time to reflect on the best means of rescuing her.

I asked for the porter. I had won his heart, as much by my
liberality to him, as by the mildness of my manner; so that,
having a disposition to serve me, he spoke of Manon's sentence
as a calamity which he sincerely regretted, since it was calculated
to mortify me. I was at first unable to comprehend his meaning.
We conversed for some minutes without my understanding
him. At length perceiving that an explanation was necessary,
he gave me such a one, as on a former occasion I wanted
courage to relate to you, and which, even now, makes my blood
curdle in my veins to remember.

CHAPTER XI

Alack! it is not when we sleep soft and wake merrily that we think on other people's sufferings; but when the hour of trouble comes, said Jeani Deans.—WALTER SCOTT.

NEVER did apoplexy produce on mortal a more sudden or terrific effect than did the announcement of Manon's sentence upon me. I fell prostrate, with so intense a palpitation of the heart that as I swooned I thought that death itself was come upon me. This idea continued even after I had been restored to my senses. I gazed around me upon every part of the room, then upon my own paralysed limbs, doubting, in my delirium, whether I still bore about me the attributes of a living man. It is quite certain that, in obedience to the desire I felt of terminating my sufferings, even by my own hand, nothing could have been to me more welcome than death at that moment of anguish and despair. Religion itself could depict nothing more insupportable after death than the racking agony with which I was then convulsed. Yet, by a miracle, only within the power of omnipotent love, I soon regained strength enough to express my gratitude to Heaven for restoring me to sense and reason. My death could have only been a relief and blessing to myself, whereas Manon had occasion for my prolonged existence, in order to deliver her,—to succour her,—to avenge her wrongs. I swore to devote that existence unremittingly to these objects.

The porter gave me every assistance that I could have expected at the hands of my oldest friend: I accepted his services with the liveliest gratitude. Alas! said I to him, you then are affected by my sufferings! The whole world abandons me; my own father proves one of the very cruellest of my persecutors; no person feels pity for me! You alone, in this abode of suffering and shame,—you alone exhibit compassion for the most wretched of mankind! He advised me not to appear in the street until I had recovered a little from my affliction. Do not stop me, said I, as I went out; we shall meet again sooner than you imagine: get ready your darkest dungeon, for I shall shortly become its tenant.

In fact, my first idea was nothing less than to make away with the two G—— M——s, and the lieutenant - general of police; and then to attack the Hospital, sword in hand, assisted by all whom I could enlist in my cause. Even my father's life was hardly respected, so just appeared my feelings of vengeance; for the porter had informed me that he and G—— M—— were jointly the authors of my ruin.

But when I had advanced some paces into the street, and the fresh air had cooled my excitement, I gradually viewed matters in a more rational mood. The death of our enemies could be of little use to Manon; and the obvious effect of such violence would be to deprive me of all other chance of serving her. Besides, could I ever bring myself to be a cowardly assassin? By what other means could I accomplish my revenge? I set all my ingenuity and all my efforts at work to procure the deliverance of Manon, leaving everything else to be considered hereafter when I had succeeded in this first and paramount object.

I had very little money left; money, however, was an indispensable basis for all my operations. I only knew three persons from whom I had any right to ask pecuniary assistance,—M. de T——, Tiberge, and my father. There appeared little chance of obtaining any from the two latter, and I was really ashamed again to importune M. de T——. But it is not in desperate emergencies that one stands upon points of ceremony. I went first to the seminary of St. Sulpice, without considering whether I should be recognised. I asked for Tiberge. His first words showed me that he knew nothing of my latest adventure: this made me change the design I had originally formed of appealing at once to his compassion. I spoke generally of the pleasure it had given me to see my father again; and then begged of him to lend me some money, under the pretext of being anxious before I left Paris to pay a few little debts, which I wished to keep secret. He handed me his purse, without a single remark. I took twenty or twenty-five pounds, which it contained. I offered him my note of hand, but he was too generous to accept it.

I then went to M. de T——: I had no reserve with him. I plainly told him my misfortunes and distress: he already knew everything, and had informed himself even of the most trifling circumstance, on account of the interest he naturally took in young G—— M——'s adventure. He, however, listened to me, and seemed sincerely to lament what had occurred. When I consulted him as to the best means of rescuing Manon, he answered that he saw such little ground for hope, that, without some extraordinary interposition of Providence, it would be folly to expect relief; that he had paid a visit expressly to the Hospital since Manon had been transferred from the Châtelet, but that he could not even obtain permission to see her, as the lieutenant-general of police had given the strictest orders to the contrary; and that, to complete the catastrophe, the unfortunate train of convicts, in which she was to be included, was to take its departure from Paris the day but one after.

I was so confounded by what he said, that if he had gone on speaking for another hour, I should not have interrupted him. He continued to tell me, that the reason of his not calling to see me at the Châtelet was, that he hoped to be of more use by appearing to be unknown to me; that for the last few hours since I had been set at liberty, he had in vain looked for me in order to suggest the only plan through which he could see a hope of averting Manon's fate. He told me it was dangerous counsel to give, and implored me never to mention the part he took in it; it was to find some enterprising fellows gallant enough to attack Manon's guard on getting outside the barrière. Nor did he wait for me to urge a plea of poverty. Here is fifty pounds, he said, presenting me his purse; it may be of use to you; you can repay me when you are in better circumstances. He added, that if the fear of losing his character did not prevent him from embarking in such an enterprise, he would have willingly put his sword and his life at my service.

This unlooked-for generosity affected me to tears. I expressed my gratitude with as much warmth as my depressed spirits left at my command. I asked him if there were nothing to be expected from interceding with the lieutenant-general of police: he said that he had considered that point; but that he looked upon it as a hopeless attempt, because a favour of that nature was never accorded without some strong motive, and he did not see what inducement could be held out for engaging the intercession of any person of power on her behalf; that if any hope could possibly be entertained upon the point, it must

be by working a change in the feelings of old G—— M—— and
my father, and by prevailing on them to solicit from the
lieutenant-general of police the revocation of Manon's sentence.
He offered to do everything in his power to gain over the
younger G—— M——, although he fancied a coldness in that
gentleman's manner towards him, probably from some suspicions
he might entertain of his being concerned in the late affair;
and he entreated me to lose no opportunity of effecting the
desired change in my father's mind.

This was no easy undertaking for me; not only on account of
the difficulty I should naturally meet in overcoming his opinion,
but for another reason which made me fear even to approach
him; I had quitted his lodgings contrary to his express orders,
and was resolved, since I had learned the sad fate of my poor
Manon, never again to return thither. I was not without
apprehensions indeed of his now retaining me against my will,
and perhaps taking me at once back with him into the country.
My elder brother had formerly had recourse to this violent
measure. True, I was now somewhat older; but age is a feeble
argument against force. I hit upon a mode, however, of
avoiding this danger, which was to get him by contrivance to
some public place, and there announce myself to him under an
assumed name: I immediately resolved on this method. M. de
T—— went to G—— M——'s, and I to the Luxembourg,
whence I sent my father word, that a gentleman waited there
to speak with him. I hardly thought he would come, as the
night was advancing. He, however, soon made his appearance,
followed by a servant: I begged of him to choose a walk where
we could be alone. We walked at least a hundred paces without
speaking. He doubtless imagined that so much precaution could
not be taken without some important object. He waited for my
opening speech, and I was meditating how to commence it.

At length I began.

Sir, said I, trembling, you are a good and affectionate parent;
you have loaded me with favours, and have forgiven me an infinite number of faults; I also, in my turn, call Heaven to witness
the sincere, and tender, and respectful sentiments I entertain
towards you. But it does seem to me, that your inexorable
severity——

Well, sir, my severity! interrupted my father, who no doubt
found my hesitation little suited to his impatience.

Ah, sir, I replied, it does seem to me that your severity is excessive in the penalty you inflict upon the unfortunate Manon. You have taken only M. G—— M——'s report of her. His hatred has made him represent her to you in the most odious colours: you have formed a frightful idea of her. She is, on the contrary, the mildest and most amiable of living creatures. would that Heaven had but inspired you at any one moment with the desire of seeing her! I am convinced that you would be not less sensible of her perfections than your unhappy son. You would then have been her advocate; you would have abhorred the foul artifices of G—— M——; you would have had pity on both her and me. Alas! I am persuaded of it; your heart is not insensible; it must ere now have melted with compassion.

He interrupted me again, perceiving that I spoke with a warmth which would not allow me to finish very briefly. He begged to know with what request I intended to wind up so fervent an harangue.

To ask my life at your hands, said I, which I never can retain if Manon once embark for America.

No! no! replied he, in the severest tone; I would rather see you lifeless, than infamous and depraved.

We have gone far enough, then said I, catching hold of his arm; take from me, in common mercy, my life! weary and odious and insupportable as it henceforward must be; for in the state of despair into which you now plunge me, death would be the greatest favour you could bestow,—a favour worthy of a father's hand.

I should only give you what you deserve, replied he; I know fathers who would not have shown as much patience as I have, but would themselves have executed speedy justice; but it is my foolish and excessive forbearance that has been your ruin.

I threw myself at his feet: Ah! exclaimed I, if you have still any remains of mercy, do not harden your heart against my distress and sorrow. Remember that I am your child! Alas! think of my poor mother! you loved her tenderly! would you have suffered her to be torn from your arms? You would have defended her to the death! May not the same feeling then be pardoned in others? Can persons become barbarous and cruel after having themselves experienced the softening influence of tenderness and grief?

Breathe not again the sacred name of your mother, he

exclaimed, in a voice of thunder; the very allusion to her memory rouses my indignation. Had she lived to witness the unredeemed profligacy of your life, it would have brought her in pain and sorrow to her grave.—Let us put an end to this discussion, he added; it distresses me, and makes not the slightest change in my determination: I am going back to my lodgings, and I desire you to follow me.

The cool and resolute tone in which he uttered this command, convinced me that he was inexorable. I stepped some paces aside, for fear he should think fit to lay hands upon me.

Do not increase my misery and despair, said I to him, by forcing me to disobey you. It is impossible for me to follow you; and equally so that I should continue to live, after the unkind treatment I have experienced from you. I, therefore, bid you an eternal adieu. When you know that I am dead, as I shall soon be, the paternal affection which you once entertained for me may be perhaps revived.

As I was about to turn away from him: You refuse then to follow me, cried he, in a tone of excessive anger. Go! go on to your ruin. Adieu! ungrateful and disobedient boy.

Adieu! exclaimed I to him, in a burst of grief, adieu, cruel and unnatural father!

I left the Luxembourg, and rushed like a madman through the streets to M. de T——'s house. I raised my hands and eyes as I went along, invoking the Almighty Powers: O Heaven, cried I, will you not prove more merciful than man! The only hope that remains to me is from above!

M. de T—— had not yet returned home; but he arrived before many minutes had elapsed. His negotiation had been as unsuccessful as my own. He told me so with the most sorrowful countenance. Young G—— M——, although less irritated than his father against Manon and me, would not undertake to petition in our favour. He was, in great measure, deterred by the fear which he himself had of the vindictive old lecher, who had already vented his anger against him for his design of forming a connection with Manon.

There only remained to me, therefore, the violent measures which M. de T—— had suggested. I now confined all my hopes to them. They were questionless most uncertain; but they held out to me, at least, a substantial consolation, in the certainty of meeting death in the attempt, if unsuccessful. I

left him, begging that he would offer up his best wishes for my
triumph; and I thought only of finding some companions, to
whom I might communicate a portion of my own courage and
determination.

The first that occurred to me was the same guardsman whom
I had employed to arrest G—— M——. I had intended indeed
to pass the night at his rooms, not having had a moment of
leisure during the afternoon to procure myself a lodging. I
found him alone. He was glad to see me out of the Châtelet.
He made me an offer of his services. I explained to him in
what way he might now do me the greatest kindness. He had
good sense enough to perceive all the difficulties; but he was
also generous enough to undertake to surmount them.

We spent part of the night in considering how the plot was to
be executed. He spoke of the three soldiers whom he had made
use of on the last occasion, as men whose courage had been
proved. M. de T—— had told me the exact number of archers
that would escort Manon; they were but six. Five strong and
determined men could not fail to strike terror into these fellows,
who would never think of defending themselves bravely, when
they were to be allowed the alternative of avoiding danger
by surrendering; and of that they would no doubt avail themselves. As I was not without money, the guardsman advised
me to spare no pains or expense to ensure success. We must
be mounted, he said, and each man must have his carbine and
pistols; I will take care to prepare everything requisite by to-
morrow. We shall also want three new suits of regimentals for
the soldiers, who dare not appear in an affray of this kind in
the uniform of their regiment. I handed him the hundred
pistoles which I had got from M. de T——: it was all expended
the next morning, to the very last sou. I inspected the three
soldiers; I animated them with the most liberal promises; and
to confirm their confidence in me, I began by making each man
a present of ten pistoles.

The momentous day having arrived, I sent one of them at
an early hour to the Hospital, to ascertain the exact time when
the police were to start with their prisoners. Although I merely
took this precaution from my excessive anxiety, it turned out
to have been a prudent step. I had formed my plans upon
false information, which I had received as to their destination;
and believing that it was at Rochelle this unhappy group was

to embark, all my trouble would have been thrown away in waiting for them on the Orleans road. However, I learned, by the soldier's report, that they would go out towards Rouen, and that it was from Havre-de-Grace they were to sail for America.

We at once went to the gate of St. Honoré, taking care to go by different streets. We assembled at the end of the faubourg. Our horses were fresh. In a little time we observed before us the six archers and the two wretched caravans, which you saw at Passy two years ago. The sight alone almost deprived me of my strength and senses. Oh fate! said I to myself, cruel fate! grant me now either death or victory.

We hastily consulted as to the mode of making the attack. The cavalcade was only four hundred paces in advance, and we might intercept them by cutting across a small field, round which the high road led. The guardsman was for this course, in order to fall suddenly upon them while unprepared. I approved of the plan, and was the first to spur my horse forward —but fate once again relentlessly blasted all my hopes.

The escort, seeing five horsemen riding towards them, inferred that it was for the purpose of attacking them. They put themselves in a position of defence, preparing their bayonets and guns with an air of resolution.

This demonstration, which in the guardsman and myself only inspired fresh courage, had a very different effect upon our three cowardly companions. They stopped simultaneously, and having muttered to each other some words which I could not hear, they turned their horses' heads, threw the bridles on their necks, and galloped back towards Paris.

Good heavens! said the guardsman, who appeared as much annoyed as I was by this infamous desertion, what is to be done? we are but two now.

From rage and consternation I had lost all power of speech. I doubted whether my first revenge should not be in pursuing the cowards who had abandoned me. I saw them flying, and looked in the other direction at the escort: if it had been possible to divide myself, I should at once have fallen upon both these objects of my fury; I should have destroyed all at the same moment.

The guardsman, who saw my irresolution by my wandering gaze, begged of me to hear his advice. Being but two, he said, it would be madness to attack six men as well armed as ourselves, and who seem determined to receive us firmly. Let us return to Paris, and endeavour to succeed better in the choice of our comrades. The police cannot make very rapid progress with two heavy vans; we may overtake them to-morrow without difficulty.

I reflected a moment on this suggestion; but seeing nothing around me but despair, I took a final and indeed desperate resolution: this was to thank my companion for his services, and, far from attacking the police, to go up with submission and implore them to receive me among them, that I might accompany Manon to Havre-de-Grace, and afterwards, if possible, cross the Atlantic with her. The whole world is either persecuting or betraying me, said I to the guardsman; I have no longer the power of interesting anyone in my favour; I expect nothing more either from fortune or the friendship of man; my misery is at its height; it only remains for me to submit, so that I close my eyes henceforward against every gleam of hope. May Heaven, I continued, reward you for your generosity! Adieu! I shall go and aid my wretched destiny in filling up the full measure of my ruin! He, in vain, endeavoured to persuade me to return with him to Paris. I entreated him to leave me at once, lest the police should still suspect us of an intention to attack them.

CHAPTER XII

The pauses and intermissions of pain become positive pleasures; and have thus a power of shedding a satisfaction over the intervals of ease, which few enjoyments exceed.—PALEY.

RIDING towards the cortège at a slow pace, and with a sorrowful countenance, the guards could hardly see anything very terrific in my approach. They seemed, however, to expect an attack. Be persuaded, gentlemen, said I to them, that I come not to wage war, but rather to ask favours. I then begged of them to continue their progress without any distrust, and as we went along I made my solicitations. They consulted together to ascertain in what way they should entertain my request. The chief of them spoke for the rest. He said that the orders they had received to watch the prisoners vigilantly were of the strictest kind; that, however, I seemed so interesting a young man, that they might be induced to relax a little in their duty; but that I must know, of course, that this would cost me something. I had about sixteen pistoles left, and candidly told them what my purse contained. Well, said the gendarme, we will act generously. It shall only cost you a crown an hour for conversing with any of our girls that you may prefer,—that is the ordinary price in Paris.

I said not a word of Manon, because I did not wish to let them know of my passion. They at first supposed it was merely a boyish whim, that made me think of amusing myself with these creatures: but when they discovered that I was in love, they increased their demands in such a way, that my purse was completely empty on leaving Mantes, where we had slept the night before our arrival at Passy.

Shall I describe to you my heart-rending interviews with Manon during this journey, and what my sensations were when I obtained from the guards permission to approach her caravan? Oh! language never can adequately express the sentiments of the heart; but picture to yourself my poor mistress, with a chain round her waist, seated upon a handful of straw, her head

resting languidly against the panel of the carriage, her face
pale and bathed with tears, which forced a passage between
her eyelids, although she kept them continually closed. She
had not even the curiosity to open her eyes on hearing the
bustle of the guards when they expected our attack. Her
clothes were soiled, and in disorder; her delicate hands exposed
to the rough air; in fine, her whole angelic form, that face,
lovely enough to carry back the world to idolatry, presented a
spectacle of distress and anguish utterly indescribable.

I spent some moments gazing at her as I rode alongside the
carriage. I had so lost my self-possession, that I was several
times on the point of falling from my horse. My sighs and
frequent exclamations at length attracted her attention. She
looked at and recognised me, and I remarked that on the first
impulse, she unconsciously tried to leap from the carriage
towards me, but being checked by her chain, she fell into her
former attitude.

I begged of the guards to stop one moment for the sake of
mercy; they consented for the sake of avarice. I dismounted
to go and sit near her. She was so languid and feeble, that she
was for some time without the power of speech, and could
not raise her hands: I bathed them with my tears; and being
myself unable to utter a word, we formed together as deplorable
a picture of distress as could well be seen. When at length we
were able to speak, our conversation was not less sorrowful.
Manon said little: shame and grief appeared to have altered
the character of her voice; its tone was feeble and tremulous.

She thanked me for not having forgotten her, and for the
comfort I gave her in allowing her to see me once more, and
she then bade me a long and last farewell. But when I assured
her that no power on earth could ever separate me from her,
and that I was resolved to follow her to the extremity of the
world,—to watch over her,—to guard her,—to love her,—and
inseparably to unite my wretched destiny with hers, the poor
girl gave way to such feelings of tenderness and grief, that I
almost dreaded danger to her life from the violence of her
emotion: the agitation of her whole soul seemed intensely
concentrated in her eyes; she fixed them steadfastly upon me.
She more than once opened her lips without the power of giving
utterance to her thoughts. I could, however, catch some expressions that dropped from her, of admiration and wonder at my

excessive love,—of doubt that she could have been fortunate enough to inspire me with a passion so perfect,—of earnest entreaty that I would abandon my intention of following her, and seek elsewhere a lot more worthy of me, and which, she said, I could never hope to find with her.

In spite of the cruellest inflictions of Fate, I derived comfort from her looks, and from the conviction that I now possessed her undivided affection. I had in truth lost all that other men value; but I was the master of Manon's heart, the only possession that I prized. Whether in Europe or in America, of what moment to me was the place of my abode, provided I might live happy in the society of my mistress? Is not the universe the residence of two fond and faithful lovers? Does not each find in the other, father, mother, friends, relations, riches, felicity?

If anything caused me uneasiness, it was the fear of seeing Manon exposed to want. I fancied myself already with her in a barbarous country, inhabited by savages. I am quite certain, said I, there will be none there more cruel than G—— M—— and my father. They will, at least, allow us to live in peace. If the accounts we read of savages be true, they obey the laws of nature: they neither know the mean rapacity of avarice, nor the false and fantastic notions of dignity, which have raised me up an enemy in my own father. They will not harass and persecute two lovers, when they see us adopt their own simple habits. I was therefore at ease upon that point.

But my romantic ideas were not formed with a proper view to the ordinary wants of life. I had too often found that there were necessaries which could not be dispensed with, particularly by a young and delicate woman, accustomed to comfort and abundance. I was in despair at having so fruitlessly emptied my purse, and the little money that now remained was about being forced from me by the rascally imposition of the gendarmes. I imagined that a very trifling sum would suffice for our support for some time in America, where money was scarce, and might also enable me to form some undertaking there for our permanent establishment.

This idea made me resolve on writing to Tiberge, whom I had ever found ready to hold out the generous hand of friendship. I wrote from the first town we passed through. I only alluded to the destitute condition in which I foresaw that I should find myself on arriving at Havre-de-Grace, to which place I acknowledged that I was accompanying Manon. I asked him for only fifty pistoles. You can remit it to me, said I to him, through the hands of the postmaster. You must perceive that it is the last time I can by possibility trespass on your friendly kindness; and my poor unhappy mistress being about to be exiled from her country for ever, I cannot let her depart without supplying her with some few comforts, to soften the sufferings of her lot, as well as to assuage my own sorrows.

The gendarmes became so rapacious when they saw the violence of my passion, continually increasing their demands for the slightest favours, that they soon left me penniless. Love did not permit me to put any bounds to my liberality. At Manon's side I was not master of myself; and it was no longer by the hour that time was measured; rather by the duration of whole days. At length, my funds being completely exhausted, I found myself exposed to the brutal caprice of these six wretches who treated me with intolerable rudeness — you yourself witnessed it at Passy. My meeting with you was a momentary relaxation accorded me by fate. Your compassion at the sight of my sufferings was my only recommendation to your generous nature. The assistance which you so liberally extended, enabled me to reach Havre, and the guards kept their promise more faithfully than I had ventured to hope.

We arrived at Havre. I went to the post-office: Tiberge had not yet had time to answer my letter. I ascertained the earliest day I might reckon upon his answer: it could not possibly arrive for two days longer; and by an extraordinary fatality, our vessel was to sail on the very morning of the day when the letter might be expected. I cannot give you an idea of my despair. Alas! cried I, even amongst the unfortunate, I am to be ever the most wretched!

Manon replied: Alas! does a life so thoroughly miserable deserve the care we bestow on ours? Let us die at Havre, dearest chevalier! Let death at once put an end to our afflictions! Shall we persevere, and go to drag on this hopeless existence in an unknown land, where we shall, no doubt, have to encounter the most horrible pains, since it has been their object to punish me by exile? Let us die, she repeated, or do at least in mercy rid me of life, and then you can seek another lot in the arms of some happier lover.

No, no, Manon, said I; it is but too enviable **a lot, in** my estimation, to be allowed to share your misfortunes.

Her observations made me tremble. I saw that she was overpowered by her afflictions. I tried to assume a more tranquil air, in order to dissipate such melancholy thoughts of death and despair. I resolved to adopt the same course in future; and I learned by the results, that nothing is more calculated to inspire a woman with courage than the demonstration of intrepidity in the man she loves.

When I lost all hope of receiving the expected assistance from Tiberge, I sold my horse; the money it brought, joined to what remained of your generous gift, amounted to the small sum of forty pistoles; I expended eight in the purchase of some necessary articles for Manon; and I put the remainder by, as the capital upon which we were to rest our hopes and raise our fortunes in America. I had no difficulty in getting admitted on board the vessel. They were at the time looking for young men as voluntary emigrants to the colony. The passage and provisions were supplied gratis. I left a letter for Tiberge, which was to go by the post next morning to Paris. It was no doubt written in a tone calculated to affect him deeply, since it induced him to form a resolution, which could only be carried into execution by the tenderest **and** most generous sympathy for his unhappy friend.

CHAPTER XIII

Sunt hic etiam sua præmia laudi,
Sunt lachrymæ rerum, et mentem mortalia tangunt.

VIRGIL.

E'en the mute walls relate the victim's fame,
And sinner's tears the good man's pity claim.

DRYDEN.

WE set sail; the wind continued favourable during the entire
passage. I obtained from the captain's kindness a separate
cabin for the use of Manon and myself. He was so good as to
distinguish us from the herd of our miserable associates. I
took an opportunity, on the second day, of conciliating his
attentions, by telling him part of our unfortunate history.
I did not feel that I was guilty of any very culpable falsehood
in saying that I was the husband of Manon. He appeared to
believe it, and promised me his protection; and indeed we
experienced, during the whole passage, the most flattering
evidences of his sincerity. He took care that our table was
comfortably provided; and his attentions procured us the
marked respect of our companions in misery. The unwearied
object of my solicitude was to save Manon from every inconvenience. She felt this, and her gratitude, together with a
lively sense of the singular position in which I had placed
myself solely for her sake, rendered the dear creature so tender
and impassioned, so attentive also to my most trifling wants,
that it was between us a continual emulation of attentions and
of love. I felt no regret at quitting Europe; on the contrary,
the nearer we approached America, the more did I feel my heart
expand and become tranquil. If I had not felt a dread of our
perhaps wanting, by and by, the absolute necessaries of life, I
should have been grateful to fate for having at length given so
favourable a turn to our affairs.

After a passage of two months, we at length reached the banks
of the desired river. The country offered at first sight nothing
agreeable. We saw only sterile and uninhabited plains, covered

with rushes, and some trees rooted up by the wind. No trace either of men or animals. However, the captain having discharged some pieces of artillery, we presently observed a group of the inhabitants of New Orleans, who approached us with evident signs of joy. We had not perceived the town: it is concealed upon the side on which we approached it by a hill. We were received as persons dropt from the clouds.

The poor inhabitants hastened to put a thousand questions to us upon the state of France, and of the different provinces in which they were born. They embraced us as brothers, and as beloved companions, who had come to share their pains and their solitude. We turned towards the town with them; but we were astonished to perceive, as we advanced, that what we had hitherto heard spoken of as a respectable town, was nothing more than a collection of miserable huts. They were inhabited by five or six hundred persons. The governor's house was a little distinguished from the rest by its height and its position. It was surrounded by some earthen ramparts, and a deep ditch.

We were first presented to him. He continued for some time in conversation with the captain; and then advancing towards us, he looked attentively at the women one after another: there were thirty of them, for another troop of convicts had joined us at Havre. After having thus inspected them, he sent for several young men of the colony who were desirous to marry. He assigned the handsomest women to the principal of these, and the remainder were disposed of by lot. He had not yet addressed Manon; but having ordered the others to depart, he made us remain. I learn from the captain, said he, that you are married, and he is convinced by your conduct on the passage that you are both persons of merit and of education. I have nothing to do with the cause of your misfortunes; but if it be true that you are as conversant with the world and society as your appearance would indicate, I shall spare no pains to soften the severity of your lot, and you may on your part contribute towards rendering this savage and desert abode less disagreeable to me. I replied in the manner which I thought best calculated to confirm the opinion he had formed of us. He gave orders to have a habitation prepared for us in the town, and detained us to supper. I was really surprised to find so much politeness in a governor of transported convicts. In the presence of others he abstained from inquiring about our past adventures. The conversation was general; and in spite of our degradation, Manon and I exerted ourselves to make it lively and agreeable.

At night we were conducted to the lodging prepared for us. We found a wretched hovel composed of planks and mud, containing three rooms on the ground, and a loft overhead. He had sent there six chairs, and some few necessaries of life.

Manon appeared frightened by the first view of this melancholy dwelling. It was on my account much more than upon her own, that she distressed herself. When we were left to ourselves, she sat down and wept bitterly. I attempted at first to console her; but when she enabled me to understand that it was for my sake she deplored our privations, and that in our common afflictions she only considered me as the sufferer, I put on an air of resolution, and even of content, sufficient to encourage her.

What is there in my lot to lament? said I; I possess all that I have ever desired. You love me, Manon, do you not? What happiness beyond this have I ever longed for? Let us leave to Providence the direction of our destiny; it by no means appears to me so desperate. The governor is civil and obliging; he has already given us marks of his consideration; he will not allow us to want for necessaries. As to our rude hut and the squalidness of our furniture, you might have noticed that there are few persons in the colony better lodged or more comfortably furnished than we are: and then you are an admirable chemist, added I, embracing her; you transform everything into gold.

In that case, she answered, you shall be the richest man in the universe; for, as there never was love surpassing yours, so it is impossible for man to be loved more tenderly than you are by me. I well know, she continued, that I have never merited the almost incredible fidelity and attachment which you have shown for me. I have often caused you annoyances, which nothing but excessive fondness could have induced you to pardon. I have been thoughtless and volatile; and even while loving you as I have always done to distraction, I was never free from a consciousness of ingratitude. But you cannot believe how much my nature is altered; those tears which you have so frequently seen me shed since quitting the French shore, have not been caused by my own misfortunes. Since you began to share them with me, I have been a stranger to selfishness: I only wept from tenderness and compassion for you. I am inconsolable at the thought of having given you one instant's pain during my past life. I never cease upbraiding myself with my former inconstancy, and wondering at the sacrifices which love has induced you to make for a miserable and unworthy wretch, who could not, with the last drop of her blood, compensate for half the torments she has caused you.

Her grief, the language, and the tone in which she expressed herself, made such an impression, that I felt my heart ready to break within me. Take care, said I to her, take care, dear Manon; I have not strength to endure such exciting marks of your affection; I am little accustomed to the rapturous sensations which you now kindle in my heart. Oh Heaven! cried I, I have now nothing further to ask of you. I am sure of Manon's love. That has been alone wanting to complete my happiness; I can now never cease to be happy: my felicity is well secured.

It is indeed, she replied, if it depends upon me, and I well know where I can be ever certain of finding my own happiness centred.

With these ideas, capable of turning my hut into a palace worthy of earth's proudest monarch, I lay down to rest. America appeared to my view the true land of milk and honey, the abode of contentment and delight. People should come to New Orleans, I often said to Manon, who wish to enjoy the real rapture of love! It is here that love is divested of all selfishness, all jealousy, all inconstancy. Our countrymen come here in search of gold; they little think that we have discovered treasures of inestimably greater value.

We carefully cultivated the governor's friendship. He bestowed upon me, a few weeks after our arrival, a small appointment which became vacant in the fort. Although not one of any distinction, I gratefully accepted it as a gift of Providence, as it enabled me to live independently of others' aid. I took a servant for myself, and a woman for Manon. Our little establishment became settled: nothing could surpass the regularity of my conduct, or that of Manon; we lost no opportunity of serving or doing an act of kindness to our neighbours. This friendly disposition, and the mildness of our manners, secured us the confidence and affection of the whole colony. We soon became so respected, that we ranked as the principal persons in the town after the governor.

The simplicity of our habits and occupations, and the perfec
innocence in which we lived, revived insensibly our early feeling
of devotion. Manon had never been an irreligious girl, and
was far from being one of those reckless libertines who deligh
in adding impiety and sacrilege to moral depravity: all th
disorders of our lives might be fairly ascribed to the natura
influences of youth and love. Experience had now begun witl
us to do the office of age; it produced the same effect upon us a
years must have done. Our conversation, which was generall
of a serious turn, by degrees engendered a longing for virtuou
love. I first proposed this change to Manon. I knew th
principles of her heart; she was frank and natural in all he
sentiments, qualities which invariably predispose to virtue
I said to her that there was but one thing wanting to complet
our happiness: it is, said I, to invoke upon our union the bene-
diction of Heaven. We have both of us hearts too sensitive
and minds too refined, to continue voluntarily in the wilfu
violation of so sacred a duty. It signifies nothing our having
lived while in France in such a manner, because there it was a
impossible for us not to love, as to be united by a legitimate tie
but in America, where we are under no restraint, where we ow
no allegiance to the arbitrary distinctions of birth and aristo-
cratic prejudice, where besides we are already supposed to be
married, why should we not actually become so,—why should
we not sanctify our love by the holy ordinances of religion? As
for me, I added, I offer nothing new in offering you my hand
and my heart; but I am ready to ratify it at the foot of the altar

This speech seemed to inspire her with joy. Would you
believe it, she replied, I have thought of this a thousand times
since our arrival in America? The fear of annoying you has
kept it shut up in my breast. I felt that I had no pretensions
to aspire to the character of your wife.

Ah! Manon, said I, you should very soon be a sovereign's
consort, if I had been born to the inheritance of a crown. Let
us not hesitate; we have no obstacle to impede us: I will this
day speak to the governor on the subject, and acknowledge that
we have in this particular hitherto deceived him. Let us leave
added I, to vulgar lovers the dread of the indissoluble bonds
of marriage [1]; they would not fear them if they were assured

[1] Some say that Love, at sight of human ties,
    Spreads his light wings, and in a moment flies.

s we are, of the continuance of those of love. I left Manon
nchanted by this resolution.

I am persuaded that no honest man could disapprove of this
ntention in my present situation; that is to say, fatally enslaved
s I was by a passion which I could not subdue, and visited by
ompunction and remorse which I ought not to stifle. But
vill any man charge me with injustice or impiety if I complain
f the rigour of Heaven in defeating a design that I could only
ave formed with the view of conciliating its favour and comply-
ng with its decrees? Alas! do I say defeated? nay punished
s a new crime. I was patiently permitted to go blindly along
he high road of vice; and the cruellest chastisements were
eserved for the period when I was returning to the paths of
virtue. I now fear that I shall have hardly fortitude enough
eft to recount the most disastrous circumstances that ever
ccurred to any man.

I waited upon the governor, as I had settled with Manon,
o procure his consent to the ceremony of our marriage. I should
ave avoided speaking to him or to any other person upon the
ubject, if I had imagined that his chaplain, who was the only
minister in the town, would have performed the office for me
vithout his knowledge; but not daring to hope that he would
o so privately, I determined to act ingenuously in the matter.

The governor had a nephew named Synnelet, of whom he
vas particularly fond. He was about thirty; brave, but of a
eadstrong and violent disposition. He was not married.
Manon's beauty had struck him on the first day of our arrival;
nd the numberless opportunities he had of seeing her during
he last nine or ten months, had so inflamed his passion, that he
vas absolutely pining for her in secret. However, as he was
onvinced in common with his uncle and the whole colony that
was married, he put such a restraint upon his feelings, that
hey remained generally unnoticed; and he lost no opportunity
f showing the most disinterested friendship for me.

He happened to be with his uncle when I arrived at the
overnment house. I had no reason for keeping my intention
secret from him, so that I explained myself without hesitation
n his presence. The governor heard me with his usual kindness.
 related to him a part of my history, to which he listened with
vident interest; and when I requested his presence at the intended
eremony, he was so generous as to say, that he must be

permitted to defray the expenses of the succeeding entertainment. I retired perfectly satisfied.

In an hour after, the chaplain paid me a visit. I thought he was come to prepare me by religious instruction for the sacred ceremony; but, after a cold salutation, he announced to me in two words, that the governor desired I would relinquish all thoughts of such a thing, for that he had other views for Manon.

Other views for Manon! said I, as I felt my heart sink within me; what views then can they be, chaplain?

He replied, that I must be, of course, aware that the governor was absolute master here; that Manon, having been transported from France to the colony, was entirely at his disposal; that, hitherto he had not exercised his right, believing that she was a married woman; but that now, having learned from my own lips that it was not so, he had resolved to assign her to M. Synnelet, who was passionately in love with her.

My indignation overcame my prudence. Irritated as I was, I desired the chaplain instantly to quit my house, swearing at the same time that neither governor, Synnelet, nor the whole colony together, should lay hands upon my wife, or mistress, if they chose so to call her.

I immediately told Manon of the distressing message I had just received. We conjectured that Synnelet had warped his uncle's mind after my departure, and that it was all the effect of a premeditated design. They were, questionless, the stronger party. We found ourselves in New Orleans, as in the midst of the ocean, separated from the rest of the world by an immense interval of space. In a country perfectly unknown, a desert, or inhabited, if not by brutes, at least by savages quite as ferocious, to what corner could we fly? I was respected in the town, but I could not hope to excite the people in my favour to such a degree as to derive assistance from them proportioned to the impending danger: money was requisite for that purpose, and I was poor. Besides, the success of a popular commotion was uncertain; and if we failed in the attempt, our doom would be inevitably sealed.

I revolved these thoughts in my mind; I mentioned them in part to Manon; I found new ones, without waiting for her replies; I determined upon one course, and then abandoned that to adopt another; I talked to myself, and answered my own thoughts aloud; at length I sank into a kind of hysterical stupor that I can compare to nothing, because nothing ever equalled it. Manon observed my emotion, and from its violence, judged how imminent was our danger; and, apprehensive more on my account than on her own, the dear girl could not even venture to give expression to her fears.

After a multitude of reflections, I resolved to call upon the governor, and appeal to his feelings of honour, to the recollection of my unvarying respect for him, and the marks he had given of his own affection for us both. Manon endeavoured to dissuade me from this attempt: she said, with tears in her eyes, You are rushing into the jaws of death; they will murder you— I shall never again see you—I am determined to die before you. I had great difficulty in persuading her that it was absolutely necessary that I should go, and that she should remain at home. I promised that she should see me again in a few moments. She did not foresee, nor did I, that it was against herself the whole anger of Heaven, and the rabid fury of our enemies, was about to be concentrated.

I went to the fort: the governor was there with his chaplain. I supplicated him in a tone of humble submission that I could have ill brooked under other circumstances. I invoked his clemency by every argument calculated to soften any heart less ferocious and cruel than a tiger's.

The barbarian made to all my prayers but two short answers, which he repeated over and over again. Manon, he said, was at his disposal: and he had given a promise to his nephew. I was resolved to command my feelings to the last: I merely replied, that I had imagined he was too sincerely my friend to desire my death, to which I would infinitely rather consent than to the loss of my mistress.

I felt persuaded, on quitting him, that it was folly to expect anything from the obstinate tyrant, who would have damned himself a hundred times over to please his nephew. However, I persevered in restraining my temper to the end; deeply resolved, if they persisted in such flagrant injustice, to make America the scene of one of the most horrible and bloody murders that even love had ever led to.

I was, on my return home, meditating upon this design, when fate, as if impatient to expedite my ruin, threw Synnelet in my way. He read in my countenance a portion of my thoughts. I before said, he was brave. He approached me.

Are you not seeking me? he inquired. I know that my intentions have given you mortal offence, and that the death of one of us is indispensable: let us see who is to be the happy man.

I replied, that such was unquestionably the fact, and that nothing but death could end the difference between us.

We retired about one hundred paces out of the town. We drew: I wounded and disarmed him at the first onset. He was so enraged, that he peremptorily refused either to ask his life or renounce his claims to Manon. I might have been perhaps justified in ending both by a single blow; but noble blood ever vindicates its origin. I threw him back his sword. Let us renew the struggle, said I to him, and remember that there shall be now no quarter. He attacked me with redoubled fury. I must confess that I was not an accomplished swordsman, having had but three months' tuition in Paris. Love, however, guided my weapon. Synnelet pierced me through and through the left arm; but I caught him whilst thus engaged, and made so vigorous a thrust that I stretched him senseless at my feet.

In spite of the triumphant feeling that victory, after a mortal conflict, inspires, I was immediately horrified by the certain consequences of his death. There could not be the slightest hope of either pardon or respite from the vengeance I had thus incurred. Aware, as I was, of the affection of the governor for his nephew, I felt perfectly sure that my death would not be delayed a single hour after his should become known. Urgent as this apprehension was, it still was by no means the principal source of my uneasiness. Manon, the welfare of Manon, the peril that impended over her, and the certainty of my being now at length separated from her, afflicted me to such a degree, that I was incapable of recognising the place in which I stood. I regretted Synnelet's death: instant suicide seemed the only remedy for my woes.

However, it was this very thought that quickly restored me to my reason, and enabled me to form a resolution. What, said I to myself, die, in order to end my pain! Then there is something I dread more than the loss of all I love! No, let me suffer the cruellest extremities in order to aid her; and when these prove of no avail, fly to death as a last resource!

I returned towards the town; on my arrival at home, I found Manon half dead with fright and anxiety: my presence restored her. I could not conceal from her the terrible accident that had happened. On my mentioning the death of Synnelet and my own wound, she fell in a state of insensibility into my arms. It was a quarter of an hour before I could bring her again to her senses.

I was myself in a most deplorable state of mind; I could not discern the slightest prospect of safety for either of us. Manon, said I to her, when she had recovered a little, what shall we do? Alas, what hope remains to us? I must necessarily fly. Will you remain in the town? Yes, dearest Manon, do remain; you may possibly still be happy here; while I, far away from you, may seek death and find it amongst the savages, or the wild beasts.

She raised herself in spite of her weakness, and taking hold of my hand to lead me towards the door: Let us, said she, fly together, we have not a moment to lose; Synnelet's body may be found by chance, and we shall then have no time to escape. But, dear Manon, replied I, to what place can we fly? Do you perceive any resource? Would it not be better that you should endeavour to live on without me; and that I should go and voluntarily place my life in the governor's hands?

This proposal had only the effect of making her more impatient for our departure. I had presence of mind enough, on going out, to take with me some strong liquors which I had in my chamber, and as much food as I could carry in my pockets. We told our servants, who were in the adjoining room, that we were going to take our evening walk, as was our invariable habit; and we left the town behind us more rapidly than I had thought possible from Manon's delicate state of health.

Although I had not formed any resolve as to our future destination, I still cherished a hope, without which I should have infinitely preferred death to my suspense about Manon's safety. I had acquired a sufficient knowledge of the country, during nearly ten months which I had now passed in America, to know in what manner the natives should be approached. Death was not the necessary consequence of falling into their hands. I had learned a few words of their language, and some of their customs, having had many opportunities of seeing them.

Besides this sad resource, I derived some hopes from the fact, that the English had, like ourselves, established colonies in this part of the New World. But the distance was terrific.

In order to reach them, we should have to traverse deserts of many days' journey, and more than one range of mountains so steep and vast as to seem almost impassable to the strongest man. I nevertheless flattered myself that we might derive partial relief from one or other of these sources: the savages might serve us as guides, and the English receive us in their settlements.

We journeyed on as long as Manon's strength would permit, that is to say, about six miles; for this incomparable creature, with her usual absence of selfishness, refused my repeated entreaties to stop. Overpowered at length by fatigue, she acknowledged the utter impossibility of proceeding farther. It was already night: we sat down in the midst of an extensive plain, where we could not even find a tree to shelter us. Her first care was to dress my wound, which she had bandaged before our departure. I, in vain, entreated her to desist from exertion: it would have only added to her distress if I had refused her the satisfaction of seeing me at ease and out of danger, before her own wants were attended to. I allowed her therefore to gratify herself, and in shame and silence submitted to her delicate attentions.

But when she had completed her tender task, with what ardour did I not enter upon mine! I took off my clothes and stretched them under her, to render more endurable the hard and rugged ground on which she lay. I protected her delicate hands from the cold by my burning kisses and the warmth of my sighs. I passed the livelong night in watching over her as she slept, and praying Heaven to refresh her with soft and undisturbed repose. You can bear witness, just and all-seeing God! to the fervour and sincerity of those prayers, and Thou alone knowest with what awful rigour they were rejected.

You will excuse me, if I now cut short a story which it distresses me beyond endurance to relate. It is, I believe, a calamity without parallel. I can never cease to deplore it. But although it continues, of course, deeply and indelibly impressed on my memory, yet my heart seems to shrink within me each time that I attempt the recital.

We had thus tranquilly passed the night. I had fondly imagined that my beloved mistress was in a profound sleep, and I hardly dared to breathe lest I should disturb her. As day broke, I observed that her hands were cold and trembling;

I pressed them to my bosom in the hope of restoring animation. This movement roused her attention, and making an effort to grasp my hand, she said, in a feeble voice, that she thought her last moments had arrived.

I, at first, took this for a passing weakness, or the ordinary language of distress; and I answered with the usual consolations that love prompted. But her incessant sighs, her silence, and inattention to my inquiries, the convulsed grasp of her hands, in which she retained mine, soon convinced me that the crowning end of all my miseries was approaching.

Do not now expect me to attempt a description of my feelings, or to repeat her dying expressions. I lost her—I received the purest assurances of her love even at the very instant that her spirit fled. I have not nerve to say more upon this fatal and disastrous event.

My spirit was not destined to accompany Manon's. Doubtless, Heaven did not as yet consider me sufficiently punished, and therefore ordained that I should continue to drag on a languid and joyless existence. I willingly renounced every hope of leading a happy one.

I remained for twenty-four hours without taking my lips from the still beauteous countenance and hands of my adored Manon. My intention was to await my own death in that position; but at the beginning of the second day, I reflected that, after I was gone, she must of necessity become the prey of wild beasts. I then determined to bury her, and wait my own doom upon her grave. I was already, indeed, so near my end from the combined effect of long fasting and grief, that it was with the greatest difficulty I could support myself standing. I was obliged to have recourse to the liquors which I had brought with me, and these restored sufficient strength to enable me to set about my last sad office. From the sandy nature of the soil there was little trouble in opening the ground. I broke my sword and used it for the purpose; but my bare hands were of greater service. I dug a deep grave, and there deposited the idol of my heart, after having wrapt around her my clothes to prevent the sand from touching her. I kissed her ten thousand times with all the ardour of the most glowing love, before I laid her in this melancholy bed. I sat for some time upon the bank intently gazing on her, and could not command fortitude enough to close the grave over her. At length, feeling that my strength was giving way, and apprehensive of its being entirely exhausted before the completion of my task, I committed to the earth all that it had ever contained most perfect and peerless. I then lay myself with my face down upon the grave, and closing my eyes with the determination never again to open them, I invoked the mercy of Heaven, and ardently prayed for death.

You will find it difficult to believe that, during the whole time of this protracted and distressing ceremony, not a tear or a sigh escaped to relieve my agony. The state of profound affliction in which I was, and the deep settled resolution I had taken to die, had silenced the sighs of despair, and effectually dried up the ordinary channels of grief. It was thus impossible for me, in this posture upon the grave, to continue for any time in possession of my faculties.

After what you have listened to, the remainder of my own history would ill repay the attention you seem inclined to bestow upon it. Synnelet having been carried into the town and skilfully examined, it was found that, so far from being dead, he was not even dangerously wounded. He informed his uncle of the manner in which the affray had occurred between us, and he generously did justice to my conduct on the occasion. I was sent for; and as neither of us could be found, our flight was immediately suspected. It was then too late to attempt to trace me, but the next day and the following one were employed in the pursuit.

I was found, without any appearance of life, upon the grave of Manon: and the persons who discovered me in this situation, seeing that I was almost naked and bleeding from my wounds, naturally supposed that I had been robbed and assassinated. They carried me into the town. The motion restored me to my senses. The sighs I heaved on opening my eyes and finding myself still amongst the living, showed that I was not beyond the reach of art: they were but too successful in its application.

I was immediately confined as a close prisoner. My trial was ordered; and as Manon was not forthcoming, I was accused of having murdered her from rage and jealousy. I naturally related all that had occurred. Synnelet, though bitterly grieved and disappointed by what he heard, had the generosity to solicit my pardon: he obtained it.

I was so reduced, that they were obliged to carry me from

the prison to my bed, and there I suffered for three long months under severe illness. My aversion from life knew no diminution. I continually prayed for death, and obstinately for some time refused every remedy. But Providence, after having punished me with atoning rigour, saw fit to turn to my own use its chastisements and the memory of my multiplied sorrows. It at length deigned to shed upon me its redeeming light, and revived in my mind ideas worthy of my birth and my early education.

My tranquillity of mind being again restored, my cure speedily followed. I began only to feel the highest aspirations of honour, and diligently performed the duties of my appointment, whilst expecting the arrival of the vessels from France, which were always due at this period of the year. I resolved to return to my native country, there to expiate the scandal of my former life by my future good conduct. Synnelet had the remains of my dear mistress removed into a more hallowed spot.

It was six weeks after my recovery that, one day walking alone upon the banks of the river, I saw a vessel arrive, which some mercantile speculation had directed to New Orleans. I stood by whilst the passengers landed. Judge my surprise on recognising Tiberge amongst those who proceeded towards the town. This ever-faithful friend knew me at a distance, in spite of the ravages which care and sorrow had worked upon my countenance. He told me that the sole object of his voyage had been to see me once more, and to induce me to return with him to France; that on receipt of the last letter which I had written to him from Havre, he started for that place, and was himself the bearer of the succour which I solicited; that he had been sensibly affected on learning my departure, and that he would have instantly followed me, if there had been a vessel bound for the same destination; that he had been for several months endeavouring to hear of one in the various seaport towns, and that, having at length found one at St. Malo which was weighing anchor for Martinique, he embarked, in the expectation of easily passing from thence to New Orleans; that the St. Malo vessel having been captured by Spanish pirates and taken to one of their islands, he had contrived to escape; and that, in short, after many adventures, he had got on board the vessel which had just arrived, and at length happily attained his object.

I was totally unable adequately to express my feelings of

gratitude to this generous and unshaken friend. I conducted him to my house, and placed all I possessed at his service. I related to him every circumstance that had occurred to me since I left France; and in order to gladden him with tidings which I knew he did not expect, I assured him that the seeds of virtue which he had in former days implanted in my heart, were now about to produce fruit, of which even he should be proud. He declared to me, that this gladdening announcement more than repaid him for all the fatigue and trouble he had endured.

We passed two months together at New Orleans whilst waiting the departure of a vessel direct to France; and having at length sailed, we landed only a fortnight since at Havre-de-Grace. On my arrival I wrote to my family. By a letter from my elder brother, I there learned my father's death, which, I dread to think, the disorders of my youth might have hastened. The wind being favourable for Calais, I embarked for this port, and am now going to the house of one of my relations who lives a few miles off, where my brother said that he should anxiously await my arrival.

CARMEN

*Translated from the French of Prosper Mérimée
by* EDMUND H. GARRETT, *with a Memoir of
the author by* LOUISE IMOGEN GUINEY

MÉRIMÉE

Born at Paris 28th September 1803. Educated for bar, but entered public service instead. Published what purported to be the dramatic works of a Spanish lady, Clara Gazul, 1825, but which in reality he had written himself. 1827, *La Guzla* supposed to be translated from the Illyrian of a certain Hyacinth Maglanovich. In 1828 appeared short dramatic romance *La Jacquerie, Chronique de Charles IX* (1829); *Les Espagnols en Danemark, Une femme est un diable, L'Amour africain, le ciel et l'enfer, Le Théâtre de Clara Gazul*, augmented by two pieces: *L'Occasion, Le Carosse de Saint-Sacrement*, 1830. Visits Spain, and on his return, after the July revolution, was appointed *chef de cabinet*. Letters addressed from Madrid and Valences to "Revue de Paris," October to November 1830. *La Double Méprise, Mosaïque*, 1833. Collected stories and *nouvelles* which had already appeared in the "Revue de Paris": *Mateo Falcone, La Vision de Charles XI, L'Enlèvement de la Redoute, Tamango, Le Perle de Tolède, La Partie de Trictac, Le Vase étrusque, Les Mécontents, Corresp.* and *Les Ames de Pingatorie*, which appeared in the "Revue des Deux Mondes," 1834.

Appointed inspector-general of historical monuments, 1834. In that capacity he travelled all over France and Corsica. *Notes d'un voyage dans le midi de la France*, 1835; *Notes d'un Voyage dans l'ouest de la France*, 1836; *La Venus d'Ille*, 1837; *Notes d'un Voyage en Auvergne*, 1838; *Notes d'un Voyage en Corse*, 1840; *Colomba*, 1841 (appeared in "Revue des Deux Mondes," July 1840); *Monuments historiques, Report au Ministre de l'Intérieur*, 1843; *Etudes sur l'histoire romaine, Guerre sociale, Conjuration de Catalina*. Elected to the Academy, and also to Academy of Inscriptions, 1844. *Peintures de l'église Saint-Savin*, 1844; *Carmen*, 1847; *Histoire de Don Pedre roi de Castille*, 1848; *Nouvelles* published, containing *Arsène Guillot, L'Abbé Anboin, Le Dame de Pique* (translations of Pushkin), *Les Bohémiens* (Pushkin), *Le Hasard* (Pushkin), and a Study on Gogol, 1852; *Le faux Démetrius, épisode de l'histoire de Russie*. Made Member of Senate, 1853. *Les deux Héritages* (Mag), 1852. *Mélanges historiques et littéraires* (collection of articles published in "Revue de Deux Mondes"). An edition of the works of Brantome, 1855. President of commission for the reorganisation of the Imperial Library, 1858. *Nouvelles Muscovites* (three tales of Turgenev's translated), 1868. Died at Cannes 23rd September 1870.

POSTHUMOUS PUBLICATIONS.—*Lettres à une Inconnue*, 1873. Translation of Gogol's *Inspector General, The Overcoat*.

Œuvres complètes in process of publication under direction of Pierre Trahard and Edouard Champion, 1927. M. Trahard is also the biographer of Mérimée; his work appeared in four parts from 1925 to 1930. *See also Mérimée inconnu*, edited by Ferdinand Bac, 1939, and A. M. Ruppé: *Mérimée*, 1945.

MEMOIR

OPPORTUNITY was always at Mérimée's elbow; he had a smooth career, a competence, leisure varied by agreeable occupations, exquisite resources. Whatever he did was done admirably, and at no expense to himself. Distinction and sense, wit and breeding, were his in their highest degree. Cousin said of him that he knew nothing imperfectly. He was a critic of men and women, and a finished archæologist; he had a distinct turn for art; he was master of six languages, and of the history and poetry of each of them, and was the founder of the modern appreciation of Russian literature. An old and most discerning traveller, he looked, wherever he went, into the heart of things. Fishermen, bull-fighters, shepherds, bandits, pleased him more than Academicians. In fact, he frankly announces somewhere that after old friends who have no affectations, he prefers an assorted society of peasants. Mérimée was able to astonish the lean Spanish gipsies with his command of Romany slang, and *Blackwood's* thought it the greatest pity in the world he had never gone off on a tour with George Borrow, allowing the public to profit by the report of two such apposite and opposite observers.

With all his gifts, Mérimée lacked "the material for mental happiness." He was too timid, too restless, and though without vanity, too fearful of ridicule and misconception. Something of the feminine-bitter pervaded both his temperament and his talent; a direct inheritance, perhaps, from his clever and devoted mother, who gave her boy for motto the satanic talisman: Μέμνησο ἀπιστεῖν, Remember to mistrust. His apprehension turned, as often as not, into satires against himself. He is faithfully outlined in his Arthur, Darcy, St. Clair, and Bernard de Margy, in the elegantly invertebrate heroes born of nineteenth-century France, who are recognisable enough in his books, though dispersed over various latitudes and periods. Of direct autobiography Mérimée gives us nothing. The publication of the *Letters to an Incognita* excited prodigious interest, because no one thitherto had any accurate knowledge of their author.

He hated folk who feel obliged to make poetic remarks while the moon is shining. He could not be expected to reveal, with Leigh Hunt, how he sat at his desk, and how his breath came and went in the heat of composition. It is curious, on the other hand, that he should have been so communicative concerning his health; he is fond of picturing himself to his robust English correspondents as lying upon the sofa, with a skin the colour of scorched grass; melancholy, vacant, and bored to death. It is certain that despite this quality of secretiveness, he never hid the evil which was in him, but carefully cherished and catalogued it, beating it out thin and broad, in the super-sincere manner of his country. His fatal disease, fatal in all cases, was indifferentism. You feel wroth at him that he went out of the world, not like a veteran from a battle-field, but like a girl from the ball-room, in smiling weariness, and without a scar. M. Jules Lemaître considers that a most distinguished attitude toward life! Mérimée surely had no monopoly of it; it is the dream of every sophomore before he has begun to think.

A mask is very irritating when its wearer is a man of genius. Unlike Hamlet, who "knew not seems," Prosper Mérimée knew little else; his whole character was encased in reserve one may rightly call ungenerous. Such diffidence as his can suggest no new worthlessness in the race, but it bespeaks weakness at once in himself. Are we not here to bluff and be bluffed? The ultimate verdict on "the visionary in humanity, the fool of virtue," is that he is a most blessed person. He is no miser, he has spent his immortal patrimony of energy and faith.

Moreover, Mérimée's withholding of his real self did him severe injustice. He was spirited and scrupulous, and a proud truth-speaker, and he had a capacity for deep affections. So much repression is upon his own natural moods throughout that it is a satisfaction to find him pleading with enthusiastic zeal for the preservation of the church of St. Savin, and a much greater one to be told during the war, at the very end, that his dying heart is sore for France, and solicitous for "those imbecile Frenchmen." He had one literary pretence, along with fifty personal ones; he would not be thought to be a serious lover of his art. With beautiful skill and ease, at his caprice and on chosen subjects, he produced twenty-two slim book in all: memoirs and critical sketches; free living historic studies, worth so many encyclopædias; comments on antique sculpture and architecture: golden burlesques, boldly successful; and, among these, the six or seven short stories which will always preserve his name from oblivion. Artist that he is, he worries his reader through them all, with some sudden ever-recurring chill, absent only from the close of *Arsène Guillot*, lest his reader, poor simple wight! should believe his chair to be safe and comfortable, and give himself over to a possible emotion. Mérimée wrote, says M. Maurice Tourneaux, "comme un Gentleman," that is, without undue interest in what he was doing, which is exactly what Pope said, long ago, in an erroneous application, of Crashaw. An outright man of letters like Mr. Stevenson prefers to go to the more affectionate extreme, and cheerfully specify "my trade," a noun which would have made Prosper Mérimée shiver. For this one Parisian, at least, has no bravado, no outward stir and sparkle. He is sick through and through with wilfully imposed cynicism which has little enough to do with the nobler cynicism of Clough's verse:

> I have seen higher, holier things than these,
> And therefore must to these refuse my heart.

Mérimée was no visionist, no spiritual nomad homesick for ideals. A dilettante to the marrow, he amused himself by producing a few masterpieces, and ended by becoming the callous, inscrutable Mephisto he had all his life tried to be. He suffered from his innate discord, and he makes others suffer. His deftest handling gets to be occasionally abnormal and meretricious. "It is," as Mr. Pater remarks in his illuminating manner, "as if there were nothing to tell of in the world but various forms of hatred, and a love that is like lunacy." *Wuthering Heights*, a crude and sincere thing, is smooth water beside much of Mérimée. His joy is to shock and vex: the conscious audacity of little minds. According to Baudelaire, it is a delicate luxury to rub people the wrong way, or to achieve, in his own more classic phrase, "le plaisir aristocratique de déplaire." Mérimée is not without his hit at *Tom Jones*, "as immoral a book as all of mine put together." His complacency, playful as it is, indicates sufficiently how hopeless it would be to confute him in his mistake. For though Fielding splash his reader, he does not sting him; his sin is not spite against humanity, but only a too liberal laughing report of it. It may be worth while to quote the Count d'Haussonville's summing-up: "Mérimée does not appeal altogether to simple natures; he is himself the fine fruit of the decadence, and to relish him very greatly, one must, perhaps, be of a sophisticated mind, and æsthetically a little depraved. . . . The painful circumstance of his novels is that he is ever likely to deflower what he creates by some jeering or even soiling touch." Nothing severer can be urged against Mérimée, and nothing truer.

He is said to have looked like an Englishman, all save the smile. What an astute Latin smile it was! never concealed except under the big, transient moustache grown in Asia Minor on the journey with the younger Ampère; a smile not unlike that of Leonardo da Vinci's women as we perceive it under the head-dress of the deceased playwright Clara Gazul, who was Mérimée's masquerading self. And it shows again, "aux lèvres malicieuses," in a water-colour copy of Mérimée the child; a portrait whose uncertain elfish beauty bids you forecast the future of an only darling, secluded from schoolfellows and reared on negations. His genial father, Léonor Mérimée, was a painter in good standing at the capital; the mother, Anna Moreau, whom the son resembled, painted also, and was a free-thinkeress, and, therefore, naturally a more significant family figure than her husband, who was merely a free-thinker. The little fellow with the auspicious name, born in 1803, was, of course, never baptised; the only bit of bad taste one can attribute to him is that he was given to boasting of that omission, albeit in the dubiously Christian salons of the Second Empire. His parents were pleased with him when he had reached the age of eighteen, and commended, somewhat prematurely, his moral sense. That same year Prosper met Henri Beyle (Stendhal) at Madame Pasta's; a momentous encounter to him. He worshipped Beyle, and quarrelled and made up with him, even as he did with the Incognita, and learned much philosophy of various kinds from his elder and exemplar; but an unprejudiced spectator may confess that the companionship reminds him ticklishly of Steerforth and David Copperfield. Mérimée, who was intended for the law, was a known writer at twenty-two, having perpetrated and sustained two superior jests, in offering purported translations to the hungry romanticists of his generation, and won the regard of Goethe, who saw Gazul in Guzla and fun in both. Mérimée's youth had its emotional scurry, ending in a comedy, with Georges Sand: he was not blighted as were Chopin and De Musset. Before 1830, he was challenged and wounded in the left arm by an old expert, who had fallen across a letter addressed to his wife. This is one of the very few scarlet episodes in a rather grey life. The young man, with his arm in a sling, was accosted by sympathising friends: who could have hurt him? "A person who does not admire my prose": nothing further. Reticence which began to bear verbal fruit of this sort is not to be deprecated. The incident which caused the duel, and the abandonment of his deepening love affair, sank into Mérimée's heart. His first journey to Spain, as Secretary of the Embassy, followed soon after; it proved a joyous and memorable experience. One of the welcome things it brought him was an acquaintance with the Count and Countess of Montijo and their two little daughters, one of whom, Eugénie, was Mérimée's pet and fast friend from the beginning. After the deposition of Charles X, Mérimée became Chef-de-cabinet in the Ministry of the Interior, and, in 1834, Inspector of National Monuments, thus securing a post which exactly suited him; ten years later, he was elected to Charles Nodier's seat in the Academy. All this time he was writing at intervals, as the whim took him; travelling in England and elsewhere, diffusing the aroma of his culture and fine, tart wit in appreciative drawing-rooms, and making epistolary confidences to the nameless young femininity who, long after, was to serve him as Fanny Brawne served John Keats. A subsequent incident does Mérimée much honour. His friend Libri, the learned son of Italy known to his sponsors as Guglielmo-Brutus-Icilius-Timoleon de Libri-Carrucci d'alla Sommaja, Member of the Academy of Sciences and Professor at the Sorbonne, was charged with the appropriation of curios and manuscripts from the collections which came under his official examination. M. Boucly complained of him to M. Guizot in March of 1848, and these secret advices were found and published. When Libri, proven to be a perfectly magnificent thief, was convicted, and given ten years' imprisonment, Prosper Mérimée, who still believed in him, came forth as his champion in the *Revue des Deux Mondes*. The immediate mundane reward of his fidelity was a fine of a thousand francs, and fifteen days in jail. A pleasingly dramatic circumstance connected with the sentence was the offer of a certain Corsican who had read and warmly admired Colomba, to start a vendetta on behalf of the author against the judge who condemned him. But Mérimée went gracefully to his cell, and sat there studying Russian, while charitable ladies arrived, of afternoons, with roses and *marrons glacés*. Nay, more; he reverted, with cool courage, to the defence of Libri many years after, and supported, though in vain, his wife's petition to the Senate: from first to last implacably steadfast and loyal, as was his wont.

In a preface, printed at the time, he apologised with good-humoured sarcasm for having been delayed a whole fortnight on his work in a place where the sun's heat is not in the least oppressive, and where one may always enjoy a profound leisure.

Meanwhile revolutions were not idle, and Louis Napoleon and his wife Eugénie, the child Mérimée had devotedly loved, were on the throne; and he himself, chiefly to gratify her, and quite aware of his own incongruous position, sat as Minister of Marine in the Imperial Senate. History does not record any unusual activity on his part; his characteristic there was absence or silence. In fact, superfluous rhetoric was by no means his delight. When the good bald president of a society of antiquaries once rose to propose the health of Prosper Mérimée, did not that ungrateful guest yearn greatly, according to his own avowal, to fire a plate of rum jelly at his head? But if Mérimée was no sham statesman, he proved to be a publicist with a conscience. He might have drawn the two salaries to which he was legally entitled, but he contented himself with the revenues of his less congenial work, and gave up his inspectorship of monuments. In all money matters he was exceedingly upright, and refused rewards for services of moment to the Emperor, "mon bourgeois," as he called him now and then. When he was fifty, he lost his mother, to whom he was tenderly attached, and from whom he had never lived apart. His time, thenceforth, coursed with dullness in a dull conniving court, and his health was breaking. He remained much at Cannes, reading, drawing landscapes and cats, and going feebly about on the breezy beaches, attended, like Cowper, by two old tacit English gentlewomen, who grieved truly for him when he died in his sleep in September of 1870. He was weary of art and of humanity, and he had seen the floods of disaster break in upon his sovereign lady, and the charming spirited prince who was dear to him for her sake. In the English cemetery at Cannes, Mérimée's ashes still lie.

He has a style of gold and steel, this "Première Prose" of Victor Hugo's lucky anagram. And how he can tell a tale, be it only that of the black-eyed boy and his presumable mamma, in one of the letters to Mrs. Senior! He had a unique grasp of narrative and a right sense of the incomparable value of biography. Declaring for what we call the humanist theory, he would have given the whole of Thucydides for an authentic memoir of Aspasia, or even of one of Pericles' slaves. Familiar with various walks of literature, and original in them all, he is yet best represented by his fiction, a term which may well include the *Jacquerie* and the *Chronicles of Charles IX*. It is notable that so apparently finical a temperament as Mérimée's should stand for results so vital and male in art. His imagination, like Mr. Hardy's and Mr. Kipling's, is concerned often with the primal major passions of mankind, breaking bonds and spreading ruin; and these themes are permeated in every case with unerring local colour and atmosphere. But Mérimée, who has Kipling's power, and in addition, his own scholar's sensitiveness and finish, has none of Kipling's fresh tenderness. In letters as in life, it must be the loving spirit which wins. Now, Mérimée is a ruthless writer. His details bite in like an etching. He deals in an economy both of emotions and of words, and in a sort of shorthand diction of consummate elegance, informed with wonderful terseness, austerity, and compression. He did not write for the mob, and he despised Macaulay, who knew not how to employ half-lights, nor to leave inferences to the reader. His matter is elementary, and he uses it with a large loose hand in small space; history in a hint, tragedy at a stroke, to be received with approval and awe by the instructed eye. There is nothing exaggerated or superfluous in Mérimée's work; neither is there evidence of striving, for it is scornfully quiet. It is all founded on essentials, on the lasting and stern generalities, and digs deep into the bed-rock of human nature. Short and acrid are these masterly things: *Matteo Falcone* and the incomparable *Storming of the Redoubt* are scarce five minutes long; *Tamango*, *The Trictrac Party*, *The Venus of Ille*, *The Etruscan Vase*, *Colomba*, *The Twofold Mistake*, *Arsène Guillot*, are brief as a breath. *Carmen* too is little, but *Carmen* is great. A text romantic in choice, it holds the norm of all realism; in Prosper Mérimée's sinister coronet it is the captain jewel. What says M. Taine in his famous sympathetic study? "Many dissertations on our primitive savage instincts, many knowing treatises like Schopenhauer's on the metaphysics of love and death, cannot hold a candle to the hundred pages of *Carmen*." And the novelist knew well his ground: his rich southern skies, his inscrutable women, his street life, with its smell of oranges and click of swords, his fierce smouldering plot and counterplot of amorous, revengeful Spain. The narration seems to go of itself, with its swart faces peering in as if hunting one another between the leaves. By an ingenious device the whole drama, in its rival parts, may still be told in the first person. Its perfect effect can never come from seeing it acted, but merely from reading it as Mérimée wrote it, with interludes, perhaps, of Bizet's ominously gay music. The heroine herself, the light bright tiger-moth, is enchanting and appalling; she is purely consistent, and tramples upon pity; tears are not to be shed for her. She will not assume the yoke, and so quits life like the invincible gipsy minx she is. Don José may bungle and waver, and make conditions, and proffer peace, and even take sardonic forethought for her inconceivable soul, but not she. She trades not with temporisers. As Mérimée himself once said gallantly of Henry the Scarred, Duke of Guise (in the *Mixed Historic and Literary Essays*), "Who would cling to an existence which thenceforth could only be employed in devising means to preserve it?" Death has become, at last, for Carmencita, the artistic necessity; and she chooses it, in her beauty, as she might choose a fresh ribbon for her bodice.

LOUISE IMOGEN GUINEY.

PART I

Πᾶσα γωὴ χόλος ἐστίν ἔχει δ' ἀγαθάς δύο ὥρας,
Τὴν μίαν ἐν θαλάμῳ, τὴν μίαν ἐν θανάτῳ.

PALLADAS.

I HAVE always suspected the geographers of not knowing what they were talking about when they placed the battle-field of Munda within the country of the Bastuli-Pœni, near the modern Monda, a few leagues north of Marbella. According to my own conjectures, based on the text of the anonymous author of *Bellum Hispaniense,* and some information gathered in the excellent library of the Duke of Ossuna, I decided that one must seek in the environs of Montilla the memorable spot where, for the last time, Cæsar played double or quits against the champions of the Republic. Finding myself in Andalusia at the commencement of autumn in 1830, I made a rather long excursion to dispel a few lingering doubts. A pamphlet that I shall soon publish will dispel, I trust, any uncertainty in the minds of all honest archæologists. While waiting for my dissertation to solve at last the geographical problem which holds all scientific Europe in suspense, I wish to tell you a short story. It will in no wise prejudice you on the interesting question of the site of Munda.

I had hired at Cordova a guide and two horses, and had taken the field—my sole baggage a few shirts and the Commentaries of Cæsar. One day, while wandering in the higher parts of the plain of Cachena, weary with fatigue, parched with thirst, broiling under a noonday sun, I was heartily consigning Cæsar and the sons of Pompey to the devil, when I saw at some distance from the path I was following a little green space dotted with reeds and rushes. This showed me that a spring was near. In fact, on drawing nearer I saw that the seeming greensward was a little bog, in which a rivulet lost itself after issuing apparently from a narrow gorge between two high buttresses of the Sierra de Cabra. I concluded that by following it up I should find cooler water, fewer frogs and leeches, and perhaps a little shade amidst the rocks. At the entrance of the gorge my horse neighed and was immediately answered by another horse that I could not see. I had scarcely gone a hundred paces when the gorge suddenly widened and displayed a sort of natural amphitheatre wholly shaded by the height of the enclosing cliffs. It would have been impossible to find a nook which promised to the traveller a more agreeable halting-place. At the foot of perpendicular cliffs the spring gushed bubbling forth, and tumbled into a little basin lined with sand as white as snow. Five or six beautiful green oaks, ever sheltered from the wind and watered by the spring, rose from its banks and spread over it the curtain of their deep shade; and finally, around the basin a fine lustrous grass offered a bed better than could be found in any inn ten leagues round.

To me did not belong the honour of discovering so beautiful a spot. A man was already resting there, no doubt asleep when I entered. Aroused by the neighing of the horses, he had arisen and approached his steed, which had profited by his master's slumber to make a good meal from the surrounding grass. He was a young gallant of medium height but robust make, with a look haughty and sad. His complexion, which might have been good, was from exposure to the sun become even darker than his hair. In one hand he held the bridle of his horse, and in the other a brass blunderbuss. I admit that at first the blunderbuss and the fierce air of its owner startled me a little; but I believed no more in brigands, from having heard so much talk about them and yet having never seen a single one. Besides, I had seen so many honest farmers arm themselves to the teeth when only going to market, that the sight of fire-arms did not warrant me in doubting the honesty of the unknown. And then, thought I, what in the world could he do with my shirts and my Elzevir Commentaries? So I saluted the man with the blunderbuss with a familiar nod, and asked with a smile if I had disturbed his siesta. Without answering he surveyed me searchingly from head to foot, and then, seemingly satisfied by his examination, he considered with the same attention my advancing guide. I saw the latter turn pale, and pause in evident terror. An unlucky meeting! said I to myself. But prudence counselled me at the same time to show no uneasiness. So I dismounted, and telling my

guide to unbridle, I knelt beside the spring and plunged into it
my head and hands; then I took a good long drink lying flat
on my belly like the bad soldiers of Gideon.

Meanwhile I kept an eye on my guide and the stranger. The
former came forward plainly against his will, and the latter
seemed to intend us no evil, for he had released his horse, and
his blunderbuss, which he had before held ready, now pointed
peacefully to the ground.

Not thinking it worth while to take offence at the slighting
manner in which I was received, I stretched myself upon the
grass, and nonchalantly asked the man with the blunderbuss
if he had not a tinder-box about him. At the same time I took
out my cigar-case. Still silent, he fumbled about in his pocket,
brought forth his tinder-box and set eagerly at work to strike
me a light. Evidently he was becoming more civilised, for he
sat down opposite me, yet never laid down his weapon. My
cigar lighted, I chose the best one remaining and asked him
if he smoked.

"Yes, señor," he replied. They were his first words, and
I noticed that he did not pronounce the *s*'s after the manner
of the Andalusians.[1] From which I concluded that he was a
traveller like myself, only less archæologically inclined.

"You will find that pretty good," said I, giving him a real
Havana regalia.

He made me a slight bow, lighted his cigar from mine,
thanked me with another bow, and began to smoke with every
sign of pleasure.

"Ah!" cried he, letting the smoke of his first puff stream
forth from his lips and nostrils, "how long it is since I have
smoked!"

In Spain, a cigar offered and accepted establishes hospitable
relations, as in the East does the sharing of bread and salt.
My man became more talkative than I had hoped. Although
he claimed to be a native of the province of Montilla, he knew
little about the neighbourhood. He could not tell the name of
the charming valley in which we were; he could not name any
neighbouring village; and finally, when I asked him if about
there he had seen any old broken-down walls, large flanged

---

[1] The Andalusians aspirate the *s*, and confound it with the soft *c* and *z*
which the Spaniards pronounce like the English *th*. By the word *señor*
alone one may distinguish an Andalusian.

tiles, or sculptured stones, he confessed that he had never noticed any such things. To make amends, however, he showed himself an expert in horse-flesh. He criticised mine, which was not a difficult task, and then gave me the pedigree of his own, which came from the celebrated steed of Cordova, a noble animal—in fact, of such endurance, his master asserted, that he had once ridden him thirty leagues in a day at a gallop, or fast trot. In the middle of his tirade, my unknown suddenly checked himself, as if surprised and vexed at having said too much. "You see, I was in great haste to get to Cordova," resumed he with some embarrassment. . . . "I had a lawsuit there." . . . In speaking he looked searchingly at Antonio, who kept his eyes fixed on the ground.

The shade and the spring so charmed me that I remembered some slices of ham that some friends of mine at Montilla had put in my guide's wallet. I had them brought, and invited the stranger to share with us the impromptu collation. If he had not smoked for a long time, it seemed to me that he had not eaten for at least forty-eight hours. He fell to like a famished wolf, and I considered that our meeting must have been providential for the poor devil. My guide meanwhile ate little, drank less, and spoke not at all; though at the commencement of our journey he had shown himself a regular old gossip. The presence of our guest seemed to annoy him, and a certain mutual distrust kept them apart, without my being able to positively divine the cause.

When the last crumbs of bread and ham had disappeared, and we had each smoked another cigar, I ordered my guide to bridle our horses; and was just going to bid our new friend adieu, when he asked me where I expected to pass the night.

Before I could heed a sign that my guide made me, I had answered that I was going to the Venta del Cuervo.

"A poor shelter for a person like you, señor. I am going there, too, and if you will permit it we will go together."

"With pleasure," said I, mounting my horse. My guide, who held my stirrup, made me another sign with his eyes. I replied by shrugging my shoulders to assure him of my tranquillity, and we set out.

Antonio's mysterious signs, his uneasiness, the few words which had escaped the unknown,—particularly his famous ride of thirty leagues, and the doubtful explanation he had given of it,—had already formed my opinion of our new travelling companion. I had no doubt but that I had to do with a smuggler, perhaps a robber; but what did it matter? I knew the Spanish character well enough to fear no evil of a man with whom I had smoked and eaten. His company even was a sure protection against all evil comers. Besides, I was glad to know what a real brigand was like. One does not meet them every day, and there is a certain charm in being near a dangerous being, above all when one finds him good-natured and subdued.

I hoped that by degrees I might win the confidence of the unknown; so despite my guide's winks I turned the conversation to the subject of highwaymen. You may imagine with what respect I spoke of them. At that time there was in Andalusia a famous bandit named José-Maria, whose exploits were the talk of the country. Suppose I am really with José-Maria! thought I. Then I told all the stories I knew of that hero—but all to his credit, you may be sure; and I expressed my great admiration for his bravery and his generosity.

"José-Maria is only a rogue," the stranger replied coldly.

Does he do himself justice, or is it mock modesty? I asked myself; for from examining so closely my companion I had come to identify him with the description of José-Maria that I had seen posted on the gates of many towns of Andalusia. Yes, thought I, it is he indeed: blond hair, blue eyes, large mouth, beautiful teeth, small hands, fine linen, a velvet vest with silver buttons, gaiters of white skin, and a bay horse—there is no doubt of it; but let us respect his incognito.

We arrived at the venta. It was just what he had described to me, one of the worst I had yet seen. One large room served as kitchen, dining-room, and chamber. On a stone flag in the middle of the room the fire was made, and the smoke passed out through a hole cut in the roof, or rather hung in clouds a few feet above the floor. Along the wall five or six old mule blankets were stretched out upon the floor. These were the beds for travellers. About twenty paces from the house, or rather from the single room I have just described, was built a kind of shed used for a stable. In this charming retreat there were no other persons just then except an old woman and a little girl, both as black as soot and horribly ragged. Behold! cried I to myself, all that remains of the population of the ancient Munda Bætica! O Cæsar! O Sextus Pompey! amazed would you be, could you come back to this world!

When she saw my companion the old woman gave a cry of surprise, "Ah! Señor Don José."

Don José frowned, and raised his hand with a gesture of command which stopped the old woman at once. I turned to my guide, and by a covert sign I made him understand that he could tell me nothing about the man with whom I was going to pass the night. The supper was better than I had anticipated there. They served us, upon a little table about a foot high, an old cock fricasseed with rice and pimentos, then pimentos in oil, and finally *gaspacho*—a sort of salad of pimentos. Three courses thus seasoned forced us to have recourse very often to a skin of Montilla wine which seemed delicious. After supper, seeing a mandolin hanging from the wall—there are mandolins everywhere in Spain—I asked the little girl, who had waited upon us, if she could play.

"No," she answered, "but Don José can play—oh, so well!"

"Will you be so good as to sing me something?" said I to him. "I love passionately your national music."

"I can refuse nothing to so polite a man, who gives me such good cigars," cried Don José with an air of good humour; and being given the instrument, he sang and accompanied himself. His voice was harsh, but nevertheless agreeable; the air sad and weird; as for the words, I did not understand a single one.

"If I am not mistaken," I said, "that is not a Spanish song which you have just sung. It resembles the *zorzicos* which I have heard in the Provinces,[1] and the words seem to be Basque."

"Yes," answered Don José with a sombre air. He laid the mandolin on the ground and, with folded arms, contemplated the embers of the dying fire with a singular expression of sadness. Illumined by a lamp on the little table, his face, at once noble and ferocious, reminded me of Milton's Satan. Like him, perhaps, my companion dreamed of the abode he had left, of the exile he now suffered for his sin. I tried to reanimate the conversation, but he did not reply, so absorbed was he in his sad thoughts. Already the old crone had retired to a corner of the room screened off by a tattered old blanket stretched

---

[1] The privileged provinces, enjoying peculiar *fueros*; that is to say, Alava, Biscay, Guipuzcoa, and a part of Navarre. Basque is the language of these countries.

across a rope; and the little girl had followed her to this retreat reserved for the fair sex. Then my guide, rising, asked me to accompany him to the stable; but at this Don José, as if suddenly awakened, asked in a brusque tone where he was going.

"To the stable," replied the guide.

"What for? The horses are fed. Sleep here. The gentleman will permit it."

"I am afraid that the gentleman's horse may be ailing. I want him to see it; perhaps he will know what to do."

Evidently Antonio wished to speak to me in private, but I cared not to arouse Don José's suspicions; in our position it seemed to me better to show the greatest confidence. I answered Antonio, then, that I had no fear for the horses and that I was sleepy. Don José followed him to the stable, and soon came back alone. He told me that the horse was all right, but that the guide valued the beast so highly that he was rubbing it down with his vest to make it perspire, and that it was to be expected he would pass the night in this delightful occupation. I had stretched myself out upon the mule blankets, taking care to wrap myself carefully in my mantle, so that I should not touch them. After asking pardon for the liberty of lying near me, Don José lay down before the door, after he had placed a fresh cap on his blunderbuss, which he took care to place beneath the wallet which served him for a pillow. Five minutes after, having wished each other good night, we were both sound asleep.

I thought I was tired enough to sleep even in such a hovel, but in an hour's time I was awakened from my first nap by a disagreeable itching. As soon as I discovered the cause I got up, persuaded that it would be better to pass the night under the stars than under such an inhospitable roof. On tiptoe then I reached the door, stepping over Don José, who was sleeping the sleep of the just, and I managed so well that I left the house without disturbing him. Near the door was a large wooden bench. I stretched myself out upon it and arranged myself as comfortably as possible to pass the rest of the night. I was about to shut my eyes for the second time, when it seemed to me that there passed before me the shadow of a horse and the shadow of a man, both walking without the least noise. I sat up, and thought that I recognised Antonio. Surprised to find him outside the stable at that time, I jumped up and went to meet him. He had stopped, having seen me first.

"Where is he?" asked Antonio in a whisper.

"In the inn, sleeping; he doesn't mind the fleas. Why have you taken the horse out?"

I noticed then, that in order to make no noise in coming out of the shed, Antonio had carefully wrapped his horse's feet in the remnants of an old blanket.

"Speak lower, for God's sake," said Antonio. "You don't know who that man is. 'Tis José Navarro, the most notorious bandit in Andalusia. All day have I been making you signs which you would not understand."

"Bandit or not," I answered, "what does it matter to me? He hasn't robbed us, and I'll wager he does not intend to."

"So much the better, but there is a reward of two hundred ducats for his arrest. I know where there is a post of lancers, a league and a half from here, and before the break of day I'll bring back a squad of stout fellows. I would have taken his horse, too, but it is so vicious that no one but the Navarro can come near it."

"What the devil are you up to?" said I. "What wrong has this poor fellow done you that you should betray him? Besides, are you sure he is the brigand you pretend?"

"Perfectly sure. Just now he followed me to the stable and said, 'You seem to know me; tell this gentleman who I am, and I will blow your brains out.' Stay with him, señor; lie down beside him and fear nothing. So long as he knows you are there he will suspect nothing."

While we were thus talking we had gone so far from the inn that the horse's hoofs would be out of hearing. In the twinkling of an eye, Antonio had torn the rags from his horse's feet and was preparing to mount. I tried both prayers and threats to detain him.

"I am a poor devil, señor," said he; "two hundred ducats are not to be thrown away, especially when it helps to rid the country of such vermin. But take care! If the Navarro awakes he will jump for his gun, so look out for yourself! As for me, I have gone too far to turn back; shift for yourself as best you can."

The rascal was in the saddle and, driving both spurs into his horse, was soon lost to my sight in the obscurity of night.

I was very angry with my guide and quite uneasy. After a moment of reflection I determined to return to the inn. Don José still slept, recuperating, no doubt, from the fatigues and vigils of many adventurous days. I was obliged to shake him roughly to awaken him. Never shall I forget the ferocious look, and the movement he made to seize his gun, which I had taken the precaution to remove a short distance from his couch.

"Señor caballero," said I, "I have a silly question to ask: Would you care to see a half-dozen lancers ride up here?"

He sprang to his feet and in a terrible voice cried out, "Who told you that?"

"What matters it whence comes the advice, provided it is good?"

"Your guide has betrayed me, but he shall pay for this. Where is he?"

"I do not know. In the stable, I think—but someone told me——"

"Who, who?—not the old woman?"

"Someone whom I know not. But, without further words, have you, yes or no, reasons for not awaiting the soldiers? If you have, lose no time; and so good-bye, and I beg pardon for having disturbed you."

"Ah, your guide! your guide! I mistrusted him from the first. But I will pay him back! Adieu, señor; God requite you what I owe you. I am not so bad as you believe me; yes, there is yet something in me to merit the pity of a gallant man. Adieu, señor—I have only one regret: that I cannot repay you for this service."

"For payment, Don José, promise me to suspect no one, and dream not of vengeance. Wait a moment; take these cigars for your trip. A pleasant journey!" and I offered him my hand.

He shook it without speaking, grasped his weapon and his wallet, and after he had spoken a few words to the old hag in an argot which I did not understand, he ran to the stable, and in a few moments I heard him gallop off into the open country.

As for me, I lay down again on my bench, but I could not get to sleep. I asked myself if I had done right in saving a robber, perhaps a murderer, from the gallows, and solely because I had eaten with him a little ham and some rice à la valencienne. Had I not betrayed my guide who upheld the law? Had not I exposed him to the vengeance of a ruffian? But the laws of hospitality! Prejudice of a savage, said I to myself; I must now answer for all the future crimes of this bandit. And yet, is it a prejudice—this instinctive conscience which defies all reasoning? Perhaps, in such a delicate case, may I not be able to extricate myself without remorse? Thus I vacillated in the greatest uncertainty in regard to the morality of my action, when I saw approaching a half-dozen cavaliers, with Antonio prudently bringing up the rear. I went to meet them, and informed them that the bandit had taken flight more than two hours before.

The old crone, questioned by the corporal, answered that she knew the Navarro when he came to her house, but that, living alone, she had never dared to risk her life by denouncing him. She added that his habit was, when at her house, always to depart in the dead of night. As for me, I was obliged to go several leagues from there, show my passport, and sign a declaration before a magistrate; after which I was permitted to resume my archæological researches. Antonio nursed a grudge against me, for he suspected me of having prevented his earning the two hundred ducats. However, we parted good friends at Cordova, and there I gave him as generous a tip as the state of my purse permitted.

PART II

I SPENT several days at Cordova. I had been told of a certain manuscript in the library of the Dominicans, in which I ought to find interesting information about the ancient Munda. Cordially received by the good priests, I spent several days in their monastery, and in the evenings I strolled about the city.

At sunset, in Cordova, there are many idlers on the quay which borders the left bank of the Guadalquivir. There one still breathes the odours from a tannery which preserves the ancient renown of the country for the manufacture of leather; but to compensate for this, one enjoys there a spectacle which has its merits. Some moments before the Angelus, a great number of women congregate on the bank of the stream, at the foot of the quay, which is quite high. Not a man dares to mingle with this troop. As soon as the Angelus rings it is supposed to be night. At the last stroke of the bell all the women undress and plunge into the water. Then such cries, such laughter, such an infernal uproar. From the top of the quay the men contemplate the bathers, straining their eyes, but seeing little. Nevertheless, these white and uncertain forms, traced on the sombre azure of the flood, set working a poetic mind, and with a little imagination it is not difficult to imagine Diana and her nymphs at the bath, without fearing the fate of Actæon.

I was told that several wretched scapegraces once made up a purse to bribe the bell-ringer of the cathedral to ring the Angelus twenty minutes before the legal time. Though it was still broad daylight, the nymphs of the Guadalquivir did not hesitate, and trusting more to the Angelus than to the sun, in perfect innocence they made their toilette for the bath, and 'tis always of the most simple description. I was not there. In my time the bell-ringer was incorruptible, the twilight dim, and only a cat could have told the oldest orange-peddler from the prettiest grisette of Cordova.

One evening, at the hour when one can see no more, I was

leaning upon the parapet of the quay, smoking, when a woman
ascended the staircase which leads to the river and came to sit
near me. In her hair she wore a large bunch of jasmin, the
petals of which exhaled an intoxicating odour. She was simply,
perhaps poorly clad, all in black, like most of the grisettes in
the evening. Women of fashion wear black only in the morning; in the evening they dress *à la francesa*. When near me,
my bather let slip to her shoulders the mantilla which covered
her head, and by the faint light of the stars I saw that she was
petite, well formed, and had very large eyes. I threw my
cigar away at once. She understood this attention, a politeness
wholly French, and hastened to tell me that she was very fond
of the odour of tobacco, and that she even smoked herself when
she could find any very mild *papelitos*. Luckily, I had some
such mild cigarettes in my case, and I eagerly offered her some.
She deigned to accept one, and lighted it at the end of a burning
cord which an urchin brought us for a sou. Smoking together,
we chatted so long, the beautiful bather and I, that we found
ourselves almost alone on the quay. I did not think it indis-
creet to ask her to take an ice with me at the *neveria*.[1]   After
a moment's modest hesitation she accepted; but, before accepting, she wished to know what time it was. I made my repeater
strike the hour, and this seemed to astonish her greatly.

"What inventions you have in your countries, you foreigners!
From what country are you, señor?   English, without doubt?"[2]

"French, and your humble servant.   And you, mademoiselle,
or madame, you are probably of Cordova?"

"No."

"At least of Andalusia?   I think I detect that from your
soft accent."

"If you note everyone's accent so well, you should be able
to divine what I am."

"I think that you are from the country of Jesus, two steps
from Paradise."   I had learned this figure of speech, which
designates Andalusia, from my friend Francisco Sevilla, the
well-known picador.

---

[1] A café provided with an ice-house, or, rather, with a supply of snow.
There is hardly a village which has not its *neveria*.

[2] In Spain every traveller who does not lug around samples of calico
or silk passes for an Englishman, *Inglesito*.   It is the same in the East.
At Chalcis I have had the honour of being introduced as a Μιλόρδος
Φραντζέσος.

"Bah! Paradise—— People here say that it is not for such as we."

"Why, then you must be a Moor, or——" I hesitated, not daring to say a Jewess.

"Oh, come now! you know well enough that I am a gipsy: shall I tell you *la baji*? [1] Have you never heard of La Carmencita? I am she."

I was at that time—it is fifteen years ago—such a miscreant that I did not draw back in horror at finding myself beside a sorceress. Good! thought I. Last week I supped with a highway robber; now I am going to take an ice with a servant of the devil. When travelling, one should see everything. I had still another motive for cultivating her acquaintance. When I left college, I confess to my shame that I had already lost some time in studying the occult sciences; several times, even, I had tried to conjure up the spirit of darkness. Cured long ago of the passion for such pursuits, I retained, nevertheless, a certain curiosity about all superstitions, and I congratulated myself on the chance of learning just how much the black art had flourished among the gipsies.

While chatting we had entered the *neveria*, and had seated ourselves at a little table which was lighted by a candle burning in a glass globe. I had time then to examine my gitana, whilst several respectable citizens, eating their ices, stared in amazement to see me in such company.

I doubt very much whether Mademoiselle Carmen was of pure blood; at least, she was infinitely prettier than any of her race that I have ever met. That a woman may be beautiful, say the Spaniards, she must unite thirty *si*, or, if you please, she must merit description by the use of ten adjectives, each of them applicable to three parts of her person. For example, she should have three things black: eyes, lashes, and eyebrows; three things elegant: hands, lips, and tresses—etc. For the rest, see Brantôme. My gipsy could not pretend to so many perfections. Her skin, though otherwise free from blemish, was nearly the colour of copper; her eyes oblique, but large and full; her lips a little thick, but admirably formed, and disclosing teeth whiter than blanched almonds. Her hair, perhaps a little too coarse, was black, with blue reflections like a crow's wing, long and glossy. Not to tire you with a

[1] Fortune.

description too minute, I will say, briefly, that to each defect she joined an excellency enhanced by the contrast. It was a wild and savage beauty, a face which astonished you at first, and was never to be forgotten. Her eyes especially had an expression, at once voluptuous and fierce, that I have never met since in any other human glance. "Eye of a gipsy, eye of a wolf," is a Spanish saying which shows careful observation. If you have not time to go to the zoological gardens and study a wolf's expression, look at your cat while she is watching a bird.

As everyone knows, it would have been ridiculous to have your fortune told in a café, so I asked the pretty witch to permit me to accompany her home; she consented without trouble, but she wished again to know how the time was passing, and asked me to again make my repeater strike the hour.

"Is it really gold?" she asked, while she examined it with an excessive interest.

When we resumed our walk it was really night; most of the shops were closed, and the streets nearly deserted. We crossed the bridge over the Guadalquivir, and at the end of the suburb we stopped before a house which, to say the least, did not look like a palace. A child let us in. The gipsy spoke to him a few words in a language I did not understand, but which I have since learned was the *rommani*, or *chipe calli*, the idiom of the gipsies. The child immediately left us in a good-sized room furnished with a small table, two stools, and a chest. I should not forget, however, a jar of water, a pile of oranges, and a string of onions.

As soon as we were alone the gipsy took from the chest a pack of cards which had evidently seen long service, a magnet, a dried chameleon, and several other objects necessary to her art. Then she told me to make a cross in my left hand with a piece of money, and the magic ceremonies commenced. It is useless to repeat to you her predictions, and as to her manner, it was evident that she was no 'prentice hand.

Unfortunately we were soon interrupted. Suddenly the door was opened violently, and a man, wrapped to his eyes in a brown mantle, strode into the room apostrophising my gipsy in no gentle terms. I did not understand what he said, but the tone of his voice indicated that he was in a very bad humour. At sight of him the fortune-teller showed neither anger nor surprise, but ran to meet him, and with an extraordinary volubility she addressed him in that tongue which she had already used before me. The word *payllo*, often repeated, was the sole word that I understood. I knew that the gipsies thus designated men not of their own race. Supposing that it was all about me, I was expecting a rather delicate explanation; already I had grasped the leg of one of the stools, and was communing with myself as to the exact moment when it would be expedient to hurl it at the intruder's head. The latter pushed the gipsy rudely aside and strode toward me; then, recoiling a step, he exclaimed:

"Ah! señor, it is you, then!"

I looked in my turn and recognised my acquaintance, Don José, and at that moment I regretted a little that I had saved him from hanging.

"Eh? so it is you, my good fellow!" I cried, laughing with the best grace I could summon. "You have interrupted mademoiselle just as she was revealing to me the most interesting things."

"Always the same! This shall end," said he between his teeth, fixing upon her a ferocious look.

Nevertheless the gipsy continued to talk to him in her own tongue. By degrees she became more and more excited. Her eyes became bloodshot and terrible; her features contracted; she stamped with her foot. It seemed to me that she was urging him to do something at which he hesitated. What this was I thought that I understood only too well from seeing her pass and repass her little hand under her chin. I was tempted to believe that there was a throat that needed cutting, and I had a strong suspicion that it was no other than mine own.

To all this torrent of eloquence Don José answered only by two or three words sharply spoken. The gipsy flashed at him a look of profound contempt; then, sitting down *à la turque* in a corner of the room, she peeled an orange and commenced to eat it. Don José took me by the arm, opened the door, and led me into the street. We went about two hundred paces in deep silence. Then, extending his hand, "Keep straight on," he said, "and you will come to the bridge."

At the same time he turned his back and walked quickly away. I returned to my inn, a little abashed and in very bad humour. The worst of it was, that when I undressed I found that my watch was missing.

Several reasons prevented me from going to reclaim it the following day, or to put the police upon the look-out. I finished my work upon the Dominicans' manuscript, and departed for Seville. After several months' wandering in Andalusia, I wished to return to Madrid, and it was necessary to pass through Cordova. I had no intention to make a long wait there, for I had taken a strong dislike to that beautiful city and the nymphs of the Guadalquivir. Nevertheless, several friends to visit, some commissions to execute, would keep me at least three or four days in the ancient capital of the Mussulman princes.

As soon as I reappeared at the monastery of the Dominicans, one of the fathers, who had always shown a great interest in my researches concerning the site of Munda, welcomed me with open arms, crying:

"Blessed be the name of the Lord! Welcome, dear friend! We thought you dead; and I, who am now talking to you, I have recited many *Paters* and *Aves*, which I regret not, for the salvation of your soul. So! you have not been assassinated, but we know that you have been robbed."

"What do you mean?" I asked, a little surprised.

"Yes, you remember—the beautiful watch! the one you used to make strike in the library when we used to tell you it was time to go to the service. Ah, well! it has been recovered, and will be given back to you."

"That is to say," I interrupted, "I had mislaid it——"

"The rascal is behind bars, and as everyone knew him to be a man who would shoot a Christian for a farthing, we were terribly afraid that he had killed you. I will go with you to the *corrégidor*, and we will get you back your watch. And then consider whether you should say that justice is not done in Spain!"

"I confess," I said, "that I would rather lose my watch than give evidence which might justly bring any poor wretch to the gallows; above all, because——"

"Oh, have no fear! he is well recommended, and they can't hang him more than once. When I say hang, I say wrongly, for he is an hidalgo, your robber; so he will be garroted [1] day after to-morrow without fail. You see that a robbery more or

---

[1] In 1830 this was a privilege of the nobility. To-day, under constitutional rule, the common people have acquired the right to the garrote.

less would make little difference in his case. Would to God that he had only robbed! but he has committed several murders, each one more horrible than the last."

"What is his name?"

"He is known here as José Navarro; but he has a Basque name which neither you nor I could ever pronounce. I tell you, he is a man worth seeing, and you who like so much to see the curiosities of the country should not neglect this chance of learning how in Spain these rascals make their exit from this world. He is in the chapel,[1] and Padre Martinez will conduct you thither."

My Dominican insisted so strongly upon my seeing the apparatus for the *pepit pendement pien choli* that I could not resist him. I went then to see the prisoner, taking with me a bunch of cigars, which I hoped might lead him to excuse my intrusion.

They admitted me to the presence of Don José, whom we found at a repast. He nodded coldly, and thanked me politely for the gift I brought him. After counting the cigars in the package, he chose a certain number and gave me back the rest, observing that he had need of no more.

I asked him whether with a little money or the influence of my friends I might not in some way soften his lot. At first he shrugged his shoulders, smiling sadly; and then, thinking better of it, he begged me to have a mass said for the salvation of his soul.

"Would you," he added timidly—"would you have another said for a woman who has wronged you?"

"Surely," I replied; "but no one that I know of has wronged me in this country."

He took my hand and pressed it gravely. After a moment's silence he continued:

"Dare I also ask of you a favour? . . . When you return into your country you will perhaps pass through Navarre. At least you will pass through Vittoria, which is not far from it."

"Yes," I said, "I shall go certainly by Vittoria, and it is not unlikely that I may turn aside to visit Pampeluna; and for your sake I will willingly make this detour."

[1] [In the Spanish prisons there is usually a chapel in which the condemned prisoners are confined and prepared spiritually for death.— TRANSLATOR.]

"Well, if you go to Pampeluna you will see more than one thing to interest you. . . . It is a beautiful city. . . . I will give you this medal." He showed me a silver medal suspended from his neck. "You will wrap it in paper"— he paused a moment to master his emotion—"and you will carry it or have it sent to a good woman whose address I will give you. Say that I am dead, but say not how I died."

I promised to carry out his wishes. I saw him again on the morrow and passed a part of the day in his company. It was from his lips that I learned the sad story you are going to read.

PART III

"I was born," he said, "at Elizondo, in the valley of Baztan. My name is Don José Lizarrabengoa, and you know Spain well enough, señor, to understand from my name that I am a Basque and of the old Christian faith. If I call myself Don it is because I have that right, and if I were at Elizondo I would show you my genealogy upon parchment. I was intended for the Church, and forced to study for it; but this profited me little. I was too fond of playing paume,[1] and that was my undoing. When we play at paume, we Navarros, we forget everything else. One day when I had won, a youth of Alava picked a quarrel with me. We resorted to our maquilas,[2] and at that I again beat him; but this obliged me to leave the country. I fell in with some dragoons, and enlisted in the cavalry regiment of Almanza. The men from our mountains learn quickly a soldier's trade. I soon became a corporal, and they were promising to make me a quartermaster when, to my misfortune, I was put on guard at the tobacco factory at Seville.

"If you have ever been at Seville you must have noticed the great building outside the ramparts near the Guadalquivir. It seems to me I can see still the door and the guard-house beside it. When they are not on duty the Spaniards play cards or sleep; but I, a free Navarro, strove always to keep busy. One day I was making a chain, from brass wire, for my epinglette.[3] All at once my comrades cried: 'There's the bell ringing: the girls are coming back to work!' You know, señor, that there are as many as four or five hundred women employed in the building. It is they who roll the cigars in a great room into which no man can enter without permission from a *vingt-quatre*,[4] because the women, especially the young ones, in warm weather work in a very free-and-easy costume. After the dinner hour, when they return to work, many young men go to watch them

---

[1] [Tennis.—TRANSLATOR.]
[2] Staffs shod with iron.
[3] [Priming-needle.—TRANSLATOR.]
[4] A municipal and police magistrate.

179

pass, and they are of all sorts. There are few of these ladies who would refuse a silk mantilla, and the amateur at that sort of game has only to stoop to win the prize. While the others looked on, I remained on my bench near the door. I was young then and always dreaming of home, and did not believe that there were any pretty girls without blue skirts and hair falling in braids on their shoulders.[1] Besides, the Andalusians frightened me. I was not then accustomed to their manners —always bantering and jesting, never a word of sense or reason. There I was, busy with my chain, when I heard some of the people say: 'There comes the *gitanella*!' I looked up and saw her. It was on a Friday, and I shall never forget it. I saw that Carmen whom you know, in whose house I found you some months ago.

"She wore a red skirt, very short, which displayed her white silk stockings, with more than one hole in them, and tiny shoes of red morocco, tied with flame-coloured ribbon. She threw back her mantilla in order to show her shoulders and a great bunch of cassia-flowers that she wore in her chemise. She had also a cassia-flower in the corner of her mouth, and she came prancing along like a thoroughbred filly from the stud of Cordova. In my country, a woman in such a costume would have made everyone cross himself. At Seville, everyone paid her some gallant compliment on her figure. She answered them all with side glances, her hand on her hip, as bold as the true gipsy that she was. At first she did not please me, and I resumed my work; but she, after the custom of women and cats, who come not when called but come unasked, stopped before me and accosted me.

"'Friend,' she said, in the Andalusian manner, 'will you give me the chain to hang the keys of my strong box on?'

"'It's to hang my epinglette on with,' I answered.

"'Your epinglette!' she cried, laughing. 'Ah! the gentleman makes lace, since he has need of *épingles*.'[2] Everyone there burst out laughing, and I felt the blood rush to my cheeks, but could find nothing to reply.

"'Well, my hearty,' she continued, 'make me seven yards of

The ordinary costume of the girls in the Basque provinces and in Navarre.

[2] [Pins. The word epinglette comes from the French word *épingle*, pin; the translation of epinglette to priming-needle destroys the pun which Carmen makes on the two words.—TRANSLATOR.]

black lace for a mantilla, pinmaker of my soul.' And taking the cassia-flower from her mouth, she threw it with a twist of her thumb and struck me right between the eyes.

"It seemed to me, señor, that a bullet had hit me. . . . I did not know what to do with myself, and stood as stiff as a post. When she had gone into the factory I saw the flower, which had fallen on the ground between my feet. I do not know what possessed me, but I picked it up, unseen by my comrades, and placed it carefully in my vest. That was my first act of folly.

"Two or three hours after, while I was still thinking it over, a porter rushed into the guard-room, all out of breath and greatly agitated. He told us that a woman had been assassinated in the great room where the cigars were made, and that we must send in the guard. The sergeant told me to take two men and look into the matter.

"I took my men and went up. Imagine, señor! On entering the room I found as many as two or three hundred women *en chemise*, or with only what was absolutely necessary on, all crying, screeching, gesticulating, and making such a tumult that you couldn't have heard God's thunder. At one side, one of them sprawled on the floor, covered with blood, and with a cross cut on her face that someone had just made with two cuts of a knife. Opposite the wounded one, who was being tended by the best of the band, I saw Carmen in the hands of five or six stout dames. The wounded woman kept bawling out, 'A priest! Confess me! I am dying!' Carmen said nothing: she clenched her teeth and rolled her eyes about like a chameleon.

"'What is the matter here?' I asked. I was at great trouble to find out what had happened, for all the women talked at once. It seems that the wounded woman had boasted that she had enough money in her pocket to buy a donkey at the Triana market. 'O ho!' cried out Carmen, who had a tongue of her own, 'thou hast not then enough for a broom?'

"The other, stung by the reproach, perhaps because she felt that a reference to that article touched her in a weak spot, answered that she was not a judge of brooms, not having the honour to be either a gipsy or a daughter of Satan; but that Señorita Carmen would soon make the donkey's acquaintance when the *corrégidor* sent her out for an airing with two stout lackeys behind to beat off the flies.

"'Well, for my part, then,' said Carmen, 'I will make drinking-troughs for the flies on your cheeks, for I feel like painting a checker-board upon them.'[1] With that—criss, cross, she began, with the knife she used for trimming the ends of the cigars, to slash a St. Andrew's cross on the girl's face.

"'Twas a clear case. I took Carmen by the arm. 'Sister,' said I politely, 'you must come with me.' She gave me a look as if she remembered me, but said resignedly, 'Let us go, then. Where is my mantilla?'

"She threw it over her head so as to show only one of her great eyes, and followed my two men as gently as a lamb. When we reached the guard-house the quartermaster said it was a grave affair, and that she must be taken to prison. 'Twas I, too, who must conduct her there. I placed her between two dragoons, and I marched behind, as a corporal should in such a case. Thus we started for the city. At first the gipsy kept silence, but in the Street of the Serpent—you know the street, and how well it merits its name by all the windings it makes—in the Street of the Serpent she commenced by letting her mantilla drop upon her shoulders, so as to show me her pretty, wheedling face, and turning toward me as much as she could, she said:

"'My officer, where are you taking me?'

"'To prison, my poor child,' I replied, as gently as I could, as a true soldier should speak to a prisoner, above all to a woman.

"'Alas! what will become of me? Noble officer, have pity upon me! You are so young, so gentle.' Then, in a lower tone, 'Let me escape,' she said; 'I will give you a piece of the bar-lachi,[2] which will make you beloved of all women.'

---

[1] "Pintar un javeque"—to paint in checkers. The Spanish checker-boards are usually painted in red and white squares.

[2] ["If the Gitánas in general be addicted to any one superstition, it is certainly with respect to this stone, to which they attribute all kinds of miraculous powers. . . . They believe that he who is in possession of it has nothing to fear from steel or lead, from fire or water, and that death itself has no power over him. . . . Extraordinary things are related of its power in exciting the amorous passions, and on this account it is in great request amongst the gipsy hags; all these women are procuresses, and find persons of both sexes weak and wicked enough to make use of their pretended knowledge in the composition of love-draughts and decoctions. In the case of the loadstone, however, there is no pretence, the Gitánas believing all they say respecting it, and still more." (George Borrow, The Zincali, an Account of the Gipsies of Spain.) Thus we see that, from her standpoint, the bribe which Carmen offered Don José was not of trifling value.—TRANSLATOR.]

"The *bar-lachi*, señor, is the loadstone, with which the gipsies pretend that one can work charms if one knows how to use it. Give a woman a pinch of it grated in a glass of white wine, and she cannot resist you.

"I replied as seriously as I could, 'We are not here to talk nonsense. You must go to prison; that's the order, and there is no help for it.'

"Now we Basque people have an accent by which the Spaniards can easily tell us; but in revenge there is scarcely one of them who can learn to say even *Bài, jaona*.[1] 'Twas not hard then for Carmen to know that I came from the Provinces. You know, señor, that the gipsies, having no country of their own, and always wandering from one place to another, speak all languages; and the most of them are equally at home in Portugal, in France, in the Provinces, in Catalonia—everywhere, in fact; even with the Moors and the English they can make themselves understood. Carmen knew the Basque dialect well enough.

"'*Laguna ene bihotsarena*, comrade of my heart,' said she, suddenly, 'are you from our country?'

"Our language, señor, is so beautiful that when we hear it in a strange country it thrills our hearts. . . . I wish I might have a confessor from the Provinces," the bandit added more softly. After a silence he continued:

"'I am from Elizondo,' I answered her in Basque, very much moved to hear my native tongue.

"'And I, I am from Etchalar,' said she. That is a place some four hours' journey from us. 'I was carried away to Seville by the gipsies. I was working in the tobacco factory to gain enough to take me home to Navarre to my poor old mother, who has no one to support her but me and the little *barratcea*[2] with its twenty cider-apple trees. Ah! were I only at home before the white mountain! They insulted me because I am not one of this nation of swindlers, peddlers of rotten oranges; and these vile women are all against me because I told them that not all their *jacques*[3] at Seville with their knives could frighten one of our boys with his blue beret and his maquila. Comrade, friend, can you do nothing for a countrywoman?'

"She lied, señor, she lied always. I do not know whether in all her life that girl ever spoke one word of truth; but when

---

[1] Yes, sir.   [2] Garden.   [3] Bullies.

she spoke I believed her: she was too much for me. She spoke the Basque brokenly, yet I believed she came from Navarre; her eyes alone, her mouth, and her complexion stamped her a gipsy. I was bewitched and no longer paid attention to anything. I reflected that if the Spaniards had spoken aught against my country to me, I would have slashed them across the face as she had just treated her comrade. In brief, I was like a drunken man. I began to talk foolishly, and was ready to act likewise.

"'If I were to push you, and you tumbled down, my countryman,' she said in Basque, 'it would not be these two Castilian conscripts who could hold me.'

"Faith! I forgot my orders, everything, and I replied:

"'Well, my friend, my countrywoman, try it, and may Our Lady of the Mountain aid you!' At that moment we were passing before one of those narrow alleys of which there are so many in Seville. Suddenly Carmen turned about and struck me with her clenched fist in the chest. I fell backwards on purpose. With one bound she jumped over me and fled, showing us a pair of legs. . . . Well, they talk of 'Basque legs,' but hers surpassed them all, as fleet as they were shapely. I picked myself up quickly, but I managed to get my lance[1] crosswise in the alley, and so well did it bar the passage that at the very start my comrades were hindered for the moment from the pursuit. Then I started off running myself, and they after me; but catch her!—there was no risk of it, with our spurs, our sabres, and our lances! In less time than I can tell you, the prisoner had disappeared. Besides, all the gossips of the neighbourhood helped her flight, jeered at us, and put us on the wrong scent. After many marches and countermarches we were obliged to return to the guard-house without a receipt from the governor of the prison.

"My men, to escape punishment, said that Carmen had spoken with me in Basque, and that it did not seem natural that a blow from so slight a girl would knock down so easily a man of my strength. All this looked suspicious, or rather, too clear. When the guard was relieved, I was reduced to the ranks and sent to prison for a month. That was my first punishment since I had enlisted. Farewell, then, to the quartermaster's stripes which I deemed already in my grasp!

[1] All the cavalry in Spain were then armed with lances.

"My first days of imprisonment passed very sadly. When
I became a soldier I had pictured to myself that I should at
least become an officer. Longa, Mina, my compatriots, have
even become captain-generals; Chapalangarra, who is a negro,
and, like Mina, a refugee in your country—Chapalangarra was
a colonel, and I have played paume a score of times with his
brother, who was a poor devil like myself.[1] 'Now,' said I to
myself, 'all the time you have served without punishment is
all time lost. Here you are with a bad reputation. To regain
the good opinion of your officers, you must work ten times as
hard as when you were a raw recruit. And for what have you
brought this punishment upon yourself? For a jade of a gipsy
who mocked you, and who at this moment goes scot-free in
some quarter of the city.' Nevertheless I could not help thinking about her. Will you believe it, señor, her silk stockings,
so full of holes, and which she so freely showed in her flight,
were always before my eyes. Between my prison bars I looked
out upon the street, and amongst all the women who passed
I saw not one the equal of that little she-devil. And then, in
spite of myself, I would smell of the cassia-flower she had
thrown at me, and which, though withered, still kept its sweet
perfume. . . . If there are witches, that girl was one.

"One day the jailer entered and gave me a loaf of Alcalá [2]
bread. 'Look,' said he, 'see what your cousin has sent you.'
I took the bread, very much astonished, for I had no cousin
at Seville. Perhaps it is a mistake, I thought, regarding the
bread: but it was so appetising, and smelt so good, that without
bothering myself about where it came from or for whom it was
intended, I determined to eat it. In trying to cut it, my knife
struck against something hard. I examined it and found a
small English file which someone had slipped into the loaf
before it was baked. There was also in it a gold-piece of two
piastres. No more doubt then; it was a present from Carmen.

[1] ["No people on earth are prouder than the Basques, but theirs is a
kind of republican pride. They have no nobility amongst them, and no
one will acknowledge a superior. The poorest carman is as proud as the
governor of Tolosa. 'He is more powerful than I,' he will say, 'but I am
of as good blood: perhaps, hereafter, I may become a governor myself.'"
George Borrow, *The Bible in Spain*.)—TRANSLATOR.]
[2] Alcalá de los Panaderos, a town two leagues from Seville, where
delicious rolls of bread are made. It is claimed that their excellency is
due to the water of Alcalá, and great quantities of them are each day
carried to Seville.

To the people of her race, liberty is everything, and they would burn a city to avoid a day's imprisonment. Besides, the girl was cunning, and with bread like that one could laugh at jailers. In an hour the thickest bar might be cut with the little file, and with the two piastres at the first slop-shop I could exchange my uniform for plain clothes. You can imagine that a man who had so many times stolen the young eagles from their nests on our crags would make little of dropping to the street from a window scarcely thirty feet from the ground. Yet I still kept my honour as a soldier, and to desert seemed to me a great crime. Still, I was touched by this token of remembrance. When one is in prison, one loves to think that outside one has a friend who still thinks of you. The gold-piece offended me a little. I would have liked well to send it back; but how could I find my creditor? That did not seem so easy.

"After the ceremony of my degradation, I thought that there was nothing further for me to suffer; but there remained yet another humiliation: that was when, after my release, I was put on guard duty as a common soldier. You cannot imagine what a man of spirit feels in such a situation. I believe I would rather have been shot. Then, at least, one marches at the head of his squad; one feels like somebody; everyone looks at you.

"I was placed as sentry at the colonel's door. He was a young man—rich, a good fellow, and fond of pleasure. All the young officers were at his house, and many citizens; women also—actresses, so it was said. As for me, it seemed that the whole city had made a rendezvous at his door to stare at me. And then comes the colonel's carriage with his *valet de chambre* on the box. Whom do I see alight? *La gitanella!* She was dressed to kill this time, adorned like a Madonna, bedecked and bedizened—a spangled dress, blue shoes, also spangled, flowers and furbelows all over her. In her hand she held a Basque tambourine. With her were two other gipsy women, one young, and one old. There is always an old woman to lead them about; then an old man with a guitar, a gipsy also, to play and make them dance. You know that people of quality often amuse themselves by bidding gipsies to their parties that they may make them dance the *romalis*, their national dance—and sometimes for something quite different.

"Carmen remembered me, and we exchanged a look. I know not why, but at that moment I wished myself a hundred feet under ground. '*Agur, laguna!*'[1] said she. 'My officer, you mount guard then, like a raw recruit!' and before I could find a word to reply she was within the house.

"All the guests were in the patio, and notwithstanding the crowd, I could see through the gate[2] nearly all that happened. I heard the sound of the castanets, the tambourine, the laughter, and the applause; and at times I could see her head when she leaped with her tambourine. Then I heard the officers saying gallant things to her that made the blood rush to my cheeks. What she replied I know not. 'Twas from that day I think that I commenced to love her in earnest; for three or four times the notion came to me to rush into the patio and cut down with my sabre all those coxcombs who were flirting with her. My torment lasted a good hour; then the gipsies came out, and the carriage carried them away.

"Carmen, in passing, gave me a look with those eyes of hers —you know them—and said to me in a low voice: 'Compatriot, when one likes a good *friture*,[3] one goes to Lillas Pastia's at Triana.' As lightly as a kid she bounded into the carriage, the coachman whipped up his mules and all the joyous band drove off, I know not where.

"You will guess that as soon as I was relieved I went to Triana,[4] but first I got shaved and brushed myself up as if for parade. She was at Lillas Pastia's, an old friture-seller, a gipsy as black as a Moor, to whose house came many of the

---

[1] "Good-day, comrade!"
[2] Most of the houses in Seville have an interior open court surrounded by porticos. The people live there in summer. Over the court is spread an awning which is sprinkled with water by day and removed at night. The street door is almost always open, and the passage to the court *zaguan* is closed by an iron gate often very elegantly wrought.
[3] [Dish of small fried fish.—TRANSLATOR.]
[4] ["The faubourg of Triana, in Seville, has from time immemorial been noted as a favourite residence of the Gitanos; and here, at the present day, they are to be found in greater number than in any other town in Spain. This faubourg is indeed chiefly inhabited by desperate characters, as, besides the Gitanos, the principal part of the robber population of Seville is here congregated. Perhaps there is no part, even of Naples, where crime so much abounds, and the law is so little respected, as at Triana, the character of whose inmates was so graphically delineated two centuries and a half back by Cervantes, in one of the most amusing of his tales, *Rinconete and Cortadillo*." (George Borrow, *Gipsies of Spain*.)—TRANSLATOR.]

citizens to eat fried fish; especially, I think, since Carmen had taken up her quarters there.

"'Lillas,' she said, as soon as she saw me, 'I shall do no more to-day. To-morrow it will be day again.[1] Come, my countryman, let us take a stroll.'

"She threw her mantilla over her face, and we were in the street before I knew where I was going.

"'Señorita,' I said, 'I think I have you to thank for a present sent me while I was in prison. I have eaten the bread, the file will do to sharpen my lance—I will keep it in remembrance of you; but the money, here it is.'

"'Goodness!' she cried, bursting with laughter, 'he has kept the money. Well, so much the better, for I am none too flush; but what's the odds? a wandering dog will not starve.[2] Come along, let us eat it all. You shall treat me.'

"We had taken the road back to Seville. At the commencement of the Street of the Serpent she bought a dozen oranges, which she made me put in my handkerchief. A little farther on she bought, besides, a loaf of bread, a sausage, and a bottle of Manzanilla. Finally she entered a confectioner's shop. There she threw on the counter the gold-piece I had returned to her, with another which she had in her pocket, and some silver. Then she asked me for all I had, too. I had only a few small pieces, which I gave her, feeling much ashamed to have no more. I thought she wanted to buy out the shop. She took all there was of the finest and dearest yemas,[3] turon,[4] preserved fruits, as long as the money lasted.[5] All this I had to carry off in paper bags. Perhaps you know the Street of the Candilejo, where is a bust of the King Don Pedro, the Guardian of Justice.[6] That should have made me think what

---

[1] "Mañana serà otro dia."   Spanish proverb.

[2]   "Chuquel sos pirela,
            Cocal terela."   Gipsy proverb.

[3] *Yemas*, yolks of eggs prepared with a crust of sugar.

[4] *Turon*, a kind of nougat.

[5] [No people are so profligate in their festivals and feasts as the gipsies. Often both parties to a marriage ruin themselves for life by extravagance at the marriage festival. For a curious account of this see Borrow's *Gipsies of Spain*.—TRANSLATOR.]

[6] The King Don Pedro, whom we call The Cruel, and whom Queen Isabella the Catholic always called the Guardian of Justice, was fond of walking about the streets of Seville in the evening, seeking adventures like the Caliph Haroun al Raschid. One night, in a lonely street, he picked a quarrel with a man who was serenading. They fought, and the

I was about. We stopped before an old house in this street.
She entered the passage and rapped at the ground floor. A
gipsy, true servant of Satan, came to open it. Carmen spoke
some words in Romany to her. The old hag grumbled at
first. To appease her Carmen gave her two oranges, a fistful
of bonbons, and also a sip of wine. Then she put her cloak
on her back and led her to the door, which she secured with a
bar of wood. As soon as we were alone she commenced to
dance and laugh like one possessed, singing, 'Thou art my
rom, and I thy *romi*.' [1]

"There I stood in the middle of the room, loaded with all
our purchases, and not knowing where to put them. She
dumped them all on the floor, and clasping me round the neck,
cried out, 'I pay my debts, I pay my debts; 'tis the law of the
Calés.' [2] Ah! señor, that day! that day! . . . When I think
of it, I forget to-morrow!"

The bandit was silent a moment; then, after he had relighted
his cigar, he continued:

"We remained together the whole day, eating, drinking—
and the rest. When she had eaten bonbons like a six-year-old
child, she stuffed handfuls into the old woman's water-jar—

king killed the amorous cavalier. At the noise of the swords an old
woman stuck her head out of a window and lit up the scene with a small
lamp, *candilejo*, which she held in her hand. Now the King Don Pedro,
one must know, though otherwise strong and lusty, had a curious de-
formity. When he walked, his knee-pans "cracked" loudly. The old
woman by this "cracking" had no difficulty in recognising the king.
The next day, the magistrate in charge came to make his report to the
king. "Sire, a duel was fought last night in such a street. One of the
combatants was killed." "Have you discovered the murderer?" "Yes,
sire." "Why has he not yet been punished?" "Sire, I await your
orders." "Let the law take its course." Now the king had just issued
a decree that all duellists should be beheaded, and the head exposed on the
field of combat. The magistrate extricated himself from the affair like
a man of wit. He had the head sawn from a statue of the king and
exposed it in a niche in the midst of the street the scene of the murder.
The king and all the Sevillians thought this a very happy thought. The
street took its name from the old woman's little lamp, candilejo, the only
witness of the affair. So much for popular tradition. Zuñiga tells the
story quite differently. (See *Annals of Seville*, vol. ii, p. 136.) However
this may be, there is still at Seville a Candilejo Street, and in this street
a stone bust which they say is a portrait of Don Pedro. Unhappily,
this bust is modern. The old one was very much worn out in the seven-
teenth century, and the municipality then replaced it by the one we
see to-day.

[1] Husband, wife.

[2] Calo, feminine Calli, plural Calés; literally, "black." A name the
gipsies give themselves in their own tongue.

'to make her a sorbet,' she said. She smashed the yemas by throwing them against the wall—'so that the flies may leave us in peace,' she said. There was no trick or folly that she did not commit. I said I would like to see her dance, but what would we do for castanets? At once she took the old woman's only plate, broke it in pieces, and behold! there she was dancing the romalis, clacking the pieces of the plate together as well as if she had castanets of ebony or ivory. One would never be bored in that girl's company, I warrant you. Evening came, and I heard the drums beating the 'retreat.'

"'I must return to my quarters for roll-call,' I said.

"'To your quarters!' she cried with an air of contempt. 'Are you then a negro slave, to let yourself be driven about with a whip? You are a real canary, in character as well as clothes.[1] Get out! You are chicken-hearted.'

"Well, I stayed, resigned beforehand to the guard-room. In the morning, she was the first to speak of our parting.

"'Listen, Joseito,' she said; 'have I repaid you? According to our laws, I owed you nothing, for you are a *payllo*; but you are good-looking; you have pleased me. We are quits. Good day.'

"I asked her when I might see her again.

"'When you are less stupid,' she said, laughing.

"Then in a more serious tone she continued: 'Do you know, comrade, that I believe I love you a little bit? But that could not last. Dog and wolf can't keep house together long. Perhaps if you conformed to gipsy law I should like to become your romi. But this is all nonsense. It cannot be. Bah! my lad, believe me, you are well out of it. You have met the devil—yes, the devil; he isn't always black, and he has not twisted your neck. I am dressed in wool, but I am not a lamb.[2] Go, burn a candle before your *majari*[3]; she has earned it. Come, let us go. Good-bye once again. Think no more of Carmencita, or she may make you wed a widow with wooden legs.'[4]

"Thus speaking, she unbarred the door, and once in the street, wrapped herself in her mantilla and showed me her heels.

[1] The Spanish dragoons are uniformed in yellow.
[2] "Me dicas vriardâ de jorpoy, bus ne sino braco." Gipsy proverb.
[3] The Virgin Mary.
[4] The gallows; widow of the last one hanged.

"She spoke truly. I would have been wise had I thought no more about her; but after that day in the Street of the Candilejo I could think of nothing else. I wandered about all day long, hoping to meet her again. I inquired about her of the old woman and the friture-seller. They both said that she had gone to Laloro,[1] as they call Portugal. Probably they followed Carmen's instructions in replying thus; but I was not long finding out that they both lied. Several weeks after my day in the Street of the Candilejo, I was on guard at one of the city gates. A little distance from this gate a breach had been made in the enclosing wall; workmen were busy there during the day, and at night a sentry was placed there to guard against smuggling. During the day I saw Lillas Pastia loitering about the guard-house, chatting with several of my comrades; they all knew him well, and his fish and his fritters still better. He approached me, and asked me if I had yet heard from Carmen.

"'No,' I answered.

"'Well, you soon will, comrade.'

"He was not mistaken. That night I was placed on duty in the breach. As soon as the corporal had left, I saw a woman coming near. My heart told me that it was Carmen. Nevertheless, I cried out, 'Be off; there is no passing here.'

"'Come, don't be cross,' said she, making herself known to me.

"'What! is it you, Carmen?'

"'Yes, my countryman. Let us talk a little, but to the point. Do you wish to earn a douro? Some people are coming with packs: let them pass.'

"'No,' I replied; 'I must stop them—'tis my orders.'

"'Your orders! Your orders! You did not think of orders in the Street of the Candilejo.'

"'Ah!' I cried, quite upset by this sole reminder, 'for that it was worth while to forget my orders; but I want no smugglers' money.'

"'Let us see, then. If you don't want the money, would you like to dine again at old Dorothea's house?'

"'No,' I replied, half strangled by the effort I was making —'I cannot.'

"'Very well! Since you are so obstinate, I know whom to ask. I will offer to go to Dorothea's with your officer. He seems to be a good fellow, and he will put on duty here a lad

[1] The red land.

who will see no more than he should. Adieu, Canary; I shall laugh well when the orders are to hang you.'

"I had the weakness to call her back; and I promised to let the whole race of gipsies pass, if necessary, provided that I obtained the only reward I coveted. She immediately swore to meet me the next day, and ran to apprise her friends who were close by. There were five of them, among them Pastia, all well loaded with English goods. Carmen kept watch. She was to give the alarm with her castanets as soon as she saw the guards; but of this she had no need. The smugglers accomplished their affair in an instant.

"On the morrow I went to the Street of the Candilejo. Carmen was awaiting me, and in a very bad humour.

"'I do not like people of whom one must beg a favour,' she said. 'The first time, you rendered me a great service without the thought of gaining aught. Yesterday you bargained with me. I don't know why I have come, for I love you no more. Come, get out! There is a douro for your trouble!'

"A little more and I should have hurled the money at her head; and I was obliged to exercise great self-control to keep from beating her. After we had disputed together for an hour, I rushed out in a furious rage. I wandered a while about the city, walking here and there like a madman; at last I entered a church, and seating myself in the darkest corner, I burst into tears. Suddenly I heard a voice, saying:

"'A dragon's[1] tears. I should like to make a philtre of them.'

"I looked up; Carmen was before me.

"'Well, my countryman,' said she. 'Do you still want me? Surely I must love you, in spite of all; for since you have left me I know not what is the matter with me. Come, now! this time it is I who asks you if you wish to go to the Street of the Candilejo.'

"So we made it up. But Carmen's temper was like the weather in our country: never is the storm so nigh as when the sun is shining brightest. She had promised to meet me again at Dorothea's, but she came not; and Dorothea asserted that she had gone to Laloro on business for Egypt.

"Knowing by experience how much dependence to place on

---

[1] [A play upon the French word *dragon*, which means both dragon and dragoon.—TRANSLATOR.]

that, I searched everywhere for Carmen where she might be; twenty times a day I passed through the Street of the Candilejo. One evening I was at Dorothea's, whom I had almost tamed by treating her occasionally to a glass of anisette, when Carmen entered, followed by a young man, a lieutenant in our regiment.

"'Get out of this,' she said to me in Basque.

"I stood stupefied with rage in my heart.

"'What are you doing here?' cried the lieutenant. 'Decamp; get out of this.'

"I could not budge. I was like one paralysed. The officer, seeing that I did not move and had not even uncovered, seized me angrily by the collar and shook me roughly. I know not what I said to him. He drew his sword, and I drew mine. The old woman seized my arm and the lieutenant gave me a cut on my forehead, the scar of which I carry to this day. I stepped back, and with my elbow sent Dorothea sprawling on the floor; then, as the lieutenant followed me up, I gave him the point of my sword, and he sheathed it in his bosom. Then Carmen blew out the lamp, and called out in her own tongue to Dorothea to fly. I myself escaped to the street, and ran on I knew not whither. It seemed to me that someone was following me. When I recovered my wits, I found that Carmen had not left me.

"'You great stupid canary,' she said; 'all you know is to commit follies. I told you that I should bring misfortune upon you. Yet there is a remedy for every ill if one has for a sweetheart a Fleming of Rome.[1] Begin by tying this handkerchief about your head, and give me your belt. Wait for me in this alley. I will be back in two minutes.'

"She disappeared, and soon brought me a striped cloak, which she had found I know not where. She made me doff my uniform and put the cloak over my shirt. Thus attired, I looked enough like the peasants of Valencia as they come to Seville to sell their chufas.[2] Then she brought me to a house somewhat like Dorothea's, at the foot of a narrow court. She and another gipsy woman washed and dressed my wound better than could a surgeon-major, and gave me something to

[1] "Flamenca de Roma," a slang term for gipsies. Rome here does not refer to the Eternal City, but to the romi, or married folks, as the gipsies call themselves. Those first seen in Spain came probably from the Netherlands: hence their name of Flemings.

[2] A bulbous root, of which an agreeable drink is made.

drink, I know not what. At last they laid me upon a mattress, and I fell asleep.

"Probably these women had put in my drink one of those soporific drugs of which they know the secret, for I did not awake until very late the next day. I had a fearful headache and a slight fever. It was some time before I recalled the terrible drama in which I had been an actor the evening before. After they had dressed my wound, Carmen and her friend, both crouching by my mattress, exchanged a few words in chipe calli which seemed to be a medical consultation. Then they both assured me that I would soon be well, but that I had better quit Seville in the shortest time possible, for if I was taken I would certainly be shot.

"'My lad,' said Carmen, 'the king will no longer give you either rice or salt cod,[1] and you must do something; you must be thinking of earning your living. You are too stupid to steal *à pastesas*[2]; but you are active and strong; if you have the courage, make your way to the coast and become a smuggler. Have I not promised to get you hanged? That is better than being shot. Besides, if you know how to manage, you may live like a prince so long as the *miñons*[3] and the coast-guard do not collar you.'

"It was in this engaging manner that that devil of a girl showed me the new career for which she destined me; to tell the truth, the only one left me, now that I had incurred the penalty of death. Need I tell you that she decided me without much trouble? It seemed to me that I should bind myself more closely to her by this life of risk and lawlessness. Henceforth I thought myself sure of her love. I had often heard of a band of smugglers who infested Andalusia—well mounted, blunderbuss in hand, and their mistresses seated on the croup behind them. Already I could see myself trotting over hill and dale with this pretty gipsy behind me. When I spoke to her of this she must needs laugh till she held her sides, telling me that there was nothing so fine as a night passed in bivouac, when each rom retired with his romi beneath the little tent made of a blanket stretched over three hoops.

"'If I keep always in the mountains,' said I to her, 'I shall

---

[1] The ordinary rations of the Spanish soldiers.
[2] "Ustilar a pastesas," to rob skilfully, without violence.
[3] A kind of free corps.

be sure of you. No lieutenant will be there to share with me.'

"'Ah! you are jealous,' she replied. 'So much the worse for you. How can you be so stupid! Can you not see that I love you, since I have never asked you for any money?'

"When she talked in that fashion I felt like strangling her.

"To make a short story, señor, Carmen procured for me a civilian's dress, in which I escaped from Seville unrecognised. I went to Jerez, with a letter from Pastia to an anisette-seller at whose house the smugglers used to meet. I was presented to these gentry, whose chief, called Dancaïre, received me into his band. We departed for Gaucin, where I again saw Carmen, who had agreed to meet me there. In our expeditions she served as a spy for us men, and a better one there never was. She had just returned from Gibraltar, and had already arranged with a ship's captain for the landing of certain English goods which we were expected to receive on the coast. We waited for them near Estepona; then we hid a part of them in the mountains, and laden with the rest we proceeded to Ronda. Carmen was already there: it was she again who told us the moment when we might safely enter the town. This first expedition and some others were fortunate.—A smuggler's life pleased me better than a soldier's.—I made Carmen presents. —I had money and a sweetheart. I felt little remorse, for, as the gipsies say, the itch of pleasure does not itch at all.[1] Everywhere we were well received; my comrades treated me well, even showing me some respect. This was because I had 'killed my man,' and amongst them all there was not one with a similar exploit on his conscience. But what affected me the most in my new life was that I was often with Carmen. She showed me more friendship than ever; nevertheless, before our comrades she never admitted our intimacy, and had even made me swear with all sorts of oaths to say nothing to them on my own account. I was so feeble in the hands of this creature that I obeyed her every caprice. Besides, this was the first time she ever showed me any of the reserve of an honest woman, and I was simple enough to believe that she had really corrected her former ways.

"Our troop, which was composed of eight or ten men, seldom met together, and only at decisive moments; we were usually scattered about by twos and threes in the towns and villages.

[1] "Sarapia sat pesquital ne punzava."

Each of us pretended to follow a trade: this one was a tinker, another a horse-dealer; I was a peddler, but I seldom showed myself in the large towns because of my bad affair at Seville. One day, or rather one night, our rendezvous was at Vejer. Dancaïre and I found ourselves there before the others. He seemed very gay.

"'We are going to have another comrade,' he told me. 'Carmen has just made one of her best strokes. She has just managed the escape of her rom, who was in the presidio at Tarifa.'

"I was beginning already to understand the gipsy dialect which nearly all my comrades spoke, and this word rom gave me a chill.

"'What—her husband! Is she then married?' I asked of the captain.

"'Yes,' he replied; 'to Garcia, the One-eyed, a gipsy as "fly" as she is herself. The poor fellow was in the galleys. Carmen so bewitched the surgeon of the presidio that she obtained the liberty of her rom. Ah! that girl is worth her weight in gold. For two years she has been contriving his escape. Nothing succeeded until they took the notion to change the commandant. With this one it seems that she has come quickly to an understanding.'

"You can imagine with what pleasure I heard this news. I soon met Garcia, the One-eyed; he was the ugliest monster that Bohemia ever reared, with a black skin and a soul still blacker; he was the most thoroughbred rascal that I have ever met. Carmen came with him, and when she called him her rom before me, you should have seen the eyes she made at me and her grimaces when Garcia's back was turned. I was indignant, and did not speak to her the whole night. In the morning, we made up our bales, and were already on our way, when we discovered that a dozen horsemen were at our heels. These Andalusian braggarts, who were always talking murder, at once showed the white feather. 'Twas a regular stampede. Only Dancaïre, Garcia, a fine-looking fellow from Ecija named Remendado, and Carmen did not lose their heads. The others abandoned their mules and threw themselves into the ravines, where the horses could not pursue them. We could not save our beasts, and hastened to unstrap the most valuable of our booty and to load it on our shoulders; then we tried to escape

over the rocks by the steepest and roughest slopes. We cast
our bales before us, and followed them as best we could, sliding
along on our heels. During this time the enemy peppered us,
and for the first time I heard the whistling of bullets; but I
did not mind them. When one is under a woman's eyes there
is no merit in defying death. We all escaped except poor
Remendado, who received a bullet in his loins. I dropped
my packet and tried to carry him.

"'Fool!' cried Garcia, 'what have we to do with carrion?
Drop him, and save the cotton stockings.'

"'Drop him!' cried Carmen.

"Fatigue obliged me to lay him for a moment in the shelter
of a rock. The One-eyed advanced and discharged his blunderbuss at the poor fellow's head.

"'He will be clever who will recognise him now,' said Garcia,
regarding the face which a dozen balls had torn in fragments.

"Such, señor, was the delightful life I led. In the evening
we found ourselves in a thicket, worn out with fatigue, with
nothing to eat, and ruined by the loss of our mules. What
did that infernal Garcia do?—he pulled a pack of cards from
his pocket, and began to play with Dancaïre by the light of a
fire that they had kindled. Meanwhile I lay down, gazing at
the stars, thinking of Remendado, and wishing myself in his
place. Carmen crouched near me, and from time to time she
rattled her castanets, humming a tune. Then, approaching
me as if to whisper, she kissed me two or three times, almost
against my will.

"'You are the devil,' said I.

"'Yes,' she answered.

"After a few hours' rest she left for Gaucin, and the following
morning a little goatherd brought us some bread. We remained
there all day, and in the night moved towards Gaucin. We
waited for news from Carmen. None came. At daybreak we
saw a muleteer guiding a well-dressed woman, with a parasol,
and a little girl who seemed to be her domestic. Garcia said
to us:

"'There are two mules and two women that Saint Nicholas
sends us. I should prefer four mules; but never mind, I will
attend to this business.'

"He took his blunderbuss and went down toward the path,
hiding in the bushes. We followed him at a little distance,

Dancaïre and I. When we were within range we showed ourselves, crying to the muleteer to halt. The woman, instead of
being frightened at our appearance—and our dress should have
sufficed for that—burst into a peal of laughter.

"'Ah! the *lillipendi*; they take me for an *erani*!'[1]

"'Twas Carmen, but so well disguised that I should not have
known her had she spoken in any other tongue. She sprang
from her mule and in a low voice conversed for some time with
Dancaïre and Garcia; then, turning to me: 'Canary, we will
meet again before you are hanged. I am going to Gibraltar,
on the "affairs of Egypt." You will soon have news of me.'

"We separated after she had shown us a place where we
could find shelter for several days. That girl was the salvation
of our troop. We soon received some money she sent us, and
information which was of more value to us: this was that on
such a day two English gentlemen would pass by such a road;
a word to the wise is sufficient—they had money in plenty.
Garcia wished to assassinate them, but Dancaïre and I opposed
it. We took nothing from them but their money and watches,
except their shirts, of which we had great need.

"Señor, one becomes a rascal without thinking much about
it. You lose your head over a pretty girl, you fight for her,
misfortune comes upon you, you must needs live in the mountains, and from a smuggler you become a robber without
reflection. We judged it would not be well for us to remain
in the neighbourhood of Gibraltar, after the affair with the
English gentlemen, and we hid ourselves in the Sierra de
Ronda.

"You have spoken to me of José Maria; well, it was there
that I made his acquaintance. He took his mistress with him
on his expeditions. She was a pretty girl, wise, modest, and
good-mannered; never a vulgar word, and so devoted! . . .
In return he made her miserable. He was always running
after other girls, he bullied her, then sometimes he took the
notion to be jealous of her. Once he struck her with his knife.
Ah, well! she only loved him the more for that. Why, that
girl was proud of the scar on her arm, and showed it as if it
were the most beautiful thing on earth. And then, to crown
all, José Maria was the very worst of comrades. In an expedition that we made, he managed so well that all the profit

[1] "Ah! the fools; they take me for a real lady!"

of the affair fell to him, and to us the trouble and the blows
But I must go back to my story.

"We heard no more from Carmen. Dancaïre said: 'One ot
us must go to Gibraltar for news of her; she must have arranged
some affair. I would go willingly, but I am too well known
at Gibraltar.'

"The One-eyed said: 'Me, too; they know me there. I have
played too many tricks on the lobsters [1] there! And as I have
only one eye, it is hard for me to disguise myself.'

"'Then I must go,' I said in my turn, delighted at the very
idea of seeing Carmen again. 'Let us see! what must be done?'

"The others told me. 'You may go either by sea or by
Saint Roque, as you prefer. And when you come to Gibraltar, ask
at the port where a chocolate-vender named Rollona lives; when
you have found her, she will tell you all that is happening there.'

"It was agreed that we should all depart for the Sierra of
Gaucin; that I should leave my two comrades there, and proceed to Gibraltar disguised as a fruit-seller. At Ronda a man
who was in our interest had procured me a passport. At
Gaucin they gave me a donkey; I loaded him with melons and
oranges, and then took the road. On my arrival at Gibraltar
I found that Rollona was well known, but that she was dead
or had gone to *finibus terræ* [2]; and her disappearance explained,
to my notion, how we had lost our means of communication with
Carmen. I put up my donkey in a stable, and taking my
oranges, wandered about the city as if trying to sell them, but
in reality to see if I could not encounter some familiar face.
At Gibraltar there are many vagrants of all nations. 'Tis the
Tower of Babel over again; for one cannot go ten paces in a
street without hearing as many tongues spoken. I met plenty
of gipsies, but I did not dare to trust any of them. They
sounded me and I them; we each divined that we were rogues
—the important thing was to know if we were of the same
band. After two days of fruitless wanderings I had learned
nothing of either Rollona or Carmen, and I was thinking of
returning to my comrades after making a few purchases, when,
as I was walking down a street at sunset, I heard a woman's
voice calling to me from a window.

[1] A name given by the Spaniards to the English because of their red
uniforms.
[2] To the galleys or "to the devil."

"'Orange-seller!'

"I looked up and saw Carmen on a balcony, leaning over the rail, and beside her an officer in scarlet, with gold epaulettes, curled hair, and the bearing of a great milord. As for her, she was dressed superbly: a shawl over her shoulders, a gold comb in her hair, in silk attire, and—the darling! the same as ever—gay with laughter. The Englishman in barbarous Spanish ordered me to come up, for madame wished some oranges; and Carmen called to me in Basque:

"'Come up, and do not be astonished at anything.'

"In fact, nothing could astonish me that she did. I cannot say whether I felt more joy than sorrow at finding her. At the door there stood a big powdered English servant, who led me into a magnificent room. Carmen immediately said in Basque:

"'Remember! you do not understand a word of Spanish, nor know me.'

"Then turning to the Englishman: 'There! I told you so: I saw from the first that he was a Basque. You shall now hear a droll jargon. How stupid he looks!—ah! one would say a cat surprised in a cupboard.'

"'And thou,' said I, in mine own tongue, 'thou hast the air of a brazen-faced jade, and I have a good mind to slash thy face before thy gallant.'

"'My gallant!' she cried. 'So you have found that out all by yourself. And you are jealous of that imbecile there! Well, you are more stupid than you were before our soirées at the Street of the Candilejo. Do you not see, fool that you are, that at this moment I am arranging an affair of Egypt, and in the most brilliant style, too? This house is mine; this lobster's guineas will be mine. I lead him about by the nose, and I will soon lead him whence he will never return.'

"'And I,' I replied, 'if you arrange the affairs of Egypt after that fashion, I will arrange it so that you will never commence again.'

"'Ah! so then! Are you my rom that you command me? The One-eyed is satisfied. What business have you here? Ought not you to be content to be the only one that can call himself my *minchorro* [1]?'

"'What does he say?' asked the Englishman.

"'He says that he is dry, and that he could down a good

---

[1] Flash term for a lover.

drink,' replied Carmen. And she threw herself back on a sofa, bursting with merriment over her translation.

"Señor, when that girl laughed there was no chance to talk sense. Everyone laughed with her. The great Englishman laughed with her, like the fool that he was, and ordered that some drink should be brought me.

"While I was drinking, 'Do you see that ring on his finger?' said Carmen. 'If you wish, I will give it to you.'

"I answered: 'I would give one of my fingers to have my lord in the mountains, each of us with a maquila in his hand.'

"'*Maquila*, what does that mean?' asked the Englishman.

"'*Maquila*,' replied Carmen, laughing all the time, 'is an orange. Isn't it a droll word for an orange? He says that he would like to make you eat an orange.'

"'Yes?' replied the Englishman. 'Very well! Bring some more maquilas to-morrow.'

"While we were talking, the domestic entered and announced that dinner was ready. Then the Englishman arose, gave me a piastre, and offered his arm to Carmen—as if she could not walk in alone! Carmen, always laughing, said to me:

"'My lad, I cannot invite you to dinner; but to-morrow, as soon as you hear the drums beat for parade, come here with the oranges. You will find a chamber better furnished than that of the Street of the Candilejo, and you will see that I am as ever thine own Carmencita, and then we can talk of the affairs of Egypt.'

"I did not reply, and was already in the street when the Englishman called to me, 'Bring some maquilas to-morrow!' and I heard the peals of Carmen's laughter.

"I went out, not knowing what I was doing, and slept scarcely any; and in the morning I found myself so incensed against the traitress that I resolved to quit Gibraltar without seeing her again; but at the first roll of the drums all my fortitude deserted me: I took my basket of oranges, and ran to Carmen's. Through the half-opened blind I saw her great black eyes watching me. The powdered footman let me in at once. Carmen sent him away on an errand, and as soon as we were alone she burst into one of her peals of crocodile-laughter, and threw herself in my arms. I had never seen her so beautiful. Dressed like a madonna, perfumed, . . . silken furniture, embroidered curtains . . . ah! . . . and I, dressed like the robber that I was.

"'Minchorro!' said Carmen, 'I would like to smash everything here, set fire to the house, and fly to the sierra!'

"And then it was caresses! . . . then laughter! . . . then she danced, she tore her furbelows: never did monkey perform more gambols, make more grimaces, commit more deviltries. When she became serious again:

"'Listen,' she said; 'about Egypt. I want him to take me to Ronda, where I have a sister a nun' (here a fresh burst of laughter). 'We will pass by a place I will tell you of; you fall on him and rob him of everything. . . . The best way would be to wring his neck; but,' she added, with a diabolical smile that she sometimes had—and that smile never a soul then wished to imitate—'do you know what you must do? Let the One-eyed go first; hold back a little yourself. The lobster is brave and skilful: he has good pistols. . . . Do you understand?' . . . She interrupted herself with another peal of laughter that made my flesh creep.

"'No,' I said; 'I hate Garcia, but he is my comrade. Some day, perhaps, I will rid you of him; but we will settle our accounts after the manner of my own country. I am only an Egyptian by chance, and for certain things I shall always be a true Navarro, as the proverb says.'[1]

"She replied: 'You are a fool, an idiot, a true *payllo*. You are like the dwarf who thought himself tall because he could spit a long way.[2] You do not love me. Get out!'

"When she told me to get out I could not go. I promised to return to my comrades and await the Englishman; for her part, she promised to be indisposed until the time of departure for Ronda. I remained two days longer at Gibraltar. She had the audacity to come in disguise to see me at my inn. I departed—I also had a project. I returned to our rendezvous, knowing the hour at which the Englishman and Carmen should pass. I found Dancaïre and Garcia awaiting me. We passed the night in a wood by a fire of pine-cones which burned splendidly. I asked Garcia to play cards. He accepted. At the second game I told him he cheated; he laughed at me. I

[1] "Navarro fino."
[2] "Or esorjié de or narsichislé, sin chismar lachiaguel." Gipsy proverb.

threw the cards in his face. He tried to seize his blunderbuss; I put my foot on it, and said:

"'They say that you can handle a knife with the best knave in Malaga. Will you try it on with me?'

"Dancaïre wished to separate us. I had given Garcia two or three blows with my fist. Rage gave him courage: he had drawn his knife and I mine. We both called out to Dancaïre to give us room and to see fair play. He saw that he could not stop us, and drew back. Garcia was already crouching like a cat ready to spring on a mouse. He held his hat in his left hand, as a guard, his knife in advance. That is the Andalusian guard. I stood on guard in the Navarro manner, right in front of him, the left arm raised, the left leg advanced, the knife along the right thigh. I felt stronger than a giant. He threw himself upon me like a flash. I turned on my left foot and he found nothing before him; but I struck him in the throat, and my knife went so deep that my hand came right up under his chin. I drew back the blade so forcibly that it broke. 'Twas all over. The blade was pushed from the wound by a jet of blood as large as your arm. He fell on his face as dead as a log.

"'What hast thou done!' cried Dancaïre.

"'Listen,' said I; 'we could not live together. I love Carmen, and I wish to be the only one. Besides, Garcia was a villain, and I have not forgotten how he served poor Remendado. There are now but two of us; but we are good fellows. Come, will you be my friend for life, for death?'

"Dancaïre held out his hand. He was a man fifty years old.

"'To the devil with love affairs!' cried he. 'If you had asked him for Carmen, he would have sold her to you for a piastre. We are only two now; how shall we manage to-morrow?'

"'Leave me to manage it by myself,' I answered; 'now I care not for the whole world.'

"We buried Garcia, and pitched our tent two hundred paces farther on. The next day, Carmen and her Englishman came along with two muleteers and a servant. I said to Dancaïre, 'I will take care of the Englishman. Frighten the others, they are unarmed.' The Englishman had a stout heart. If Carmen had not pushed his arm he would have killed me. In short, I reconquered Carmen that day, and my first words were to tell her that she was a widow. When she found out how it had happened:

"'You will always be a *lillipendi*!' she said. 'Garcia should have killed you. Your Navarre guard is all nonsense, and he has sent to the other world cleverer men than thou. But his time had come. Yours will come, too.'

"'And yours,' I said, 'if you are not a true wife to me.'

"'So much the better,' she replied; 'I have often seen in the coffee-grounds that we two must die together. Bah! he who sows, reaps!' and she rattled her castanets, which she always did when she wished to drive away unpleasant thoughts.

"One is apt to forget oneself when speaking of his own affairs. All these details must bore you; but I shall soon finish. The life we led lasted long enough. Dancaïre and I joined with us several comrades more trusty than our old ones, and we busied ourselves smuggling; sometimes, I must admit, we also stopped people on the highway, but only at the last extremity, when we could not live otherwise. Besides, we did not maltreat travellers; we confined ourselves to taking their money. During several months I was content with Carmen: she continued to be useful in our operations by advising us of good strokes that we might make. She stayed sometimes at Malaga, sometimes at Cordova, and sometimes at Granada; but at a word from me she left all, and came to meet me at some isolated inn, or even in camp. Once only—'twas at Malaga—she gave me some anxiety. I knew that she had cast her wiles about a very rich merchant, with whom she proposed, probably, to repeat the pleasantry of Gibraltar. In spite of all Dancaïre could say to dissuade me, I set out and entered Malaga in plain daylight. I looked Carmen up, and brought her away at once. We had a very warm explanation.

"'Do you know,' she said, 'that since you are really my rom, I love you less than when you were my minchorro? I won't be tormented, much less commanded. What I wish is to be free, and do what I like. Take care not to push me too far. If you annoy me, I will find some good fellow who will serve you as you served the One-eyed.'

"Dancaïre reconciled us to one another. Shortly after, misfortune fell upon us. The soldiers surprised us. Dancaïre was killed, as were two others of my comrades; two more were captured. I myself was sorely wounded, and without my good horse I would have been taken by the soldiers. Worn out with fatigue, with a bullet in my body, I hid myself in a wood with the only comrade left me. I fainted when I dismounted, and I thought I was going to die like a wounded hare in the underbrush. My comrade carried me to a cave known to us, and then went to seek Carmen. She was at Granada, and came on the instant. She did not leave me a single moment for fifteen days—she did not close an eye; and nursed me with a skill and attention never shown by other woman for the man she loved best. As soon as I could use my legs, she fetched me to Granada in great secrecy. Gipsies can find safe retreats everywhere, and I passed more than six weeks in a house two doors removed from the judge who was seeking for me. More than once from behind the blinds I saw him pass. At length my strength came back; but I had reflected while on my bed of pain, and I intended to mend my ways. I spoke to Carmen of quitting Spain and trying to live honestly in the New World. She laughed at me.

"'We were not made to grow cabbages,' she said; 'our destiny is to live at the expense of the *payllos*. Come, I have arranged an affair with Nathan-ben-Joseph, of Gibraltar. He has some cotton stuffs which only await you to smuggle them in. He knows that you are alive. He counts on you. What will our correspondents in Gibraltar say if you break your word?'

"I let myself be persuaded, and resumed my wicked career.

"While I was in hiding at Granada, there were some bull-fights which Carmen attended. When she came back she talked a good deal about a very adroit picador named Lucas. She knew his horse's name, and how much his embroidered vest had cost him. I did not pay much attention to this. Juanito, my remaining comrade, told me several days afterwards that he had seen Carmen with Lucas at the house of a merchant of Zacatin. This began to alarm me. I demanded of Carmen how and why she had become acquainted with the picador.

"'He is a fellow,' said she, 'with whom one may arrange an affair. The river that makes a noise has either water or pebbles.[1] He has earned 1200 reals in the bull-ring. One of two things must happen: we must have this money; or, as he is a fine rider

---

[1] "Len sos sonsi abela
Pani o reblendani terela." Gipsy proverb

and a brave fellow, we might enrol him in our band. So-and-so are dead; you must needs replace them. Take him with you.'

"'I do not want his money or himself, and I forbid you to speak to him,' I cried.

"'Take care!' she replied. 'When one forbids me to do a thing, it is soon done.'

"Happily, the picador left for Malaga, and I set to work to smuggle in the cotton for the Jew. I had a great deal to do on that expedition, and Carmen, too; and I forgot Lucas. Perhaps she also forgot him—for the moment, at least. It was about this time, señor, that I met you—first near Montilla, then afterwards at Cordova. I will not speak to you of our last interview. You perhaps know more about it than I. Carmen robbed you of your watch; she also wanted your money —above all, the ring that I see now upon your finger, and which she said was a magic ring and of great importance to possess. We had a violent dispute, and I struck her. She turned pale and wept. 'Twas the first time I ever saw her cry, and it gave me a terrible shock. I asked her to forgive me, but she sulked all one day; and when I left for Montilla she did not wish to kiss me.

"I had a heavy heart when, three days after, she came to see me, with a laughing air as gay as a lark. All was forgotten, and we were like a pair of lovers for two days. When we were parting she said to me:

"'There is to be a fête at Cordova. I am going to see it; so I shall find out what men leave with money, and I will tell you.'

"I let her go. When alone I thought over this fête, and the great change in Carmen's humour. She must have already revenged herself, I thought, since she has given in first.

"A peasant told me that there was a bull-fight at Cordova. My blood boiled, and like a madman I set out for the place. Someone pointed out Lucas, and on a bench near the barrier I saw Carmen. I had only to look at her a minute to confirm my suspicions. Lucas with the first bull acted the gallant, as I had expected. He tore the cockade [1] from the bull and carried it to Carmen, who pinned it in her hair immediately.

---

[1] "La divisa," a knot of ribbons indicating by its colour from which pasture the bull comes. This knot is affixed to the skin of the bull by a steel hook. It is the height of gallantry to tear it from the living animal and offer it to a woman.

The bull charged him, as if to avenge me. Lucas was over-turned, with his horse on his breast and the bull on top of both. I looked for Carmen, but she was no longer in her place. As it was impossible for me to get out, I was forced to await the end of the fight. Then I went to the house which you know of, and remained there quietly all the evening and a part of the night. About two o'clock in the morning Carmen returned, and was a little surprised to see me.

"'Come with me,' I said to her.

"'Very well,' she said; 'let us go.'

"I went to fetch my horse and put her behind me, and we travelled all the night without exchanging a single word. At daybreak we halted at a solitary inn, near a little hermitage. There I said to Carmen:

"'Listen. I forget all. Of the past I will not speak a word. But swear to me one thing: that you will follow me to America, and that you will there lead a quiet life.'

"'No,' she replied in a sulky voice; 'I do not wish to go to America. I am well satisfied here.'

"''Tis because you are close to Lucas,' I said. 'But reflect well; if he recovers, 'twill be only to make old bones. Yet, after all, why should I bother myself about him? I am tired of killing your lovers; it is you whom I will kill next.'

"She regarded me fixedly, with her wild air, and said:

"'I have always thought that you would kill me. The first time I saw you I had just met a priest at the door of my dwelling, and to-night, while leaving Cordova, saw you nothing? —a hare crossed the road between your horse's feet. It is fate!'

"'Carmencita,' I asked, 'is it true that you no longer love me?'

"She did not reply. She was seated cross-legged on a mat, and tracing figures on the ground with her finger.

"'Let us change our life,' I cried, in a supplicating voice. 'Come, let us live together somewhere where we will never be parted. You know that we have a hundred and twenty onzas buried under an oak near by. . . . Besides, we still have money in the hands of Ben-Joseph the Jew.'

"She began to smile, and replied:

"'Me first, then you; I knew well 'twould happen thus.'

"'Reflect!' I continued. 'I am at the end of my patience and my courage; make up your mind, or I will make up mine.'

"I left her and walked toward the hermitage. I found the hermit at prayer. I waited until his prayer was done; I would have liked very much to pray, but I could not. When he arose I drew near him.

"'Father,' said I, 'will you pray for one who is in great peril?'

"'I pray for all the afflicted,' he replied.

"'Could you say a mass for a soul about to appear before its Creator?'

"'Yes,' he answered, regarding me fixedly. And as there was something strange in my looks, he wished to make me talk.

"'It seems to me that I have seen you before,' he said.

"I put a piastre on his bench.

"'When will you say the mass?' I asked.

"'In half an hour. The innkeeper's son from over there comes to serve it. Tell me, young man, have you not something on your conscience which torments you? Won't you listen to the counsels of a Christian?'

"I felt ready to cry. I told him I would return, and fled. I laid me down upon the grass until I heard the bell. Then I drew near, but I remained outside the chapel. When mass was said I went back to the inn. I hoped that Carmen had fled—she might have taken my horse and escaped; but I found her still there. She did not wish that anyone might say that I had frightened her. While I was away she had ripped the hem of her dress and taken out the lead. Now she was before a table, gazing into a bowlful of water at the lead, which she had melted and that moment cast in. So absorbed was she with her enchantment that she did not at first notice my return. Sometimes she took a piece of lead and turned it in every direction with a sad air; sometimes she sang one of her mystic songs, in which the gipsies invoke Marie Padilla, the mistress of Don Pedro, who was, they say, the *Bari Crallisa*, or the queen of the gipsies.[1]

"'Carmen,' I said, 'will you come with me?'

"She arose, threw away her bowl, and drew her mantilla

[1] They accuse Marie Padilla of having bewitched the King Don Pedro. A popular tradition asserts that she gave Queen Blanche of Bourbon a girdle of gold which seemed to the eyes of the bewitched king a living serpent. From that arose the repugnance that he always showed for the unhappy princess.

over her head as if ready to go. They brought me my horse. She sprang up behind me, and we departed.

"'So, my Carmen,' I said, after we had gone a little way, 'you really wish to follow me, don't you?'

"'I will follow you to death, yes; but I will never live with you again.'

"We were in a solitary gorge. I pulled up my horse.

"'Is it here?' she cried, and with one bound she sprang to the ground. She threw off her mantilla, cast it at her feet, and stood motionless, with one hand on her hip, looking me steadily in the eyes.

"'You wish to kill me, I can well see,' she said. 'It is decreed; but you shall never make me yield.'

"'I beseech you,' I said to her, 'be reasonable. Listen to me. All the past is forgotten. Nevertheless, you know well that it is you who have ruined me. 'Tis for you I have become a robber and a murderer. Carmen! my own Carmen! let me save you, and with you save myself.'

"'José,' she replied, 'you ask the impossible. I love you no more; you, you love me still, and for this you wish to kill me. I might yet tell you some lie, but I do not care to take the trouble. All is over between us. As my rom, you have the right to kill your romi; but Carmen will be always free. Calli she was born and calli she will die.'

"'So, then, you love Lucas?' I demanded.

"'Yes; I have loved him, like you, for a moment—less, perhaps, than you. Now I love nothing, and I hate myself for ever having loved you at all.'

"I threw myself at her feet, I took her hands in mine, I bedewed them with tears. I reminded her of all the happy times we had spent together. I offered to remain always a brigand, to please her. Everything, señor, everything, if only she would love me again.

"She said, 'To love you, it is impossible. To live with you, I do not wish it.'

"Fury seized me. I drew my knife. I would have liked her to be afraid or to plead for mercy; but that woman was a demon.

"'For the last time,' I cried—'will you stay with me?'

"'No! no! no!' she cried, stamping her foot; and she drew from her finger a ring I had given her, and threw it amongst the bushes.

"I struck her twice. 'Twas Garcia's knife, which I had taken when I broke mine in his throat. She fell at the second thrust, without a cry. It seems to me that I can still see her great black eyes steadily fixed on me; then they became dimmed and closed. I remained completely prostrated for a good hour beside the body. Then I remembered that Carmen had often told me that she would like to be buried in a wood. I dug her a grave with my knife, and placed her in it. I searched a long time for her ring, and at last I found it. I placed it in the grave beside her, and also a small cross. Perhaps I did wrong. Then I mounted my horse, galloped straight to Cordova, and at the first guard-house I made myself known. I told them that I had killed Carmen, but I did not wish to tell them where her body lay. The hermit was a holy man. He prayed for her. He said a mass for her soul. . . . Poor girl! It is the gipsies who are to blame, for having reared her as they did."

APPENDIX

SPAIN is one of the countries where one finds to-day, and in greater numbers too, these nomads who are scattered all over Europe, and who are known under the names of bohemians, gitanos, gipsies, zingari, etc. The most of them live in, or rather wander through, the provinces of the south and east, in Andalusia, in Estremadura, in the kingdom of Murcia; they are numerous in Catalonia. These latter often cross over into France. The men are generally horse-traders, veterinary surgeons, and mule-clippers; to these callings they add that of tinkers, to say nothing of smuggling and other unlawful pursuits. The women tell fortunes, and sell all sorts of drugs, harmless or otherwise.

The physical characteristics of gipsies are easier to distinguish than to describe; and when a single one has been seen, you can recognise amongst a thousand strangers an individual of this race. Their features, their expression above everything else, distinguishes them from the people who inhabit the same countries. Their complexion is very swarthy, always darker than that of the people amongst whom they dwell. Hence the name of *calé* (blacks), by which they so often call themselves.[1] Their eyes are set obliquely, are large and well formed, jet-black, and shaded by long thick lashes. One can only compare their expression to that of a wild animal. Boldness and timidity are both expressed there at the same time, and in this respect their eyes reveal very well the characteristics of the race—cunning, bold, but by nature afraid, as Panurge, of a blow. For the most part the men are well built, lithe, and agile. I do not think that I ever saw one who was fat. In Germany, the gipsy women are often very pretty. Beauty is very rare amongst the gitanos of Spain: when they are young they are passable looking, but when they have once become

[1] It has seemed to me that the German gipsies, although they understand perfectly the word *calé*, do not like to be called by it. They call each other *Romané tchavé*.

mothers they are absolutely repulsive. The dirty personal habits of both sexes are incredible; and he who has not seen the locks of a gipsy matron can with difficulty form any idea of them, even by imagining the most unkempt, greasy, dusty, and frowzy head possible. In some of the large cities of Andalusia, some of the young girls, a little more agreeable than the others, take better care of their persons. These dance, for hire, certain dances which resemble closely those forbidden at our public carnival balls. Mr. Borrow, an English missionary, author of two very interesting works on the gipsies of Spain, whom he has tried to convert at the expense of the Bible Society, assures us that there is no example known of a gitana yielding to a weakness for a man of another race. It seems to me that there is a great deal of exaggeration in the praise he accords to their chastity. In the first place, most of them are in the fix of the homely woman in Ovid—*Casta quam nemo rogavit*. As for the pretty ones, they are, like all Spanish women, fastidious in the choice of their lovers. One must please and also deserve them. Mr. Borrow quotes as a proof of their virtue an incident which does honour to his own virtue, and particularly to his *naïveté*. An immoral man of his acquaintance, he says, offered vainly several onzas to a pretty gitana. An Andalusian to whom I told this story declared that the rake would have had better success had he shown her a few piastres, and said that offering gold onzas to a gitana was as bad a means of persuasion as to offer a million or two to a barmaid.

However that may be, it is a fact that the gitanas show an extraordinary devotion to their husbands. There is no danger, no misery, they will not brave to assist them in their need. One of the names they give themselves, the *Romé*, or the married folks, seems to me to attest the respect of the race for the married state. As a rule, one might say that their chief virtue is patriotism, if one may so call the fidelity they display in their relations with others of their own race—their anxiety to aid each other, and the absolute secrecy which they maintain in compromising affairs. Still, in all secret and lawless associations we observe something similar.

A few months ago I visited a tribe of gipsies established in the Vosges. In the hut of an old woman, the oldest of her tribe, there was a gipsy, a stranger to her family, who was mortally ill. This man had left a hospital, where he was well cared for, to die amongst his compatriots. For thirteen weeks he had been their guest, much better treated than the rest of the family, who lived in the same hut. He had a good bed of straw and moss, with fairly white sheets, while the rest of the family, eleven in number, slept on some planks three feet long. So much for their hospitality. The same woman, so humane toward her guest, said to me, before the sick man, "*Singo, singo, homte hi mulo.*" (Soon, soon, he must die.) After all, the life of these people is so miserable that the approach of death has no terror for them.

A remarkable trait in the gipsy character is their indifference to religious matters. Not that they are free-thinkers or sceptics; never have they made any profession of atheism—far from it. The religion of the country where they live is also theirs; but they change their religion when they change their country. To the superstitions which amongst savage people replace the religious sentiments, they are equally strangers. Still, I have noticed that the Spanish gipsies have a singular fear of contact with a dead body. There are few of them who will consent, even for money, to carry a corpse to the cemetery.

I have said that most of the gipsy women concern themselves with fortune-telling. In this they acquit themselves very well. But a greater source of profit to them is the sale of charms and love-potions. Not only do they have toads' feet to keep fickle hearts faithful, and powdered loadstone to attract indifferent ones, but they employ at need powerful conjurations which oblige the devil to lend his aid. Last year a Spanish lady told me the following story:

She was passing one day through the Street of Alcala, very sad and preoccupied. A gipsy squatted on the sidewalk accosted her, saying:

"My beautiful lady, your lover has deserted you."

It was the truth.

"Do you wish me to bring him back to you?"

One can understand with what joy the offer was accepted, and what confidence must have been inspired by a person who could thus divine at a glance the innermost secrets of the heart. As it would have been impossible to proceed with the magic rites in the most frequented street of Madrid, they arranged a meeting for the next day.

"Nothing will be easier," said the gitana, "than to bring back the faithless to your feet. Have you a handkerchief, a scarf, or a mantilla that he has given you?"

Yes, she had a fichu of silk.

"Now sew with crimson silk a piastre in one corner of the fichu; in another corner a half-piastre; here a very small coin; there a piece of two reals. Then sew in the centre a gold-piece —a doubloon would be the best."

The doubloon and the other pieces were sewn in.

"Now give me the fichu: I will carry it to the cemetery at midnight. Come with me, if you wish to see a fine piece of deviltry. I promise you that to-morrow you shall see your lover again."

The gipsy went alone to the Campo Santo, for the lady was too afraid of devils to go with her. I leave you to guess whether the poor forsaken one ever again saw her lover or the silk fichu.

In spite of their wretchedness and the sort of aversion they inspire, the gipsies enjoy a certain consideration among un-enlightened people, and of this they are very proud. They feel themselves a race superior in intelligence, and cordially despise the people who entertain them.

"The gentiles are so stupid," a gipsy of the Vosges said to me, "that there is no merit in taking them in. The other day a peasant hailed me in the street, and I went into her house. Her stove smoked, and she wanted a charm to make it draw. First, I made her give me a good piece of bacon. Then I mumbled over these words in Romany: 'You are a fool,' I said; 'a fool you were born, a fool you will die.' . . . But when I came near the door I spoke in good German, and said, 'The surest way to keep your stove from smoking is never to build any fire in it,' and I skipped out."

The history of this race is yet a problem. We know surely that their first tribes, small in numbers, appeared in the eastern part of Europe about the beginning of the fifteenth century; but no one knows from whence they came, nor for what they entered Europe; and, what is strangest, we cannot tell how in such a short time they have increased in such a prodigious manner in several countries so far apart. The gipsies them-selves have preserved no tradition in regard to their origin; and if most of them speak of Egypt as their mother country, 'tis because they have adopted a fable told about them for many years.

Most Oriental scholars who have studied the gipsy language think that it originated in India. In fact, it appears that many of the grammatical roots and forms of Romany also appear in idioms derived from the Sanscrit. It is supposed that in their long wanderings they have adopted many foreign words. In all the dialects of Romany we find Greek words. For instance: *cocal*, bone, from χοχχαλον; *petalli*, horse-shoe, from πέταλον; *cafi*, nail, from χαρψί, etc. To-day, the gipsies have almost as many dialects as there are separate tribes. Everywhere they speak the language of the country they live in more easily than their own tongue, which they use only when they would speak freely among themselves before strangers. If we compare the dialect of the German and Spanish gipsies, who have been for centuries without communication, we find many words common to both; but the original tongue everywhere is strikingly altered, though in different degrees, by contact with the more cultivated tongues which these nomads have been obliged to use. German on one side, Spanish on the other, have so modified the original Romany that it would be impossible for a gipsy of the Black Forest to converse with his Andalusian brethren, though it would be necessary for them to exchange only a few sentences to perceive that they both spoke dialects derived from the same tongue. Some words in very frequent use are common, I think, to all the dialects: thus, in all the vocabularies that I have been able to see, *pani* means water; *manro*, bread; *mâs*, meat; and *lon*, salt.

The numerals are everywhere nearly alike. The German dialect seems to me much purer than the Spanish, for it has retained many primitive grammatical forms, while that of the gitanos has adopted the Castilian. Nevertheless, some words are exceptions, attesting the ancient community of language.

The preterites in the German dialect are formed by adding *ium* to the imperative, which is always the root of the verb. The verbs in Spanish Romany are all conjugated after the manner of the Castilian verbs of the first conjugation. The infinitive *jamar*, to eat, is conjugated regularly—*jamé*, I have eaten; *lillar*, to take, must be conjugated *lillé*, I have taken. Still, some old gipsies say, exceptionally, *jayon*, *lillon*. I know of no other verbs which have preserved this ancient form.

While I am thus displaying my smattering of Romany, I should note several slang French words which our thieves have borrowed from the gipsies. From the "Mysteries of Paris," polite society has learned that *chourin* means knife. This is pure Romany: *tchouri* is one of the words common to all the dialects. M. Vidocq calls a horse *grès*—again a Romany word, *gras, gre, graste, gris*. Add still another word, *romanichel*, which in Parisian slang means gipsies. It is a corruption of *rommané tchave*, gipsy lads. But an etymology of which I am proud is that of *frimousse*, face, visage, a word which all the school-children use, or did use in my time. Observe first that Oudin, in his curious dictionary, wrote in 1640, *firlimouse*. Now *firla, fila*, in Romany means face; and *mui* has the same meaning—it is exactly the *os* of the Latins. The combination *firlamui* was immediately understood by a pure gipsy, and I believe it conforms to the spirit of his language.

But this is enough to give the reader of Carmen a good idea of my study of Romany. I will conclude with this proverb, quite apropos: "*En retudi panda nasti abela macha.*" (No fly can enter a closed mouth.)

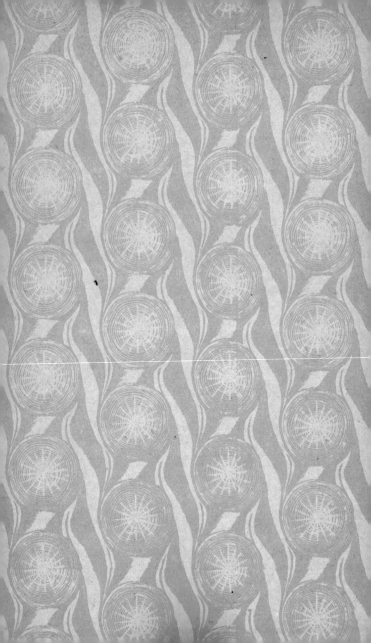